W9-DCW-714

BY LAURIE R. KING

MARY RUSSELL

The Beekeeper's Apprentice	*Pirate King*
A Monstrous Regiment of Women	*Garment of Shadows*
A Letter of Mary	*Dreaming Spies*
The Moor	"The Marriage of Mary Russell:
O Jerusalem	A Short Story"
Justice Hall	*The Murder of Mary Russell*
The Game	*Mary Russell's War and Other*
Locked Rooms	*Stories of Suspense*
The Language of Bees	*Island of the Mad*
The God of the Hive	*Riviera Gold*
"Beekeeping for Beginners:	*Castle Shade*
A Short Story"	*The Lantern's Dance*

STUYVESANT & GREY

Touchstone	*The Bones of Paris*

KATE MARTINELLI

A Grave Talent	*Night Work*
To Play the Fool	*The Art of Detection*
With Child	

AND

A Darker Place	*Lockdown*
Folly	*Back to the Garden* (a Raquel
Keeping Watch	Laing novel)
Califia's Daughters (as Leigh Richards)	

THE
LANTERN'S
DANCE

THE
LANTERN'S
DANCE

A NOVEL OF SUSPENSE FEATURING
MARY RUSSELL AND SHERLOCK HOLMES

Laurie R. King

BANTAM

NEW YORK

The Lantern's Dance is a work of fiction. Names, characters, places, and incidents are the products of the author's imagination or are used fictitiously. Any resemblance to actual events, locales, or persons, living or dead, is entirely coincidental.

Copyright © 2024 by Laurie R. King

All rights reserved.

Published in the United States by Bantam Books, an imprint of Random House, a division of Penguin Random House LLC, New York.

Bantam & B colophon is a registered trademark of Penguin Random House LLC.

LIBRARY OF CONGRESS CATALOGING-IN-PUBLICATION DATA
Names: King, Laurie R., author.
Title: The lantern's dance: a novel of suspense featuring Mary Russell and Sherlock Holmes / Laurie R. King.
Description: First edition. | New York: Bantam Books, 2024. |
Series: Mary Russell and Sherlock Holmes; 18
Identifiers: LCCN 2023039786 (print) | LCCN 2023039787 (ebook) |
ISBN 9780593496596 (hardcover acid-free paper) | ISBN 9780593496602 (e-book)
Subjects: LCSH: Russell, Mary (Fictitious character), 1900—Fiction. |
Holmes, Sherlock—Fiction. | LCGFT: Detective and mystery fiction. |
Thrillers (Fiction) | Novels.
Classification: LCC PS3561.I4813 L37 2024 (print) | LCC PS3561.I4813 (ebook) |
DDC 813/.54—dc23/eng/20230905
LC record available at https://lccn.loc.gov/2023039786
LC ebook record available at https://lccn.loc.gov/2023039787

Printed in the United States of America on acid-free paper

randomhousebooks.com

1st Printing

First Edition

Book design by Caroline Cunningham

This one is for my beloved friends at Bookshop Santa Cruz,

who have been a major part of my life for more than half a century.

THE
LANTERN'S
DANCE

CHAPTER ONE

"Let me help," he said.

"I can manage."

"Russell, I'll get the—"

"I'm *fine,* Holmes," I snapped. I was not fine. And when it came to admitting that an infirmity might require some help, I was proving nearly as cantankerous as Sherlock Holmes himself could be.

"I can—"

"Holmes, just pay the ruddy driver, I'll send someone out for the bags." Assuming they hadn't changed their minds as to the invitation. Or gone off to the South of France for the month.

"Watch the—"

"I see it!" And nearly tripped over it, one crutch-leg sliding into an ill-fitting stone on the walk.

But he let me get on with my halting progress, stumping along the walk-way towards the brightly painted door while the taxi-driver undid the rope strapping our trunks and valises in place. We'd expected to be met when we got off at the station in nearby Délieux. And though the absence of a car might have been a message of sorts—that antipathy had returned, that we should simply continue on to Paris—we had been invited, we had accepted, and we had cabled ahead with our information.

And even if the absence of greeting at the station had been due merely to the chronic forgetfulness of an artist, one would have thought that Damian's doctor fiancée, who had impressed even Holmes as being marvellously competent, would remember the arrival of her soon-to-be in-laws. (Stepmother-in-law? *Me?*)

I reached the end of the pathway without mishap, negotiated my way up the two low steps, settled my balance so I could reach out for the bell—then stopped, abruptly, three feet from the front door. After a moment, leaving the crutches tucked under my aching arms, I unfurled my fingers from the grips and raised them, hands outstretched.

Resentments, unsettled scores, and long-standing acrimony were one thing.

What I had not anticipated was being met by the sound of a break-action shotgun snapping into place behind me.

stood utterly still. So did the person with the shotgun. The voices from the lane concluded their business. A car door slammed, the taxi's engine clattered into life, the gate creaked, footsteps began— and cut short as the world's first consulting detective saw the tableau on his son's doorstep.

The sound of the motorcar faded away. Holmes and I waited, either for the man to pull down on the trigger or to decide that we were not the enemy he seemed to be anticipating.

"*Qu'est-ce que vous voulez?*" His voice was raised so as to reach both of us. It was not, to my relief, Damian.

"*Nous cherchons la famille Adler,*" I said over my shoulder. We're looking for the Adler family.

"*Vos noms?*"

"The name is Holmes," came the voice from the gate. "Sherlock Holmes."

"Ah," the man behind me said, in English this time. "Good."

The shotgun mechanism clicked. I let out a shaky breath and lowered my hands onto the crutch grips, manoeuvring myself around.

On the surface, my would-be assailant was a French agricultural worker: soft cap; tie-less, once-white shirt under a working man's waistcoat and red braces; and soil-coloured trousers of hard-wearing twill. His shirtsleeves were rolled up on meaty forearms, revealing a tattoo whose significance no doubt Holmes would read, but to me looked like a scrawl of dark chalk dissolved by time. His shoes, however, were no peasant clogs, but fit him well and had once cost a pretty centime.

The shoes led me to reconsider his status—and indeed, the set of his shoulders made it clear that this was not a gardener in the habit of tugging his forelock, or even doffing his cap. Beyond that, Damian clearly trusted this man enough to give him the name of Sherlock Holmes.

"*Bonjour,* Monsieur," I said.

"You, I think, will be Madame Holmes?"

"Er, yes."

"I most abjectly beg your good pardon, Madame. I am Gervais LaRue. Monsieur Adler said you would come. Have you hurt—ah, Monsieur," he said, holding out a hand for Holmes to shake. "I apologise for my *ambuscade* on your good wife. Please, come in—here, I shall open. Madame, you have injured yourself?"

"A minor sprain, nothing to worry about." It was a foolish injury, a combination of a small dog, a distracted mind, and some slippery tiles on a Berlin railway platform. My brusque tone of voice told him that I did not wish to talk about it.

He made sympathetic noises, but hastened to retrieve a heavy skeleton key from a pocket and fitted it into the door, fiddling it into place awkwardly around the gun draped across his other arm. "*Il faut plus d'huile,*" he muttered to himself, then grunted in relief when the key turned and the door came open.

"Where are the Adlers?" Holmes demanded.

"Ah, Monsieur, now that is a tale—come, my wife will bring food, and I will tell you all."

M. LaRue trotted ahead of us into the dim interior, ducking through one door and reappearing without the gun, then crossing the hallway to disappear through another. His footsteps went soft as he passed over carpet, then came the sounds of windows and shutters being thrown open. Holmes turned back down the path to fetch our bags. LaRue came out, squeezing past me to trot after Holmes. I decided there was little point in blocking the hallway, so stepped inside what proved to be a large sitting room, its stale air rapidly dissipating with the morning breeze.

On the outside, the Adler home was a substantial stone-walled, two-storey, red-tile-roofed French house with bright flowers along the walk and, unlike any of its neighbours in this village to the south of Paris, shutters and door painted an orange so bright, a child might have chosen it.

The inside, too, was a mix of traditional and modern, with a rococo limestone fireplace and ornate fringed ceiling lamps—once gas, now electrical—that looked askance at the brilliant blocks of colour in the carpet and the dozens of bottles lining the wall behind a cocktail bar decorated with a modernist version of Bosch's *The Garden of Earthly Delights*, its polished metal top set with ash-trays from half a dozen Parisian cafés. Gilt-framed portraits and landscapes shared the walls with art that resembled industrial schematics, primitive cave-paintings, or in one case, an artist's actual palette. The curtains were pale green linen, the seats were mostly Deco armchairs in several shades of darker green velvet, and the low table before the fireplace looked like a piece fallen off of an aeroplane. A leather settee in a startling shade of fuchsia was blessedly muted by the magnificent old Turkish rug draped across it. An elegant antique glass-fronted bookcase was stuffed with modern novels and books for children. On its top was a tangle of deer antlers, out of which peeped a child's teddy.

The orange doors, angular furniture, shin-endangering table, and avant-garde rectangles of painted canvas on the walls testified to the presence of Damian Adler: Surrealist artist, occasional murder suspect, and consequence of the affair between an American contralto and the world's most eminent English consulting detective, some thirty years before.

The children's books and teddy bear were signs of one Estelle Adler, Damian's four-and-a-half-year-old, disconcertingly intelligent daughter.

The pale green curtains, the modern-but-subdued wallpaper, and the pieces of furniture that looked as if they might actually be used for sitting upon demonstrated the conciliatory influence of Damian's wife-to-be, Dr Aileen Henning.

And underlying these three strong modern personalities, I caught glimpses of another strong individual: the rococo fireplace, ceiling lamps, and Turkish throw-rug were signs of the opera singer and renowned adventuress, Irene Adler. Damian's mother, my husband's long-ago . . . paramour.

This house had once belonged to her. In his early years on Baker Street, Irene Adler had come to Holmes' attention as the suspect in a case of blackmail—and promptly claimed his youthful heart by outwitting him soundly.* He eventually discovered that she was not only innocent, but that she was the wronged party, fighting to protect her future with the man she loved. She and Godfrey Norton had married, escaping with their dignity and their love—only to have it turn to ashes when he died and she was injured in an accident a few years later.

Holmes heard of the accident as he was working his way back across Europe after an enforced absence from London. He tracked her down in Montpellier, to offer his condolences. Matters progressed—only to have her briskly send him on his way home to London in April of 1894, with no more explanation than she wished to return home to America.

What she failed to mention was that she had become pregnant. Holmes' brother, Mycroft, knew—Mycroft seemed to know most things—but Holmes himself only learned of his son's existence six years ago, in the already tumultuous summer of 1919. When we met Damian, he was an ex-soldier-turned-artist whose problem

---

* "A Scandal in Bohemia," by Arthur Conan Doyle.

with drugs had led to a murder charge. Holmes and I investigated the matter and saw him freed—after which he, like his mother before him, disappeared from view, only in his case, to Shanghai.

So far as I knew, Holmes had never been inside this house that was now Damian's.

I heard voices from outside: a woman calling a question, answered by a shout from M. LaRue, coming in the front door and going past the sitting room with our bags. Holmes followed, his arms also full. Their two voices came from deeper in the house, then returned up the hallway. I turned on my crutches and followed, finding them in the kitchen—a room where the traditional French furnishings of burnished copper, hand-hewn wood, and practical fabrics gave no ground to modern life. M. LaRue was unlatching a side door onto a tree-lined terrace whose lines I remembered from one of Damian's sketchbooks, seen long ago.

The woman whose voice I'd heard—who indeed had not ceased to mutter to herself, despite Monsieur's attempt at explanation—bustled in, pounced on the kettle, filled it from the old tap, slapped it down on an electrical ring that was the most modern thing in the room, crossed the kitchen to give my hand two brisk pumps—down, up, down—then did the same to Holmes, before hurrying out of the door and into the garden. Her ongoing monologue faded along with the sound of her heels on the gritty stone.

"My wife," M. LaRue offered. "Pauline."

I looked at the kettle, and at the very British tea-pot beside it. Tea was not a French habit.

Two minutes later, she was back, carrying a heavy-laden basket that she proceeded to unpack onto the wooden table: a baguette, two pieces of cheese (one hard, one soft), half a roast chicken, a bottle of wine with no label, a small pot of liver pâté, and a gorgeous smooth-skinned melon whose late-summer aroma I could smell even over the garlic and cheese.

Holmes surveyed the growing banquet with disapproval, and turned to the husband.

"Do you generally greet strangers with a shotgun?"

"As I said, your son's absence is a tale, to be told at length."

Son?

A weighty pause lay across Mme LaRue's ongoing monologue— *the baguette was lamentably stale and the chicken was left-overs, there would be better cheese tomorrow after the Délieux Wednesday market*— while Holmes and I contemplated the fact that Damian had not only given this man the name Sherlock Holmes, but had disclosed how they were related.

"Tell me now," Holmes demanded.

"Oh, Monsieur, I did not mean to alarm—they are fine; merely, it was thought that between the questions and the intruder—"

... that the grapes were not quite ripe yet so perhaps we could make do today with the melon from the garden, Mme LaRue maundered on.

Two men facing off, one woman attempting to ease tensions with hospitality, another woman whose irritation with herself and apprehension with the situation had been building for days—

I abruptly saw that things had got off to a poor start here. And that alienating these two people—people intimate with the Adler household—by demanding facts before food would not be a helpful way to proceed. In any event, the stuffy air in the sitting room indicated that the family had been gone for a while. What difference would another half hour make?

"Holmes," I cut in, "perhaps we might want to eat first."

I held his gaze for a moment, then deliberately picked up the melon in both hands and lifted it to my face, filling my lungs with an exaggerated degree of appreciation. M. LaRue smiled and fetched a corkscrew; Mme LaRue fell silent at last and fetched some plates; and Holmes, after a hesitation, accepted my recommendation and pulled out a chair.

In fact, it proved little hardship to act out the greed of two people who had spent too many days subjected to train schedules across the width of Europe.

The wine was the work of M. LaRue—from vines, he told us, that his father had planted during the reconstitution of France's devastated vineyards. This opened polite conversation concerning the wickedness of *phylloxera vastatrix* and the inferiority of modern wine grown on American stock. I quietly drank, and made no attempt to defend my countrymen.

The melon was sublime.

When the feast was nothing but bones, crumbs, and a pot scraped empty of pâté, Mme LaRue asked—in French again, although she seemed to understand English well enough—if we preferred coffee or tea, and said that she would bring it out onto the terrace, where we could talk.

Her husband dragged chairs and a small metal café table into the dappled shade of a plane tree growing over the little pond, and we sat.

The respite, I could see, had achieved the goal of setting the LaRues at ease.

"*Alors*," he said. "You will want to know of your son, and why he is not here."

"If you would," Holmes said. He drew out his pipe, M. LaRue his cigarettes. I satisfied myself with a tiny cup of madame's *café fort* and a glance at Holmes.

He did not meet my eyes.

CHAPTER THREE

H olmes did not speak much about his son.

After we had freed Damian in 1919, years had gone by with no word. We had both resigned ourselves to the thought of him dead. He had, after all, a troubled history of drugs and drunken arguments, and although in actual fact he was both alive and productive, his work becoming well known even outside of Shanghai, it was under a pseudonym that Mycroft's agents had not caught.

And then a year ago, Damian turned up at the door of our Sussex home, reluctantly asking Holmes to find his missing wife.[*] Yolanda was a native of Shanghai he had met, married, and had a daughter with.

I shall never forget the look on Holmes' face when Damian told him about the child, who was also missing: Sherlock Holmes— a grandfather?

By the time Damian came to us, his marriage was more by way of a business partnership than a romance, with most of Yolanda's energy and enthusiasms dedicated to a man named Thomas Broth-

---

[*] See *The Language of Bees* and *The God of the Hive*.

ers, leader of a religious cult, the Children of Lights. We had not managed to save Yolanda, but we had preserved the lives of Damian and little Estelle, picking up an odd assortment of friends along the way—including a tiny red-haired Scots physician named Aileen Henning.

That particular friendship began as little less than outright abduction—polite, and entirely for her medical skills, that she might deal with the bullet in Damian's shoulder—but nonetheless, abduction it was. To our surprise, Aileen had chosen not to return to her hard-fought practice in a remote Scottish fishing town. Instead, she had come to France with Damian and the child, and a letter over the summer had informed us that a wedding was in the works. In fact, the letter went on to say, young Estelle was already addressing her father's intended as "Mama Aileen."

The letter had come from Aileen, not Damian. And although it included her blithe note that Damian was looking forward to our visit, neither Holmes nor I were entirely reassured. The relationship had never been easy.

Still, ancient animosities aside, I looked forward to seeing how a fiery Scots lady doctor and a devoutly idiosyncratic Surrealist painter of nightmares might formalise their relationship in a French village, accompanied by half the French Bohemian art world, with the bride attended by the small, wickedly smart, grey-eyed, half-Chinese granddaughter of Sherlock Holmes.

M. LaRue finished building his cigarette, lit one end, handed it over to his wife, and began to assemble a second one as he started to tell us why none of the Adlers were at home.

"This is a small village, Madame, Monsieur. Strangers are noticed. When M. Damian and his daughter and *la belle docteur* came here last year, they were the first new faces since the end of the War. For the most part, our young people leave, for Paris or beyond. But of course we knew M. Damian. He was small when Mme Adler came, so he grew up with our children. When she died, before the War, my wife and I were instructed to hold the house in waiting for him.

"He would come, from time to time. He spent some weeks here after the War, recovering from injuries, but after that, we did not hear from him for years. However, we had no reason to think that he had died, so we continued to maintain it for him. Madame and I live next door. Her brother, Pierre, has a small cottage that Mme Adler built for him at the back. Pierre was ... disfigured in the War, and is grateful that M. Damian has agreed for him to stay. Pierre works," LaRue hastened to explain. "The garden is mostly his, and he has clever hands for repairing all manner of things. But the way he looks, not everyone would be willing ...

"At any rate, this has been the situation, until finally, last year, M. Damian returned. And despite the undeniable oddness of M. Damian and his living arrangements—and some of his parties, although those have gone quieter since the *conseil* sent a letter— the village has come to look upon the family with affection, even humour. And the child is lovely and *Madame la docteur* is both charming and willing to turn out for a sick or injured neighbour."

"The Prodigal returns," Holmes said. He was being remarkably tolerant, although I could feel him quivering with impatience.

"*Exactement.* And therefore, when strangers come and begin to ask about them, even the village children know to turn a puzzled face on the questioner."

At last.

"Strangers? When?"

"It began the middle of last week—not here but in Délieux. Two men came off the Paris train. One was thirty or so years old, hand-some, in a well-tailored suit. The other was older, and more foreign. Neither looked entirely French."

"You saw them?"

"Not the older man, but the younger one came here—not here to the house, but to Sainte Chapelle—in a motorcar, a day or two later."

"Jour du marché," Madame LaRue contributed.

"That's right, it was market day, which makes it Friday. He stood out, not just because of his shiny motorcar."

"Not French, you think. Then what?"

"From one of the colonies, perhaps, although he spoke almost like a Parisian."

"Africa?" France had colonies across the African continent, and faces in all the multiplicity of browns were common in the larger cities, especially those with busy ports. But LaRue was shaking his head.

"Not from *l'Afrique,* no. From the East, I would say."

I shot Holmes a glance. The East—as in Shanghai?

"China?" he suggested.

LaRue thought for a moment, then looked to his wife, who gave one of those eloquent French shrugs indicating the vast extent of what she did not know. He shook his head. "I think not, but I am not certain I could judge. Black hair and eyes, and dark skin, both of them. I heard that the older man was darker."

"What questions did they ask?"

"In Délieux, I understand, they were looking for an artist named Adler. I suppose someone there gave them the name of this village, and the younger man came to Ste Chapelle, to ask at the market. As I say, no-one here would give them information, but Délieux is a larger town, without our loyalties. When the man came, he knew of a red-headed lady in the house. He wanted to know how long had they been here, where did they come from, which house was theirs. Oh, and he asked about *la famille* Vernet."

Holmes stiffened.

Arthur Conan Doyle had given the world precisely three facts about Sherlock Holmes' background. First, that he had an older brother named Mycroft, who was something high and enigmatic in the British government (read: a spymaster). Next, that the Holmes family were English "country squires" (that is, not quite aristocracy). Finally, that his grandmother was "the sister of Vernet, the French artist." Doyle never specified which of the half-dozen artists Vernet was meant, but in fact, Holmes' grandmother had been Horace Vernet's sister, Camille Vernet-Lecomte.

But virtually no one outside of Holmes' immediate circle knew that he was in any way related to Damian Adler. There was no reason why the name Vernet should have been heard in the village.

"Did they say why they wanted a member of the Vernet family?" he asked LaRue.

"Not so far as I heard. Although I understand the Vernets are distant relations of M. Damian. He was in Paris last month, and when he returned, he told us that he had gone to see the place where his uncle used to work."

"His *uncle?*" This time, Holmes could not hide his alarm. The only uncle Damian Adler possessed was Mycroft Holmes. Not only had Holmes' older brother never worked in Paris, but if that connexion was becoming known, we might be in trouble.

"*Grand-oncle.*" This was from Mme LaRue. "*Ou peut-être arrière.*"

Her correction made it slightly less worrisome. A great-uncle could be one of the lesser late-Victorian Vernets—or if "*arrière,*" then the previous generation, possibly Horace himself.

LaRue waved away any concerns about the generational divide. "Some uncle or other. M. Damian was amused at the thought—he showed us the man's work in a book, so very, very different from his, *n'est ce pas?* At any rate, when he took the family to Paris for a few days, that they might see the *Exposition des Arts,* he went past *l'Academie* and asked to see the uncle's rooms. Others are there now of course, but the building itself has not changed. And it seemed that a concierge who has worked there since *La Belle Époque* remembered another Vernet who painted there, who died

THE LANTERN'S DANCE 17

twenty, twenty-five years ago. So clearly," he finished up, "M. Damian must have told the people at *l'Institut* of the family link."

Which was not ideal, although a family as wide-spread as the Vernets could be claimed by any number of descendants.

"*Les caisses,*" Madame prompted.

"Ah yes—the crates! Some days after the family returned to Ste Chapelle, a letter arrived to say that the concierge had got to thinking and remembered that once, long ago, some Vernet possessions had been left in a storage attic, and when he went to look, he was astonished to discover the boxes still piled together in a distant corner. Since they had never been claimed and there was some desire to clear the storage, did M. Damian want them? Naturally M. Damian said yes, and that he would pay for the shipping, and so they came here."

"When did all this happen?"

After some consultation, the LaRues agreed: the trip to Paris had been the first week of August, with the family's return the 11th or 12th. The *Institut*'s letter had come on August 14. M. LaRue had collected the four crates at the train station two and a half weeks later, on the first of September—one day before the foreign men had shown up in Délieux, and three days before the younger one came to Ste Chapelle on market day.

Nearly a month went by between Damian's visit to his artist ancestor's rooms and the men asking after a Vernet descendant.

"What was in the boxes?" I asked.

"Nothing of importance. A dozen or so small paintings. Sketches, some journals and letters, odd things collected during travels. Personal memorabilia, you understand? The sort of things that servants hesitate to throw out completely, when clearing rooms that have been vacated. At least, nothing that seemed of any great interest under a preliminary look. They have yet to be properly unpacked, as M. Damian was *préoccupé* with a new painting and *Madame docteur* was busy with renovations to the plumbing and decorating. She was determined that the two of you should have a proper bathroom, when you arrived."

"*Et alors—*"

"And *then*," LaRue cut in, overriding his wife, "the lascar broke in."

Holmes nearly dropped his pipe. "A *lascar*? Why on earth would an Indian sailor come out here?"

I had to agree. Even in England, one rarely saw lascars outside of port cities. But I had a question of my own: "How did you know he was a sailor?"

LaRue laughed. "I know nothing—it was M. Damian who saw him. It was the middle of the night, and *la petite* had wakened him. She is a restless sleeper, I understand. When she was asleep again, he made his way downstairs in the dark—he broods over his paintings some nights, though he takes care not to wake the others. But he heard a sound as he went past the sitting room. Something moving, he thought, perhaps the shutters were loose, so he turned on the switch to see and found himself face to face with this ... foreign stranger. The man turned and dove out of the window he'd just climbed in, and ran off into the night."

"And Damian said he was a lascar?"

"It was a sort of joke, perhaps, because the man looked Indian and his feet were bare. It sounded to me like one of his Bohemian friends—as you can imagine, we have had all sorts here, since they arrived—but M. Damian said he did not know him, and that the man's appearance made him think of the sailors who would climb up and down the rigging. At first, he was angry, and I think frightened. Then he said, perhaps the lascar had nothing to do with the two nosey men and was merely a house-breaker looking for something of value. And then he decided that perhaps my explanation was the right one, and he tried to convince Mme Aileen that it could be one of their friends playing games—you know, the kinds of idiot *blagues* and trickeries that young people play these days. I believe he was trying to reassure himself as much as *Mme la docteur*. But in truth, he looked to me a touch *inquiet*. And madame did not find it at all a joke."

"*Il a fait un dessin*," contributed our one-woman Greek chorus.

But then, Damian's hands were constantly producing sketches, and Holmes had a more immediate concern than his son's artistic inspirations. "Is that why the family is away? Because of this lascar?"

The LaRues looked at each other, and Monsieur rose and went into the house, coming back with a knife, or more accurately, a machete. It resembled a Gurkha's kukri, but heavier. And, we saw when he laid it on the table, dull enough to shame any Gurkha.

"He dropped it as he fled. In the garden bed outside."

A knife put a very different face on the matter. A person could slaughter an entire family with this blade, in no time at all, and in utter silence.

As it was, the smears along the last few inches of the blade were merely soil. Holmes bent to examine the marks, without touching it.

"You suppose there's any chance of prints?" I asked him.

"We can try. When did the man break in?" he asked LaRue.

"Sunday night—or early Monday morning, I suppose. They packed and were on the train by noon."

"Where did they go?"

"To Nîmes. M. Damian has friends who run an hotel there—La Petite Bohème. He said to tell no one but you."

No one but us, I thought, *and any of the dozens of artists who might be travelling down to the Riviera.*

"When is the next train down there?"

LaRue fished out a large brass pocket watch and popped it open. "Forty . . . three minutes. That is for *l'Express*. The next one is not until evening."

Holmes stood. "Is there someone who can drive me to the station?"

"Pierre could run you in."

"Leave the knife there," Holmes told him. "Russell?"

"I'll deal with it."

He had crossed the terrace and disappeared into the house before I'd retrieved my crutches. Well, I thought, that decision had certainly been made without much contribution from me.

CHAPTER FOUR

Our room—fortunately—was on the ground floor. When I got there, Holmes was busily yanking things out of bags and shoving them into a valise.

I stepped out of my shoes to sit on the bed, studying my strapped-up ankle. There was no denying that it interfered with my mobility. "I take it that you intend to leave me behind."

"Don't you think it best?"

"No. Well, not really."

"I doubt I'll be more than a day or two. Leave it propped up, you'll be fine by the time I return."

"Holmes, I'm sorry." The words surprised me—I hadn't planned to say them, had only meant to ask what he intended to do when he found Damian. Perhaps I had overindulged in M. LaRue's wine.

He raised his head. "Sorry for what?"

I could see the accumulation of stress in his face: my ill temper, his uncertainty about Damian, grown now into out-and-out worry. To say nothing of recent events.

"Berlin was . . . difficult," I said. "But there's no reason for me to take it out on you."

What we had found there, sent on what seemed a minor matter

by Mycroft, had been deeply disquieting. A Freudian might have said I injured my ankle deliberately, so as to remove the both of us from the situation.

Holmes shook his head. "The current relative calm seems to have even Mycroft misled. He has a great deal of ground to make up there."

Without us, I sincerely hoped. "What will you do with Damian?"

"Put him and his two womenfolk in a safe place. I will then return, and we can find out what is going on."

"Thank you for saying 'we.'"

He grinned, and slapped a pair of clean shirts into the valise—which in my case would have meant a myriad of wrinkles, but in his, merely a sharpening of the crisp folds.

"Could this . . ." I paused, and climbed off the bed to close the door. "Could this be one of that madman's followers, the Children of Lights, come for revenge? I'd have thought that, without Brothers, they would simply go looking for someone else to adore."

"Revenge does seem unlikely, but I'd rather not take a chance."

"You'd say it has to do with that question about the Vernets rather than with the Children of Lights."

"Almost certainly."

"*Almost.*"

He did not reply, being occupied with folding a pair of trousers under his chin.

"It could be nothing," I pointed out. "Even Damian said it could be one of his more thoughtless friends, playing a joke on him. Or a newspaper reporter, after a clever scoop about the artistic antecedents of Damian Adler."

"A reporter who broke in with a machete in hand?"

"He didn't actually use it."

He cocked an eyebrow at that, and dropped to his heels over the bag that held our books. "There are those who would relish finding a means of harming me through my family."

"Surely Damian can protect himself?"

"And Dr Henning, and the child? While he is preoccupied with his work?" He dropped a book into the valise, frowned, and went to fetch his shaving kit.

"Holmes, Damian was a soldier, and he's far from stupid."

"True. On the other hand, the lad sounds halfway to convincing himself that the matter means nothing. That horrific events in his past do not mean that the future holds the same thing. And, incidentally, that the work his father has spent his life doing has nothing to do with the real world of Damian Adler."

"He couldn't be that foolish."

"I won't know until I speak with him." He tucked a packet of tobacco into the case and started to buckle it shut.

"Holmes? Take the revolver."

"You may need it."

"I'll sleep with M. LaRue's shotgun."

After a moment, he nodded and retrieved it from its concealed pocket. He then fastened the buckles and picked up the valise, giving me a very nearly apologetic smile. "Perhaps you'll be able to raise some fingerprints from the knife."

He detoured long enough to deliver a brief kiss to the top of my head, and went out of the door.

"Or perhaps," I called at his retreating form, "the lascar and his two associates will come back, and I'll have them all nicely bound and gagged when you return."

CHAPTER FIVE

The sound of the motor faded from the kitchen. Mme LaRue and I looked at each other.

"Have you a sheet of newspaper?" I asked.

She fetched one from the stove-side kindling box, and I carried it outside to the café table, wrapping up the knife and bringing it back to the kitchen.

"Mme LaRue, you said Damian made a drawing. Was it of the lascar—the burglar?"

"*Oui*," she said, and went on to tell me—in French—how he'd thought perhaps someone in the village might have seen the man, but although she and her husband had shown it among the neighbours, no one had recognised him.

"Do you still have the drawing?"

"*Bien sûr. Un moment.*" She walked out and came back to lay the torn-out page of a sketching block on the table.

Rendered in pencil, it showed a man in the kind of loose garments worn anywhere from North Africa to India. *More Bengal than Shanghai*, I thought. He was bare-headed, and stood in a slightly crouched stance, as if startled and about to bolt and run. Both hands were visible: no knife, and if he'd been wearing it through his belt, it was well hidden by his tunic-length shirt. There was something in his left hand, but it looked more like a small torch than a weapon. His feet were bare, the toes splayed on the floor tiles.

Most of Damian's attention had been spent on the face: angular features, heavy eyebrows over dark eyes, thick black hair. No beard or moustache. He had shaded the skin to indicate a darker tone, like the two men who had been asking for information, although the face could be from anywhere between Istanbul and North India.

Small exaggerated patches of graphite suggested smallpox scars, along with a thin, crescent-shaped scar along his right cheekbone.

The drawing was precise and alive, although I had to wonder at the expression Damian had given him. The man seemed more alarmed than threatening—which could be actuality, or it could be an artist sacrificing exactitude to his need to deny fear. Or even to the wish of avoiding the cliché of a bloodthirsty foreigner. Still, I had no doubt that I would recognise the man if I passed him in the street.

"Is there a photographic studio in the village?" I asked. "I should like to have reproductions made of this."

Mme LaRue regretted that there was not such a thing in Ste Chapelle, but the town of Délieux had one, and M. LaRue could easily take this when he returned from the train station.

I thanked her, and set the drawing aside until I could find a protective envelope. When she had finished tidying away the lunch things, I assured her that I did not need any help getting around, but accepted her offer to bring me some of the dinner she was cooking for her husband. She urged me to keep the doors and shutters locked, lest the lascar return, then paused on the doorstep.

"*Mon frère,*" she began, and then ran aground on an uncomfortable silence.

"Who lives in the back," I prompted.

Her brother, it seemed, was among other things what passed for a night-watchman, *chez* Adler. Her brother was appalled that he had not kept the house from being invaded. He felt responsible. I should be aware, therefore, that Pierre was likely to be outside at all hours of the night, by way of protecting the house. I should not concern myself, were I to see a strange man. One with ... injuries.

"From the War, yes?" She gave a vague gesture to her face, and nodded. I assured her that I had seen such injuries, that I appreciated his diligence, and that I was not about to be frightened, now that she had warned me.

"Though he probably shouldn't try to come in without knocking." I wouldn't want to club the poor fellow with a crutch.

"*Oh, non! Non non, il n'entrerait jamais!*"

"Well, that's fine, then. It's very good of him to keep an eye on things."

She was grateful that I understood, and explained again that Pierre was so happy to be permitted to continue in his small house, that he had loved Mme Adler when she was alive and he was honoured to be invited to serve her son, and she herself had been afraid that M. Damian's wife-to-be and small daughter might be frightened by Pierre's face and manner, but they had been so generous and ...

She was still speaking as I gently pushed her out of the kitchen door. I closed it. After a moment's silence, her voice came through, reminding me to lock it. I turned the latch; her footsteps retreated.

Had Holmes been there, I would not have admitted that my foot ached. But he was not, and it did, so I swung my way down the hallway to the rooms we'd been given, tossed Holmes' strewn possessions into one corner, found a book, and stretched out on the bed with a sigh.

It was a very pleasant room, an addition to the house so recent, one could smell the paint. The practicality and decisiveness of the building project made me smile. Over the course of six weeks the previous year, Dr Henning—Aileen, she'd said I was to call her—had gone from under-employed lady doctor to involuntary partner-in-crime to romantic interest of a wildly avant-garde artist, ending up in this patch of French countryside where she divided her time between treating the ailments of local farmers and bringing her fiancé's inherited home into the twentieth century. I suspected that Damian Adler's free-thinking way of life did not mean that he took over many of the household drudgeries.

And now, it seemed, poor Aileen was on the run again. Truly, one never knew where one would find oneself when in the company of a Holmes.

Or occasionally, where one might find oneself abandoned to her own devices.

I opened the book, read half a page, and found my thoughts returning to Pierre, the Adler gardener, handyman, and self-appointed night-watchman. A nation full of damaged young men, left to eke out a living where they could, including a hut in the back garden of his sister's neighbour. Though he'd lived there before he was injured, acting as resident muscle to an elderly American opera singer. Well, not elderly—she was only in her fifties when she died. She'd been three years older than Holmes, so would have been thirty-seven when Damian was born. Remarkably old for a first baby, perhaps, but plenty young enough to be . . . appealing.

Holmes claimed he'd never suspected. That he'd been offended by her haughty declaration that she was going home to America, and had secretly agreed that it was past time for him to get back to his work in London. I believed him—although I suspected that, had it been a man who showed such uncharacteristic behaviour, he might have enquired further. Women had always been a blind spot in Holmes' generally suspicious approach to the world—a consequence of his Victorian upbringing, perhaps, or of his mother's early death by suicide and having spent his adolescence with a bereft father. A father who, come to that, had been even more catastrophically abandoned by the woman he loved.

I'd always been curious about Irene Adler. Interest in one's predecessor was only natural—but not exactly a comfortable topic of discussion with one's husband. I hoped to learn a little more about her on this visit to the house that had been hers for twenty years. Just as I looked forward to learning more about her son, my (still such an odd thought) stepson who was five years older than I. Very probably the only child Holmes would have. Window into a life that might have been.

And with the house lying empty around me, surely twenty minutes was enough to prop up a twisted ankle? I lowered my feet to the bedroom floor and retrieved the crutches to set off for a survey of the house—or at least its ground floor. Not the kitchen, though I might snoop through the cabinets at some point. I started with the sitting room which, beneath the modern trappings, had been laid out by Irene Adler.

CHAPTER SIX

The sitting room took up one corner of the house, with two sets of wide casement windows on each of its outer walls. The windows, which M. LaRue had opened in order to push back the shutters and give the room light, had then been carefully locked again, as if an army of lascars waited to invade. The air was now stuffy, although I imagined that on Sunday night, the household had done as most French residents would do, namely leave the windows open but the louvred shutters locked, allowing the house to cool. As I crossed the room, using caution lest the crutches stub into the carpet underfoot, I noticed marks where the intruder had come through, at the front corner window. He must have stood in the flower-bed and used the long blade of that intimidating knife to jemmy open the shutter's latch—hence a few bits of peeled-off paint and wood slivers on the floorboards.

I opened the latches so I could lean out and see where the man had stood. The ground was soft enough to be disturbed, and a couple of the plants had been crushed, either by the intruder's leap or the heavy shoes of those coming to look. I could see a pair of deep dents, some eighteen inches apart, that might have been made by naked heels leaping from window height, although they had been partly obscured by later visitors. The ground immediately below had a hole roughly the dimensions of the blade, probably where LaRue had retrieved it. I could see nothing of any interest as evidence, though I would go and look more closely later, when the sun was shining on this side of the house.

I turned my back on the garden, letting the crutches hold my weight, to study the room from the angle the intruder had seen it (albeit briefly). The moon had been four days past full, plenty of light to get inside without using the torch. He probably switched it on once inside, since even a room furnished in the minimal modernist fashion has plenty of hazards to the unwary. So what would his beam have shown? Books on shelves and tables; paintings and prints on the wall; knick-knacks, framed photos, and a time-faded daguerreotype on the mantelpiece: some of those were probably valuable, but nothing that would call out to a common or garden burglar. The objets d'art arranged in the corner-piece étagère, for example—a piece of furniture that looked like a cross between a Chinese bird-cage and a futurist chair—would seem at first glance like knick-knacks, although nestled amongst the beach-side souvenirs, bird-nests, paper flowers, and much-loved toys were an exquisite Fabergé egg daubed with a smear of what looked (and, on closer examination, smelled) like chocolate, a Tiffany clock with its XI missing, and an enamelled elephant some three inches tall whose eyes could have been actual diamonds.

Pride of place, I noticed, was given to a tiny hand-made tea set with cups fashioned from acorn caps.

The Fabergé egg alone would have made any burglar's trip worthwhile. And two or three of the smaller paintings would have been worth something. I especially liked the one of two women from the back, shoulders nearly touching, grey head and blonde bent over an infant—and I saw it was signed: "EVernet-Lecomte," and dated 1895. The artist was Camille's son, Sherlock Holmes' uncle, Charles Émile Hippolyte Lecomte (who had added the "Vernet" to his name for its saleability).

However, the intruder had already been halfway across the room when Damian came in, and Damian seemed to have heard the actual sounds of his breaking in. Which would indicate that the intruder's goal was not here, in the sitting room.

His torch, however, was.

I found it beneath a settee, flung away as he'd leapt for the window, overlooked thereafter. It was a task retrieving it, but after many curses I got one crutch behind it and pulled it into the open. With care, I lifted it onto a cushion without leaving my own fingerprints behind. Had it been on? The sliding switch appeared to be in the "off" position—even with it burning, he'd have been blinded when the room's lights went on.

I tried to reconstruct the moments following the break-in. Trip the latch, climb up to the sill—a place to check for fingerprints—and then inside. What then? Either put the knife down on the table or window-sill and take out the torch, or slide the blade into a sheath hidden by clothing. Either way, according to Damian's sketch, his right hand was free as he crossed the room to the door, which had opened before he reached it.

Then, after he and Damian stared at each other long enough for his face to imprint on the artist's memory, instead of pulling his knife—or leaping over to where he'd left it—and using it to attack the householder who had disturbed him, he flung away the torch, scrambled out of the window, dropped or knocked the knife to the flower-bed, and disappeared into the night.

Most likely, I thought, he had left the knife on the window-sill, and accidentally kicked it out as he fled.

Shoes and transport must have been somewhere nearby, but unnoticed. A resident of this quiet village would have heard a motorcar's arrival. And if he'd used a cycle, it would have been foot-powered and silent, not powered by petrol.

The whole thing demonstrated an unlikely combination of skill and panic. Was he a thief, or an assassin? If burglary, then his target was both specific and something he knew with a brief glance was not in this room. And assuming this break-in was related to the questions the two foreigners had asked, then work by more valuable artists than the Vernets—including Damian Adler himself—could be found in any French villa or Paris *hôtel particulier*.

On the other hand, if murder had been on his mind, whether he was a member of the Shanghai cult out for revenge or some enraged art critic in esoteric clothing, he had proved blessedly inexperienced and faint-hearted at the art of assassination. But what other options were there? A spy? For what purpose? Damian Adler held no secrets, had no politics at all, so far as I knew. Granted, his uncle Mycroft held political secrets enough for several families, but if an enemy had learned of the connexion and thought to use Damian to manipulate the British government through his uncle's affections—a plot even Conan Doyle might have considered far-fetched—why send a trio of distinctly foreign men into the French countryside?

What if their target wasn't Damian, but Aileen Henning? She did not strike me as a woman with mighty secrets in her past. And yes, one might speculate that some personal threat had sent her to that obscure corner of Scotland, except I knew for a fact that she had not been in hiding, since any number of her brothers, sisters, cousins, and school friends knew precisely where she was.

I shook my head. One could not construct bricks without mud, or a theory without data. The pool of data I had was so thin as to trickle through my fingers: *Time to move on, Russell.*

The rest of the sitting room contained much of interest, but nothing related to the invasion of the home, so I fetched another sheet of newspaper and wrapped up the torch, leaving it on the kitchen table with the machete.

The next room had been an office or library. It was still furnished with a heavy pigeonholed desk, reading chairs, and a peculiar mix of books, from a Victorian survey of women explorers to a racy French novel about a woman's affair with a man half her age. However, it appeared as if the shelves were in the process of being cleared, and the packets and equipment spreading out across the glass-front bookshelves declared the room now a doctor's surgery. Her patients' complaints seemed mostly to involve sore throats, eye infections, minor wounds, and broken bones, but she was prepared for something more traumatic: syringes waiting beside a new-looking safe implied that it was her drugs cabinet, while a prominently placed valise was ready-packed with the equipment and drugs needed for a major accident. I helped myself to a roll of medical strapping tape, and hobbled on.

Across the hallway from the office/surgery was a small, cheerfully tiled lavatory, either newly installed or comprehensively re-built. Beyond that were two doors. On the right was the guest suite we'd been given. I opened the door on the left.

Another brand-new space, two storeys tall and covering nearly as many square feet as the rest of the ground-floor rooms combined. High windows on the north and east showed the sky and the tops of trees, making the room bright at any time. A small cast-iron stove in one corner for the winter, a paint-splattered scullery sink in the other for cleaning up, Damian's studio would be the envy of half the artists in France.

And he'd been busy—I was relieved to see that the bullet wound to his shoulder was not creating problems. The place was a chaos of works both in progress and finished. Three canvases stood on easels. Another, ten feet tall, leaned against the west wall with a stepladder to hand. One long table was all but buried under over-sized drawings, rough and finished, realistic or not. In one corner was a stack of half a dozen drawings with a bowl on top. Curious, I went to look, and found it contained, not an abandoned meal, but a handful of things gathered from a beach—sand, three shells, a tiny dried-up crab, some threads of crisp seaweed. The drawing beneath it, despite being a quick dash of ink across the page, was clearly meant to be a seashore. And I was intrigued to find the sketches beneath it growing more realistic as they went. Or more probably, he had started with realism and been hunting for the abstract essence of the seaside experience.

On the table's other corner, the corner nearest the door, lay three thick little sketchbooks, their cheap, paperboard corners bent with wear. I'd seen Damian pull one like these from his pocket to jot down thoughts and images last year in Sussex. I opened the one on top, and looked down at Estelle, squatting in the garden to examine something at her feet. On the next page, he'd made a close study of one side of her head, capturing the way her heavy, black hair fell across her shoulder. He had written a note in one corner, saying, *That black silk from Taipei.* The next page showed a modernistic-looking rag-doll leaning against a rock: *Kiki,* it said. Then came Dr Henning striding down the path. Mme LaRue frowning into a steaming saucepan. A dead bird: *A throng of ants.* Not all had notes, but each was dated. This top book, nearly full, was no more than a week old.

I put it down and glanced through the others. The earliest of the three began with line drawings of dramatic, modern-looking buildings that I recognised from newspaper articles—the Decorative Arts exposition. Damian had gone to see it in early August, and it looked as if he'd spent the whole time planted amidst the crowds, sketching furiously. Most of these pages had notes along their margins—one showing the Japanese pavilion remarked on the gloss of lacquer and the smell of bamboo. A boxy construction with many stairs leading up to an entrance framed by a huge, decorative flare noted, in French, *The explosion of capitalism.* The Soviet Union page simply said, *Pluie!* Perhaps a rain shower provided the artist with some key memory.

The three books between them covered little more than a month. He must do ten or twelve drawings a day—and there were stacks of similar books on the shelves. I shook my head and put these back as I'd found them.

By contrast, both to the quick sketches and to the disarray of his worktable, two hyper-realistic paintings of young Estelle and one of a certain red-haired doctor, her mouth quirked in amusement, had been framed and mounted onto the high southern wall in a rare display of organisation. *Like Holmes' laboratory,* I thought with a smile. It, too, appeared chaotic—except for one wall, where Holmes had neatly displayed the painting of his mother that I had stolen for him as my wedding gift.

Unlike the Holmes work-space, one corner of Damian's had been claimed by a younger generation, with a half-sized chair and table, blocks of sketching pads, a half-sized easel, and a unit of shallow drawers with the child's artistic endeavours. I was rather relieved to find that Estelle's daunting cleverness did not extend to her drawings, which seemed no more sophisticated than those of any other infant her age (although, in an era of Picasso and Du-champ, what did I know?). It was also good to think that Damian was not fobbing his child off onto a new wife, along with the other household responsibilities.

An array of books on a shelf near the diminutive table—neatly lined up, in contrast to the rest of the room—brought a mental picture of Damian deeply immersed in his latest inspiration, paint flying and deaf to the world, while his small daughter sat and pored over *The Wonderful Wizard of Oz* and *Peter Pan.* This, too, re-minded me of Holmes, unmindful of Mrs Hudson tidying around him—or come to think of it, a painting I'd laughed over showing Holmes' great-uncle, Horace Vernet, in a studio inhabited by two dozen men, a barking dog, a monkey, and a nervous-looking white horse, with an épée duel going on in the centre while two bare-chested boxers waited their turn, accompanied by a drummer, a bugle player, three conversations—and over at the side, oblivious to it all, a man at an easel.

It would appear that, in addition to piercing eyes, aquiline nose, and the varied permutations of "art in the blood," one could also inherit an extreme ability to block out tumult, discomfort, and dis-traction.

I shuffled over to examine the recent portrait of Estelle. She had grown since last I saw her, but she still radiated brightness, from her glossy black hair to the mischief in those grey eyes. Her great-grandmother, source of that eye colour, would have turned one hundred this year. What would she have made of the tyke?

I went on.

The rest of Damian's work was either figures or city images, with—unexpectedly—some tentative ventures into the French countryside. The nightmare theme of his earlier paintings appeared to be fading, while his colours grew ever more vibrant, his shapes more electric. Even in my relative ignorance of artistic trends, I could see that Damian Adler's style was changing dramatically, from the slightly cold, hyper-real absurdity of Surrealism to something softer and more nearly Expressionist.

I wondered what the critics made of it.

Twenty minutes later, I caught myself up short. *Russell, that lascar wasn't out to steal a Damian Adler painting!* And there, off in a corner, half-hidden behind two rolls of canvas and a bundle of kiln-dried wood, I spotted some threads of excelsior and tracked them to their source: two old tea chests, one steamer trunk, and a sturdy shipping crate some thirty inches on a side. Each container had a label glued to the top, with Damian's name and telephone number, sent by the *Institut de France,* care of the railway station in Délieux.

Had the boxes been securely fastened, I might have hesitated. But the timing of the break-in, so soon after men had been asking about the name Vernet—as well as the lascar's blatant failure to use his knife on Damian—suggested that he could have been after something in one of the recently arrived *Institut* boxes.

And in any event, they'd all been recently opened—the trunk's padlock lay on a nearby shelf, while the shipping crate and one of the tea chests showed signs of having had their tops prised up, with the nails crudely straightened and shoved roughly back into place. The top of the other tea chest, which bore the stencils of a Ceylon estate, would no longer close all the way, and its nails had been hammered flat, to protect either hands or the contents.

I pulled over a wooden chair, hoping that its rainbow splatters of paint were mere accident and not some genius work of art, and used it to sit down before the crates.

I began with the Ceylon tea chest.

Beneath the top was an old, once-pretty, knocked-about Chinese lacquer box some fifteen inches square and half that deep. I rested it on the edge of the chest and worked its tarnished brass hook with a thumb-nail, lifting its hinged lid.

The box was purpose-built for what it contained, with a lining of ancient, dark blue silk following the nooks and hollows that cradled the pieces of a device that had to be some kind of lantern, or a particularly elaborate candle-holder.

The main piece, catty-corner across the top, was eight inches of Chinese cloisonné enamel-ware in old and intricate abstract designs. The curve of it invited the hand to lift it from its silken bed—but before my fingers had made contact with the worn silk around the narrow riser, I forced myself to stop, and hobbled over to wrestle a sturdy table into place.

I took out the base, enjoying the shape and texture. My fingers located a few chips out of the enamel, and repairs had been made at one point, but it was mostly intact. I stood it on the table, secure on its wide base, and set about unpacking the rest of the device, laying all the pieces out on the table.

Glass cup. The bowed wires of a lamp-shade's harp that ended in a finial with three washers and a screw cap. A metal hoop some three inches high and a dozen across with thin windows cut all along its top. A fan with half a dozen blades, slightly smaller across than the hoop—and I recognised what this was even before I came to the strips of paper. It was some kind of zoetrope, the child's toy that spun around and mimicked animated motion from the drawings on the paper strips—but this one was a far more complex machine than the one I'd had as a child.

It took some time, and several retracing of steps, before I had the thing together. It was indeed a spinning zoetrope, but it was built around a lamp—which would not only illuminate the drawings as one peered through the slots in the whirring shade, but might generate enough heat to drive the blades of a kind of fan at the top. Like a cross between a zoetrope and one of those German Christmas carousels.

I was grinning as I inserted one of the paper strips into the shade and blew the device into motion. A dancing girl tossed a long scarf into the air and caught it, again and again—but I had to see it working correctly.

I found candles in the kitchen, broke one down to a couple of inches, rested it in the glass cup, and set it alight.

At first, nothing happened. Disappointed, I nudged the shade into motion—and that was all the encouragement it needed.

It was a self-propelling zoetrope, a remarkably early form of animation. The flickers of twelve drawings, each one slightly different, fooled the eye into seeing it as motion. Up and down went the girl's scarf, the motion seamless, hypnotic, with no jump at all between the strip's final drawing and the start of its next circuit. Around and around, this precursor of Felix the Cat, by the looks of it more than a century old.

I will admit, I fed quite a few of the paper strips into the shade, going back for more candles. And even when I let the device go still, it wasn't because I'd grown disinterested in it, merely that I became aware that spending a day mesmerised by antique moving images was somewhat childish.

I was also amused to find some new paper among the strips: Damian had produced four image-strips for his daughter—a flapper performing the Charleston, a delightfully wriggling snake, an exuberant tumbling gymnast, and an egg that hatched into a bird and flew upwards, disappearing just in time for the eggshell pieces to come together and hatch again.

I held the flapper up to the light, admiring the man's technique. A child's plaything, any details of which would be rendered invisible by the blur of the spin, and yet each of the twelve drawings was an exquisite miniature, an inch of ink figure capturing the high spirits and effort of the young dancer. Her long pearl necklace rose and swung, the fringe on her skirt bounced. In the same way, the egg-to-bird progression seemed to tell a tale, from a simple oval of pure potential to a celebration of winged freedom.

I could imagine these strips perfectly framed and hung for sale in a gallery.

With some reluctance, I returned the strips to their slot and blew out the candle.

I stretched hard, to rid my shoulders of the kinks, and looked from the image-lantern to the three remaining boxes.

Delightful though the lantern might be, Damian's lascar had not broken in searching for an archaic bit of whimsy. So, what was he after?

CHAPTER SEVEN

felt an odd hesitation about violating the remaining crates. Unlike the one containing the lamp, the lids of these had been nailed down again. By Damian. Who was not even my blood relation, although the previous year, we had begun to form a relationship that was—inevitably—unique. Holmes was barely the man's father. I was not his stepmother in anything other than a roughly sketched family tree. The most I could hope for was that we might be . . . friends.

However, if there was some threat to Damian and his family, the answer might lie in these boxes. And in any event, I was here and Holmes was not and four shipping crates were what I had to investigate.

I began again with the Ceylon tea chest, pulling out what lay beneath the lamp's lacquer box. It was mostly clothing, exotic garments from all over—a silk *kurta* tunic from India, indigo blue and embroidered around the neckline; a cotton *abayya* from Egypt or Palestine, originally purple but faded to lavender on the shoulders and back; a linen cap with a band of Russian embroidery. All, I found, men's garments, but for a small man, some inches shorter than I. It had all been stuffed inside, willy-nilly, although hard fold-lines in the fabric spoke to a long storage before its recent disturbance.

When the crate was empty, I poked at the wood itself, hoping for hidden secrets. There were none. I checked the seams and pockets on the garments as I folded them away, in case of hidden treasure, but neither ring nor brooch-jewelled choker appeared—not so much as a faience bead. When I finished, the neatly-folded contents left ample room for the lantern's box back on top.

The lantern itself I left assembled on the table.

The second tea chest weighed a young ton. I prised off the top with a hefty screw-driver left conveniently nearby, and found it lined with thick velvet and filled with daguerreotype plates. These I removed with considerable caution, and was pleased to discover that, although they seemed loose, they had been packed with enough care that only two had cracks in their glass. They, like the clothing, were of the exotic, mostly capturing scenes of Egypt and Palestine, some with posed figures. One showed a slim, middle-aged European with full moustache and thinning hair, dressed in an odd combination of vernacular garments, including loose trousers, a snug shirt, and a fringed sash around his waist. Another captured a raffish man sprawled beside a campfire, his dark hair and beard giving him a Middle Eastern look, although the way he stared into the camera struck me as European. A third plate had both men, posed in Bedouin garb, from *kaffiyeh* to soft boots, reclining self-consciously in a Bedu tent with a hookah on the carpet between them.

I returned the plates in the order I'd found them, but again, they seemed loose—and I remembered the daguerreotype propped up on the mantelpiece in the sitting room. It had shown some men in native clothing, standing in front of the Great Sphinx.

I retrieved my crutches and went to the sitting room. The Sphinx daguerreotype on the mantelpiece did indeed capture that same slim European, dressed in clothing that looked like a tourist's recent purchase. Two of the other figures were clearly European, although standing behind them with the reins of a somewhat blurred donkey was a young lad, probably a local guide or assistant, dressed by contrast in an everyday *abayya*, a casual head-wrap, and plain sandals.

Was it the Sphinx or the men that had caught Damian's eye? (Though I supposed it could have been Aileen, or even Estelle, who claimed it from the box.) I imagined it was the landmark, or he'd have chosen the other photograph showing the man alone.

I went back to the studio and turned my attention to the steamer trunk.

To my surprise, it was nearly empty—at least, though the interior was fitted side-to-side with drawers and trays, most of them held nothing but stains, scrapes, and small bits of paper. It was an artist's travelling workshop, from a drift of charcoal in one of the small drawers to the smears of oil-based paint in another—and then one of the drawers slid out completely and I was holding a self-contained watercolour paint box, with palette tray, blocks of dry pigment, and its own slim drawer for brushes and such. The paint was there, cracked into desiccated bits; the brushes were not.

The sides, lining, and backs of the drawers held no hidden secrets beyond fragments of leaves and some sand picked up on its travels.

This left the one actual shipping crate. Here, Damian had tamped down the top firmly enough that I needed the screw-driver again.

Its contents echoed the daguerreotypes, although they were a different medium: paintings, standing edge-up. Unlike the glass plates, these were all different sizes, which explained the need for excelsior, although most of that seemed to have been swept up after Damian and his family looked through them.

The crate held fourteen paintings, the largest thirty inches by twenty-four, the smallest eight by twenty. All oils except one, a watercolour version of the Sphinx photograph that had been romanticised by the addition of three camels and an unlikely palm tree. They were difficult to judge while in the box, and I didn't want to simply pile them in a heap, so—cursing the awkwardness of a foot that jabbed pain whenever I put weight on it—I arranged them against the wall in more or less chronological order, guided by the signatures and occasional dates.

I knew something about the Vernets, and could generally distinguish one from another in a museum. The dynasty had begun with Joseph Vernet—more fully, Claude Joseph—whose dramatic seascapes and moonlit clouds were greedily sought after by young eighteenth-century blades doing the Grand Tour. Joseph's son, Carle (his full name was Antoine Charles Horace Vernet), had turned from horses to Napoleonic battles after his beloved sister was executed by the Revolution in 1794. Then came Carle's son, Horace (strictly, Émile Jean-Horace, not to be confused with his nephew Carle Émile—the number of recurrent names found in this family could give a genealogist a headache). Horace Vernet was also hugely popular for his vast battle scenes, but in his middle years he began to travel, and expanded the usual European themes to the romantic (often biblical) possibilities of North Africa and the Middle East. Horace's sister, Camille, married an artist named Hippolyte Lecomte, starting a dynasty of their own (although their son Émile was the one who chose to confuse matters by adding the Vernet to his name). So far as I knew, none of the Vernet women had been artists—typical, in a system based on patrons and benefactors—but Camille's youngest, Louise Estelle (not to be mistaken for Horace's wife, Louise, or his daughter, Anne Elisabeth Louise, or Camille's granddaughter, Camille Elisabeth Louise, or . . .), had married an Englishman, thus bringing the Vernet "art in the blood" into a family of country squires.

The name of the English squire was Holmes.

Of the fourteen paintings in the crate, three were by Carle Vernet: a furious battle of lunging horses, raised swords, and spotless uniforms; a fabulously glossy and long-tailed Arabian stallion; and the small, affectionate portrait of a young woman with arched eyebrows and frothy blonde eighteenth-century curls. Most of the rest were by his massively prolific son, Horace, and ran the gamut from a pair of arch-necked greys in a field to a ship under fire and an unfinished study of an African soldier. The nicest one showed three proud men on caparisoned camels with the servants well hidden behind them. The man in the lead was tucking his head down, as if sharing a jest with the painter.

Then I pulled out the portrait of a face I knew.

Not personally—she'd died half a century before I was born, but the brooch Holmes had given me on my eighteenth birthday held a miniature of this same woman, his grey-eyed grandmother, Camille Vernet-Lecomte. It had been painted by her brother Horace. And though I was no expert, it looked to me as if this was by the same hand.

Either Damian had not recognised her, or he'd had his own reasons for leaving his great-grandmother Camille in the box rather than propping her on the mantelpiece.

At the end of the row of paintings, I arranged a trio of pieces that lacked signatures, whose styles were beyond my skill at identifying. One was a dark and melodramatic study of Napoleon, slumped in a chair, which I suspected had been painted in the years just prior to the emperor's 1815 exile. The next was a kitten curled up before a fireplace, an unlikely piece of domesticity after all the race-horses and battle scenes. The last showed a grey-haired woman seated looking out of a window, the head of an infant tucked into the side of her neck. The distinctive curtains declared it a pair to the Émile Vernet-Lecomte painting of the two women on the sitting-room wall, although this one was neither signed nor dated.

I stood it at the end of the row. It drew my eye as the furious horses, Egyptian countryside, and sleeping kitten did not. I wondered why he had not shown the women's faces in either painting. Perhaps they were not commissioned portraits, leaving Vernet-Lecomte free to explore the eloquent pose of the women, here

with the child's head, in the other one with the younger leaning
into the older, the echo of their hair colour and garments in the
room's background details. Indeed, the prominence of some of the
objects suggested a significance I could not begin to decipher.

After a while, I shuffled backwards so I could survey this gallery
of art by no-longer-fashionable painters. I could see absolutely
nothing that was worth breaking through a window to steal.

I decided to leave out the overlooked picture of Camille to show
to Damian. The rest I began to return to the crate, but when I tried
to slide the tallest of them back into place—a Horace Vernet desert scene of a seated falconer—it stuck up above the rest. *The excelsior must have gathered into a clump at the bottom,* I thought with
irritation, and pushed my arm down to dig the stuff out.

Only to have my fingers hit something more solid than wood
shavings.

My hand came up with a small, soft, leather-bound note-book.
The thongs that held it shut hadn't been worked open for many
years, but eventually they came loose before the dry leather broke.
I blew away the lingering wisps of wood, and opened the covers.

It was a journal—a memoir, as its introductory words said: *Ce
livre d'images est en guise de mémoire.* I thought at first the strong,
clean handwriting belonged to a young man, but by the end of the
first paragraph, I had changed my mind. A woman, almost certainly. As I read further, her words made my eyebrows rise, so that
I turned the page with considerable interest.

The second page had been written by the same assured hand,
but instead of formal French, I was looking at tidy rows of complete gibberish: they were letters, yes, but drawn from several alphabets. And some of the shapes were from no writing system I
knew.

It had to be some kind of code. Grammatical marks were the
usual mix of commas, periods, and French quotation marks. Para-
graphs began with indentations—unless the space at the front of

some lines had some other meaning. Every so often, the text would break off before the end of a page, and the next page would begin with two lines of header, as if some form of Chapter One followed by a title or descriptor.

I turned through the pages, and found that everything after that French introduction was a methodical, incomprehensible mix of letters and shapes. If not code, it was the work of a madwoman—a remarkably precise madwoman.

I jerked as a sound broke the long hours of silence. Before I could raise myself from the stool, it was followed by the house-keeper's voice.

"*Madame? Êtes-vous ici, Madame?*"

"I'm back here, Mme LaRue," I called.

The journal, I discovered, fit nicely into a pocket, and the last two paintings slid easily into their crate. When Mme LaRue came in, the only signs of my intrusion were the assembled image-lamp and the painting of Camille Vernet.

Only when she flipped on the light switch did I notice how long I had sat here—and with the realisation, my foot began to pound, my back threatened a cramp, and my inner self called out for sustenance.

Fortunately, she had brought a dinner over for me, and when I was settled—at the actual dining table this time, no longer in the informality of the kitchen—she also took care to pull up a low stool with some cushions for my foot.

As she came and went, she assured me that Holmes had caught the train for Nîmes, and that M. LaRue had taken the drawing to the photographer in Délieux for reproduction. He would pick up the prints in the morning. I in turn reassured her that there was no need to provide a cooked breakfast for me, and that indeed, I was equally happy with either a midday dinner or a cheese-and-bread luncheon, whichever was simpler for her.

The latter brought a *tut* to her lips, the idea that today's emergency rations might be taken for the norm. And I did enjoy her cooking.

Once the dishes were clean, every kitchen surface was sparkling, and every window locked and shuttered, she exhorted me to rest my foot, which looked as if it pained me, and used her key to lock the kitchen door.

I lingered over my coffee, and my thoughts.

They went, first, to Holmes. One would think I'd be well accustomed to his sudden absences, but I did feel them. And I did worry, just a little, when he went off without someone to watch his back. Someone who, unlike Damian, did not allow bitterness to taint her affection, and might not become so totally engrossed in work that she could overlook monkeys, bugles, and barking dogs.

Perhaps I was not giving Damian sufficient credit. He'd survived nearly four years as a soldier in the front-line trenches after all. And even considering the burden of shell shock that followed most soldiers home—which in Damian's case brought severe claustrophobia—his experiences would have left him not only alert to threat, but also prepared to defend his family.

However, there was a world of difference between open battle and stealthy attack. He was different from Holmes in so many ways, oblivious to matters that did not bear upon his art.

How much of that difference was due to their upbringing? I wondered. Damian was eighteen when Irene died, while Holmes lost his mother at eleven, and lived after that with a distraught father. There was a reason Holmes kept clear of his family's home. Damian, on the other hand, was happily making his mother's house his own. He would not be doing so were it not a place of good memories.

Which circled my thoughts back to Holmes: he claimed that he had come to terms with Irene's decision to push him away, leaving him in the dark about the existence of a son. But how could any man be at ease knowing that a woman he loved had made that key decision for him, had deliberately chosen to free him for his work rather than tying him down to paternity? He had to feel that he had ultimately failed her. Failed to win her trust.

So much about the man and his past that I did not know—and those things I did know, how much I did not truly understand.

My cup was empty, so I left it in the kitchen sink and climbed into my night-clothes, raising up my throbbing extremity on a pillow at the end of the bed. I switched on the bed-side reading lamp, and opened the coded journal in hopes of inspiration.

And woke at dawn to birdsong, the light still burning, the book lying open on my chest.

CHAPTER EIGHT

No telegraph flimsy awaited me, no telephone call had broken my sleep. I told myself as I dressed that Holmes had no reason to interrupt his rescue mission to reassure me.

Sitting at the kitchen table with a cup of French coffee as thick as motor oil, I opened the journal again. It seemed less of a code than a personal cipher, reminiscent of those that Holmes and I occasionally used. The previous day's survey had left me with the impression that it was built primarily out of four alphabets: the Latin one used by all European languages; Greek, which might be expected of someone with an education; Arabic, less likely; and Devanagari, a script used only in India. This last gave me pause: Holmes is not the only one to mistrust coincidences.

Now I spotted some letters that could be Cyrillic or Coptic, along with a pepperpot sprinkling of Greek lambdas and neat plus marks that stood unconnected with other letters—the sort of obvious abbreviations any undergraduate would employ, a quick way of writing "the" or "and." But what to make of the occasional squiggle? Were those runes, Pitman shorthand, or simply an uncharacteristically clumsy pen nib? Plus the occasional astrological symbol, mathematical mark, and three different characters that could be hieroglyphics.

When I had finished my breakfast—I'd been pleased, but not surprised, to find fresh bread, fruit, milk, and a newspaper left on the table for me at heaven only knows what hour—I armed myself with pencil, pad, and foot-cushions, and got to work.

I had read the introduction twice the day before, its French as clear, elegant, and old-fashioned as the handwriting itself, but this morning, with a fresh mind and a lovely day building outside, I read it again, translating it into a note-book as I went:

This book of images is by way of a memoir, and an explanation. Perhaps also a request for forgiveness, although I cannot see what I might have done with my life other than what I did. For any harm this has brought, I am sorry. Nonetheless, I swear it is nothing to the harm that would have been done, had I chosen another path.

I am well aware of the dangers inherent in committing my story to the page. I am certain that, despite all the years and all the distance, watch is still kept. At least, it was when this journal of images was written, and I imagine that, considering what is involved in the matter, it will take time for interest to fade. Memories are long when greed and resentments combine.

So, my compromise: I will set down a series of key events from my life, concealed in a manner few people will be able to unlock. Even then, this is not an autobiography, merely twelve detailed images with long gaps between them. I trust that "those that have eyes to see" might interpret them as a sequence.

If you, reading this, bear me and mine no ill will, then I can only wish you a pleasant hunt for meaning—even if you are not one of those for whom it was intended.

A woman's handwriting, definitely, strong, even, and controlled, with touches of decorative emphasis on the up-strokes. French in training rather than English or American—my brief thought that this was Irene Adler speaking, in a journal crafted for Holmes' eyes that had somehow ended up in the crate, died a quick death. There was a degree of formality that pointed to careful tutelage some long time ago, indicating that she was of the leisured classes, but one of the rare families that thought the education of women a good thing.

Her own native intelligence shone from every letter and word.

She used a good pen that left no stutters or gouges. The ink looked as black as the day it was set down, and the leather cover was supple apart from the ties, suggesting it might be contemporary with the later paintings it had been stored with—those of the 1890s—rather than those from a century earlier. The paper was thick, expensive, and very white. When I held the page up to the window, I could see a watermark, and made a mental note to sketch it when the sunlight was strong against the glass.

But what of the message itself? When a woman of intelligence, breeding, and education spoke of threat—the French word she used was *"menace,"* not *"risque"* or *"danger"*—I thought it as well to pay attention.

I suspected that it was a basic letter-substitution, since the characters were grouped in ways that resembled written words: the two lines at the top of the first page, for example, held a grouping of eight characters, a space, then five. Below it, a phrase (?) of four "words" was broken into two, seven, three, and eight "letters." And then the text itself began.

When Mme LaRue's key sounded in the kitchen door some five hours later, I was still struggling to prise any meaning at all out of the initial lines of text.

I laid down my pen gratefully, swearing to myself that, if it turned out this unknown woman of intelligence and education had been playing some elaborate game, I was going to hunt her down—hunt down her grandchildren, if need be—and give them a piece of my mind.

Holmes tends to regard meal-times as an irritant inflicted on him by landladies and other simple-minded folk, but in fact, an interruption can be useful when one has been pounding one's head against an obstinate piece of work. This particular interruption consisted not only of nutrition, in the form of Mme LaRue's fragrant casserole and all the accompanying dishes, but also of M. LaRue's report on the photographic reproductions of Damian's would-be burglar.

"I had him print twenty copies, as you said," he told me, laying a small stack on the table. "But I've left some of them there, in Délieux, with shopkeepers who have windows on the main streets, and did the same here in the village."

"Excellent, thank you." I took a copy from the stack, finding it as crisp and clear as I'd hoped. The photographer had added a telephone number at the bottom. "Whose number is this?"

"It rings here, or to our house if the family is away. *Madame la docteur* thought to have a line installed, in case someone needed her."

I'd seen the device on her desk, new-looking though without a rotary dial—no automated exchanges, here in the countryside. "I shall listen for it," I assured him.

"If you miss a call, *les Maries* will be happy to re-connect you. Our operators," he explained. "Both named Marie. They are there from first light to perhaps seven in the evening. If you try and they don't pick up, give them a few minutes to finish their coffee or return from the garden."

"One hopes there are not many medical emergencies at night."

"Oh, we bang on their door," he said, as if that was self-evident. "We all know where they live."

The LaRues left me to my meal, using their key to lock up behind them.

The food was as good as its odour had promised. I drank a glass of the wine M. LaRue had set on the table, and when I had finished, I transported the dishes into the kitchen without catastrophe and poured a cup from the pot of coffee Mme LaRue had made. I eyed the doorway, with its two steps down to the garden, and left the coffee to go back into Dr Henning's surgery.

As I thought, she had a collection of medical props leaning in the corner, including three lengths of canes. I traded my crutches for one, and gingerly hobbled back down the hallway. Having one hand free meant that I could carry my coffee into the garden, barely spilling any, and sit, letting the sun beat down on my upturned face.

An interruption, a new position, a change in surroundings. Even with eyes closed, my body knew it was not in an English garden. The odours were different, the sunlight against my eyelids more intense. The bells tracing the passage of time from the nearby church steeple sounded flat to ears accustomed to the full-throated swing of Anglican bells. The rise and fall of a half-heard conversation was not the rhythm of English; the creaks and hoofbeats from a passing cart were subtly foreign; a distant dog's monotonous bark seemed to have an accent.

Though the neighbour's cockerel sounded the same.

The woman's code used none of the standard cipher techniques—at least, not *only* one of the standards. Letter-substitution would not account for the odd scattering of symbols or marks. I'd tried ignoring everything that was not an actual letter, but what was left gave me no discernible patterns. Picking out the sequences based on the alphabets—Roman letters copied onto one page, Greek on another—had left me with sheets of unrelated letters. And if she'd been using a combination—say, letter-substitution with a random smatter of extraneous symbols—how were the eyes of her intended audience supposed to pick them out?

I could see no method to the lines on the page.

Perhaps it was in fact madness, despite the clear control in the handwriting. Or a complicated joke from a woman with far, far too much time on her hands. It reminded me of the codex snatched up by the collector Wilfrid Voynich from under the noses of the Vatican Library, just before the War. The codex was centuries old, and so many generations of scholars had flung themselves at it, only to bounce off its impenetrable pages of flowing and illuminated script, one could only reach the conclusion that the beautifully decorated text was in fact a cheerful and elaborate hoax.

Still, one had to begin with the assumption that it would make sense, once the clue to it appeared. That was the first thing Holmes had pointed out about ciphers, back in the early days when I was his apprentice: there is little reason to put something into code if no one can ever figure it out. The key is the key—something that the intended audience will either know or have to hand. This could be a pattern, a piece of knowledge, or the page of a book held in common, but whatever unlocks the cipher, it has to be something the desired reader has, while an unwanted intruder does not.

Where should I look for the clue that would open this code? It was more than possible I did not have it. And if I did not, how could we decipher what this woman had to tell us? I might put the puzzle aside for Holmes to mull over—after all, what urgency could there be in a piece of decades-old whimsy?—but . . .

But I hated to admit defeat. And I had absolutely nothing to occupy my time other than to listen to the march of bells. And I could not shake that niggling suspicion that to find Devanagari script in the same house that was invaded by a lascar, a happenstance that might be dimly possible in parts of England, was a coincidence beyond acceptance here in rural France.

Holmes might have some suggestions, but waiting for Holmes was rarely my preference. Without him, what forward step could I take? At home, in better days, I might have simply handed the thing over to Mycroft and waited for his department's cryptographers to pull it apart. Short of that, and less emotionally fraught, I could ask for help from its counterpart in Paris. What was France's Intelligence agency called? *Deuxième Bureau*, that was it—"Second Desk," which always brought to mind a row of schoolboys bent over their homework. But again, while Holmes was a *Chevalier* of the *Légion d'Honneur* and could no doubt summon the *Deuxième Bureau* to his beck and call, what luck would his wife have, doing the same? *Mais non, Madame,* please to return when your husband is here.

And inevitably, I thought, the solution would turn out to be something I should have seen, and I would be patted on the head in that aggravating way men have. Yes, one really ought to place the key in plain sight. Or at least, in the sight of "those that have eyes to see."

I frowned, and worked the journal out of the pocket where I'd thrust it, unwilling to let the thing out of my sight.

One ought to leave the key, perhaps, in the introductory words to a document, visible to anyone who can read French, but unseen by those lacking the *eyes to see.*

"This book of images," she began. And later, "twelve detailed images."

And the first line of the first coded page began with eight characters, then a space, followed by a group of five.

Première Image.

Even then, the woman didn't make it easy. Instead of a letter-to-letter substitution, where one could identify the most-often-used letters and plug in the E, the A, the T, the I, and so on, in this woman's mind, one letter could have half a dozen possible substitutes, employed in some apparently random sequence. And I would find, as I went along, that the diabolical creature kept adding to them, trading out a squiggle for a hieroglyphic, or a Greek pi for a P.

It was more like archaeological work than cryptology, painstakingly clearing each letter before moving on to the word, then to the phrase, and turning it into English from the French.

It took me until nearly midnight before I had unlocked the meaning of her first entry: *la fenêtre des sourcils.*

CHAPTER NINE

FIRST IMAGE

THE EYEBROW WINDOW

My earliest detailed memory is a picture of the moment my mother gave me away.

I can see her tears. Tears from *Maman* were always alarming, but these were terrifying, welling huge and silent to spill unchecked down her face. And while normally I would comfort her, wiping them away with my little hands and making loud kissing noises against her cheeks until she yielded to my silliness and her weeping turned to a laugh and then a long, shared embrace, this time I could not even go to her because the arms holding me belonged to the man I called Uncle Christian, and he was carrying me, one inexorable stride after another, down the rose-smelling path from the cottage to the carriage that waited in the lane.

As my point of view expanded, like a frame spreading from doorway to cottage front to the roses and trees around the front, my mother shrank, ever smaller.

I screamed, wailing and kicking, struggling to escape, but my childish muscles were no match for the arms that locked me in. *Maman* stayed on the step, her arms embracing emptiness, my village nurse, Solange, trying to console her—though that was *my* responsibility, a thing only *I* could do! My throat was ripped with frantic screams, and when I heard the creak that meant the garden gate was opening, I lunged over to clamp my sharp teeth into his ear.

His silk hat tumbled away, voices were raised, but the arms stayed tight around me as he bent to climb the carriage steps. The door closed, as startling as the harsh, hot wash of blood in my mouth.

My abductor sat, and I let go my jaws so I could turn and see . . .

The first image of my new life, framed by the carriage window: *Maman*, a doll-like figure at the end of the path, hair like gold, her dress the colour of the April sky. *Maman*, surrounded by roses that climbed over the door and around the eyebrow window, the same beloved pink roses that we had found tumbling wild in a vast nearby garden—I could smell the scent despite the distance. *Maman:* fists clenched, face shiny wet, muscles so tight I could feel them—and yet she did not leave the old stone step. She did not come after me.

Maman.

The whip cracked, the wheels creaked into motion, and the life I knew fell away.

Uncle Christian's arms continued to hold me as, one by one, the markers of home went past the window. The girl who brought eggs, still warm from the hens; the man with the missing foot; the dog with the white spot over one eye—all came up alongside, all glanced at the carriage, and all let us go by. No one reached out to stop us.

We had a house in the city, but this was home, the place I knew so well—village and fields, the small forest *Maman* and I walked in sometimes, a curve of the river that was quiet and safe and unlike the noisy, chaotic city streets. Here we could set off one way to see the hermitage on the mountain, or another if we wished to walk in the footsteps of an Empress. Or a third way—and with that idea, here came the church itself. Surely, I thought, surely the *sainte patronne* of Paris would reach out and keep me . . . but her chapel went by as well, silent and uncaring.

My sobs turned into hiccoughs, my breath began to catch in my throat.

When our wheels passed over the wide river that meant the city began, I accepted my fate. After a while, I let my head drop, to rest against his shoulder.

One arm stayed around me, lest I fling myself towards the door. The other hand, the one with the wide golden ring, came up to smooth my hair.

"I don't understand," I told him, my voice feeling ragged.

"I know." His head came down, so that he was speaking into my hair. "It is complicated, but I will do my best to help you make sense of it. In the meantime, sweet girl?" I pulled away so I could look into his dark face, seeing myself reflected in those brown eyes of his. He smiled. "I promise you, dear child, I will always help you. I will always protect you."

I believed him. Of all the uncles I had, Uncle Christian, the least seen and most mysterious, was the one who never treated me like a child. He never invented nice things to say about my drawings, never sent me away with Solange so he and *Maman* could talk.

I studied the state of his ear. His collar was brilliant red—*vermilion*, I thought—and although the cravat was too dark to show a stain, blood was creeping down the threads of his white shirt as well.

I turned away and nestled into his chest. The arm around me felt more natural, less like a binding. The city was growing up around us.

"Uncle Christian? I'm sorry I bit you."

"That's all right, my little warrior. Your mother would be proud of you."

As I sank into sleep, wrapped up in his warm and familiar odour, I somehow knew that Uncle Christian would no longer be a colourful visitor, but a permanent part of my life. Knew that I did not have a choice in the matter.

I was, after all, only four years old.

CHAPTER TEN

finished the first chapter, as I said, late at night. Mme LaRue had brought me a supper, and her husband had tried to tell me about the enquiry into Damian's intruder, but I had been so focused on extracting the meaning in just one more word, sentence, paragraph, that neither food nor information got through the barrier.

At last, I dropped my glasses onto the dining-room table and sank my aching eyes into my palms. It was silent, I noticed after a time. None of the usual birdsong, clucking hens, passing voices or engines. Not even a barking dog.

I raised my head and saw the blackness at the unshuttered window.

I stretched, hard, and hobbled down with the cane to the lavatory, then came back to pick over the congealed food on the plate. I washed it down with a small glass of wine and a large pot of tea, then soaked for a time in a hot bath, but when I was in bed at last, past one in the morning, the words I had translated kept sleep from taking me.

The child had been . . . what? Given to this uncle? Sold? Was the "uncle" even a blood relation, or was this the opening chapter of a harrowing tale of exploitation and scandal? I had to believe that a woman who could write with that confident and educated hand had overcome her travails, but still, a story that began with a small child being abandoned by her mother did not promise to hold much sweetness and light.

Earlier times and other places had different attitudes to the proper raising of children. In any event, I had been raised by un-usual parents—there was never any discussion of sending even my brother away to school, unlike most of the male undergraduates I'd met at Oxford, who had been sent away at what I thought a shock-ingly young age, to spend their formative years in a boarding school. Day and night, for ten months out of every year, entirely in the company of peers, servants, and schoolmasters. For some, it began when they were not much older than the child in the text.

But giving a son to a boarding school to be raised was surely a very different matter from handing over a small daughter to a man in a carriage.

I lay in the dark, thinking of Estelle Adler.

CHAPTER ELEVEN

HOLMES

Sherlock Holmes stood in the dark, alert for any motion from the street before him. He disliked being forced to choose between caution and speed, but urgency had a way of pushing other considerations aside. He'd been scrupulous—changing trains twice and train cars half a dozen times, watching the other passengers, paying close attention to any who might be mistaken for a lascar, or even a mixed-race Asian. However, his fellow travellers had been remarkably conventional, apart from a trio of Japanese students headed for Lyons and a shy Senegalese junior officer with a ticket to Marseilles. He'd caught a glimpse of a Parsi married couple, but they were still tucked away in their first-class compartment when he disembarked.

Once in Nîmes, he dove into the tangle of streets around the amphitheatre and doubled back before coming out near the Hôtel Petite Bohème. He now stood in a dark doorway down the street from the hotel, watching the wide boulevard for potential trouble.

The idea of a "lascar" coming after Damian was disturbing. They could be a rough lot—which was somewhat ironic, since in Holmes' experience, Indians as a rule tended to be more genial and law-

abiding than their English equivalents. But any man who signed
on to a long sea voyage, only to be treated like a slave, given a fraction of a white sailor's pay, and abandoned by the captain at any
convenient port—where local residents would consider him a
criminal until he was in fact driven to crime—well, the menacing
overtones of the word made him uneasy.

The lad might be an artist to his bones—impulsive, egotistical,
and often preoccupied—but he had survived the Front, and although he could be openly antagonistic towards his father and
generally touchy to the world, he had never struck Holmes as
flighty. If Damian chose the word "lascar," his eyes had perceived a
threat. And although M. LaRue's account sounded as if Damian
was trying to talk himself out of his alarm, blaming the episode on
a foolish friend or a wayward sneak-thief, Holmes would not.
Holmes would remain vigilant.

He knew, standing motionless despite his fatigue, his hunger,
and his craving for a cigarette, that any simple amateur would have
been left far behind. Even someone experienced in the surveillance
arts would have had to work to keep him in sight. But this was his
son, and his son's family. Until he knew if he was dealing with lascars or Shanghai cult members or simple burglars or, yes, even a
young blade with a badly misplaced sense of humour, Holmes
would take no chances.

Hence, the trip south that could have delivered him to Nîmes in
time for last night's dinner had instead brought him just as the
smell of the day's first loaves trickled from the bakeries.

When he was satisfied that the straight, wide, distinctly Roman
street before him held no covert watchers, he waited until a group
of men dressed in hotel uniforms came off the tram, then followed
them down the alleyway and through the kitchen door of the Petite Bohème, to present himself at Damian's second-floor suite
along with the arrival of morning tea.

Damian looked startled by his father's abrupt appearance.

Dr Henning, wearing a dressing gown, walked in from what was clearly a bedroom. She stopped dead, turned pink, and backed up, shutting the door behind her. The child who'd been standing with her nose against the window turned, and hesitated. An object tucked into her left arm might possibly have been a doll.

Damian waited until the servers had left, then said, "Hullo, Father. I didn't expect you here this soon." He came forward and offered his hand.

"It seemed expedient," Holmes said, and shook it.

"I'm glad LaRue told you where we were. I wasn't sure he would, that intruder spooked him more than a little. Estelle, you remember your *grand-père?*"

"Good morning, Grandpapa," she said in careful English, coming forward to extend her hand.

"*Bonjour, Mlle Adler,*" Holmes replied, bowing over her fingers.

"This is Kiki," she told him, holding out the object for him to take.

It was, as he had suspected, a form of cloth doll. It was mostly head, with wide-spaced eyes that quirked up at the corners, their lids painted green. Its nose was a mother-of-pearl button, its mouth was a tiny red flower, its hair a bowl of black silk yarn. It had arms and legs, disproportionate and not quite matching, but from the neck down it was swathed in an emerald-coloured silk garment akin to a kimono.

"A group project," Damian explained. "Foujita made the sketch—that's meant to be Alice Prin, also known as Kiki de Montparnasse. Sonia Delaunay transferred the drawing onto fabric, Sara Murphy sewed it, Mistinguett donated some stockings for the stuffing, and the dress is by Coco Chanel. Coco I had to pay," he noted, "although the silk is a remnant from one of Aileen's dresses. The others did it for nothing because Estelle is just so charming."

Holmes nodded solemnly at this list of notables from the Paris art scene, and handed the doll back to its child.

"Tea?" Damian asked. "Or shall I ring down for coffee? We'll go down for breakfast shortly—Estelle compared four different places yesterday, in search of the best *pain au chocolat,* only to declare the hotel's café the winner. Theirs are as large as her head."

"You've been—" Holmes caught himself: *Don't begin with criticism.* And the lad was clearly making an effort to be amiable. Instead, he took off his hat and dropped it and his coat over the back of a chair. "I see you've felt free to come and go, from the hotel."

"Why on earth not? We're a long way from Ste Chapelle."

"Of course. Tea will be fine, thank you."

"I don't have to ask if you've been up all night, I can see you have."

"How can you tell, Papa?" a small voice demanded.

"Just how he looks."

"But how does he look?"

"Persistent, isn't she?" Damian commented. The tea had been set up on a small table with four chairs, immediately beside a window. Damian cleared away some pages of the child's colouring, slid a new-looking sketchbook into his pocket, and poured out a cup of tea, laying it in front of a chair. "Here, sit."

Holmes considered the view. The curtains were completely drawn back. The morning sun poured over the table, setting the tea-cups and silver aglow, exposing them all to the dozens of windows in the office building across the street. However: if the man with the knife had not attacked Damian, then perhaps murder was not the goal—or not the only goal. Therefore, he did not need to concern himself with snipers, and so he merely sat down and took a welcome swallow of the hot beverage. He then lowered his head to meet the child's intent gaze. "How do you think your father can tell I've been up all night?"

Estelle considered this for a moment, her grey eyes travelling along his shoes, his trousers and shirt collar, his face. "There's wrinkles. And dirt on your cuffs. And you're stubby."

"Stub—oh, you mean I have stubble. You're right, I haven't shaved since yesterday. Clever eyes."

The bedroom door opened and Dr Henning came out, dressed now and chin raised, daring him to take any notice of that moment of uncharacteristic embarrassment. He'd always liked Aileen Henning, from the moment she realised that she was being abducted and reacted not with fear, but with fury. And then, when faced with a patient whose life needed saving, she'd got quietly to work.

She had changed since he'd last seen her. In the Scottish fishing village, she had been a deliberately frumpy lady doctor, attempting to win over the locals with her dull clothing and her hair bound into a knot. The knot was now a glossy red bob, her nails wore polish, and she'd found a seamstress who knew how to make the most of her diminutive figure and colouring. He could well imagine her in emerald-coloured silk.

He rose to greet her. She returned the greeting and took the empty chair, accepting the tea Damian held out to her, but not quite meeting the eyes of her soon-to-be father-in-law.

Holmes sat again, taking care to conceal any trace of amusement. They were two adults, who in any event intended to marry. Why should the current lack of a document create any awkwardness in the situation?

"You didn't bring Mary?" she asked.

"Russell is currently at your house with her foot propped on a stool. She wrenched her ankle getting off the train in Germany, painful but nothing serious."

The medical person demanded specifics, but having given a few, Holmes shook his head. "I assure you that her chagrin at a moment's clumsiness is causing her more pain than the actual injury."

"Well, Mme LaRue will take good care of her. Did they tell you about the man who came through our window?"

"They did. It is . . . concerning."

"It's the sort of nonsense one expects in Paris," Damian complained. "Who'd have imagined *Les Apaches* would find their way into the countryside? I'll need to have Gervais strengthen the latches on the shutters."

Holmes opened his mouth to object, then glanced at the small figure listening with interest and the red-headed woman listening with, he thought, a degree of anxiety. So, instead, he blandly lifted his tea-cup and drank, and raised no objection when the doctor, Estelle, and the child's collaborative Jazz-Age doll proposed to set off for the child's morning *pain au chocolat*. They would be safe enough inside the hotel, and it was urgent that he speak with Damian.

Damian, with a glance at his father, told the others that he'd join them shortly.

The moment the door clicked shut, Holmes abandoned his cup. "You cannot believe your intruder came from some common Parisian gang."

"Can't I?" The retort was automatic, and as instantly retracted. "Well, no, I suppose you're right—although even small villages like Ste Chapelle aren't as innocent as when I was growing up there."

"The LaRues said you thought it was a lascar. I took that to mean someone who appeared generally Indian, rather than specifically a sailor."

"To be honest, I'm not sure what brought that word to mind," Damian admitted. "Other than the fellow looked something like the sailors I'd see on British ships around Shanghai."

"But not from Shanghai himself?"

"Oh no, nothing like. Dark eyes and hair, yes, but not at all the same shape or skin colour. Or clothes—he was wearing those loose trousers and long shirts they wear in India. No turban, though, which the sailors usually have. I made a drawing of him—did they show you?"

Il a fait un dessin, Mme LaRue had said. Holmes kicked himself over his failure to follow that up.

But if the man—if all three men—were indeed from India, wouldn't it lessen the chances that the Children of Lights were behind this? The majority of Thomas Brothers' followers were quiet, middle-class English women. Not at all the sort to carry out their own revenge. "No, I did not see it. I needed to leave the house fairly rapidly, if I wanted to catch the Express." Although in the end, there had been little point in making haste.

"Well, I can do you another if you want—although I'm not sure how accurate a likeness I caught. Coming face to face with a man in the middle of the night, I may have been more concerned with his presence than with the details of his facial structure." He gave his father a crooked smile, and pulled out a silver cigarette case and decorative lighter. "Scared the hell out of me, to be honest. The idea that he could get into the house where Estelle and Aileen were sleeping."

"Quite understandable," Holmes replied, thinking, *Good, I'm glad you were frightened.*

"But it's got to be something ordinary. Some fool thinking that because I'm an artist and foreign, I have a house full of treasure. We'll fix the shutters. I'm beginning to be sorry I raised a fuss."

"I do not think you should disregard the threat."

"I'm not disregarding any threat. I'm here in Nîmes, aren't I? Although, I do have to wonder—the man ran like a rabbit the instant I turned on the lights. I seemed to be the one who frightened him."

"Yes," Holmes mused. "That was interesting, was it not?"

"Oh, for God's sake," Damian protested, "you're not going to make this into one of your damned enigmas, are you? There's no mystery here. Some poor Indian chap came looking for money in a drawer, mystery over."

"If that is the case, why did you leave Ste Chapelle?"

"I suppose we panicked. Everything that happened last year came rushing back. Aileen was frightened, Estelle went quiet, so I thought I'd take them to Antibes for a while. They can have a nice holiday on the beach—the Murphys have a house there, you met them, I think? I'll stay a few days then go home and get back to work. Behind stronger latches."

The boy's as obstinate as his mother, Holmes thought.

Damian frowned. "What does that expression mean?"

Holmes let his face go smooth. *And nearly as perceptive.* "I was merely thinking that you occasionally remind me of your mother." The American accent in the young man's English. His automatic rebellion against anything that resembled a command. The keen eyes and quick wit. He even had Irene's crooked smile, though in his case half-hidden by the beard.

Damian seemed to welcome the distraction. "The house reminds me of her, all the time," he confessed. "Even with all the changes Aileen's making, I keep expecting to see Mamá come through the kitchen door and scold me for tracking paint." Then the moment of accord shifted. "But you never knew that house, did you?"

"I only saw it from the outside," Holmes replied. "Six years ago." His brief alliance with Irene Adler had taken place less than thirty miles from here, during his three years' absence from Baker Street. Unexpected, eye-opening, life-changing. Not that he hadn't still intended to return to London—after all, Professor Moriarty had awaited his attentions—but the thought had begun to grow, as the days with Irene stretched to weeks, that his life there need not be solitary . . .

And then, as abruptly as it began, she'd sent him away, back to London. When he'd found out about Damian, just six years ago, Holmes had wondered if she'd sent him off before she learned she was pregnant, or because of it. If, on the day of their parting, she had known that she would not be returning to America, as she claimed, but buying a house in Ste Chapelle where she could raise her son. Their son.

Even now, he was not sure if he was grateful, or angry. Both, no doubt. Emotion could be so distracting.

"You cannot go back," he told Damian now. "Not until we have resolved the threat."

That obstinate gleam in the eyes was back. "Father, I have work to do. I've promised six new paintings by the first of the month."

"All the better to solve the problem so you can paint without interference."

"Why are you so convinced that this was anything other than a chance break-in? I know I was ... alarmed, at first. I even thought for a minute that it might be those mad followers of Thomas Brothers, out to make me pay. But once I stopped to think about it, I realised how absurd that was."

"Why?"

"What do you mean? *I* didn't kill Brothers. I barely knew the man. In any event, I was half-dead myself when he died, and not even in England."

"Facts do not matter when blame is being handed out. He died, you did not, and you were visibly connected to his final days."

"Nonsense. And anyway, the intruder was neither Chinese nor English. And he certainly didn't look anything like one of the lunatic's followers."

"What about the two foreigners who came searching for you? M. LaRue said they knew the name 'Vernet.'"

"The men in Délieux? You may not understand, dear Father, how widely known your son is in Jazz-Age Paris. We have our own versions of the *Daily Mirror* here, and there are always reporters sniffing around for a juicy scandal. If they broke the story that Damian Adler is a descendant of the Vernet family, the bonuses would keep them for the rest of the year."

"You are comfortable with the idea of coincidence?" Holmes asked sharply. "That two Indian journalists happen to come the same week an Indian breaks into your house?"

"Why would it be coincidence? They could have paid some ruffian to go through my papers, looking for dirt. But whether it's coincidence or not, the real question is, am I willing to overturn our lives again because one man breaking in and two others asking about me *might* be some indication of a threat? If I do that, where do I stop? Hire bodyguards? Leave the country? Yes, terrible things happened a year ago. 'Stella's nightmares have only begun to fade. Hell, my own nightmares still come around. But just because those things happened doesn't mean more horrible things are waiting out there for us. Unless," he said with great deliberation, "*you* have some clear cause for me to change my mind and turn my family's life upside-down, again."

Holmes dropped his head into his hands. He'd hoped to gain Damian's cooperation without inflicting his own dread on the lad—and handing him another brick for the wall that stood between them. But there seemed to be no avoiding the matter.

He sat back. "You ask if I have reason to believe those men were sent by the Children of Lights? As of yet, I do not. Do I feel that ignoring the threat invites further violence against you? It is true that the intruder could easily have used that machete on you instead of dropping it to the ground and taking to his heels. But Damian, what if he was not after you? What if his real weapon was a vial of chloroform, and his target was . . . his goal was a small, easily carried child? A child related by blood not only to a famous detective, but to his brother, a man who wields enormous power in the British government?"

The colour drained from Damian's face—then it flooded back in. "Jesus. Are you saying that this whole thing could be because of *you?* That no sooner do I finally—*finally*—create a decent life here than it all goes to—"

"Damian," Holmes said sharply, "stop. I need you to think. If someone identified you as a means of reaching either Mycroft or me, that means they know who we are to you. Who have you told?"

"What about Uncle Mycroft?" Damian demanded.

Holmes reviewed the past moments of conversation and came up with no matches. "Sorry?"

"Uncle Mycroft? Could that have been one of his men?"

"Why would Mycroft send a lascar to break into your house?"

"Why would he do anything? Is he watching us?"

"Damian, I—"

"I know he used to check on us, when Mother was alive. And last year when I was in England, I told him not to do it anymore, but sometimes, when I see strangers in the village, I wonder."

"If your uncle is sending agents to watch you, he certainly doesn't report to me."

"Aileen says I'm imagining things. I probably am." Damian made an effort to bring himself under control. "Who did I tell— about you, specifically? I haven't given your name to anyone but the LaRues, and that only because you were coming to stay and I'd have felt idiotic using one of your pseudonyms the entire time you were here. But I made it clear that they mustn't let anyone know. And I refuse to believe that either of them would do a thing to endanger Aileen or Estelle."

"When did you tell them?"

"Just a few days ago. Saturday or Sunday."

"Which was it?"

"I don't know, I've been busy. Sunday, maybe?"

That would be fast work, Holmes reflected, *to arrange a burglary in a handful of hours.* "Could you have accidentally said something to friends? Perhaps to the people at the *Institut?*"

"Only about the Vernets." Damian stubbed out the cigarette in an ash-tray, frowning in thought. "But if I haven't told anyone, and Aileen hasn't—you can be sure she hasn't—then this probably has nothing to do with you or Uncle Mycroft. And nobody was looking to use 'Stella to blackmail you two. Which would be a huge relief, but still brings us back to the question of who the hell was it?"

Holmes fixed the young man with a hard look. "I. Do. Not. Know. And I cannot know because I am here, in the south of France, helping to ensure your family's safety. Not in Ste Chapelle, where I should be, gathering the data needed for a solution."

His response might have triggered another sharp reply, had it not been for the lingering image of a lascar bundling little Estelle out of the house.

"I ... Yes, I see. I still think you're exaggerating matters, but you're right, we shouldn't risk it. We can leave Aileen and Estelle here and I'll come with you."

"That would be—" Holmes stopped to choose more discreet words. "Whatever those men are after, we do not yet know their resources or their intent. We must assume that they will not hesitate to use a threat to your family to get it. We do need to take Dr Henning and the child to a safe place. Once there, you yourself need to keep them safe. And we cannot use an hotel where you arrived openly, and where you continue to come and go with no attempt at concealment."

Damian got up to make a circuit of the room, ending up at the window. Holmes stifled a protest—if anyone was watching, they already knew where Damian was. After a minute, he opened his own cigarette case, using Damian's lighter to get the cigarette going.

"I have friends in Toulon, or Antibes," Damian said at last.

"The Riviera is the first place someone would look for an artist, and your friends would talk to their friends. You need to go west, not east, and inland. In the vicinity of a medium-sized town, where strangers are unremarkable."

"It sounds as if you have a place in mind."

"I do."

"I have to work. The shows I have coming up are important. As it is, we ran off in such a panic that I left my sketchbooks behind. I need them."

"You have a sketchbook."

"It's not the paper I want, it's the ideas."

"I'll have them sent to you. And yes, there will be space to set up your easel and paints."

"When do you want to go?"

"Immediately. As immediately as we can get your things together."

"You're coming with us?"

"You will need me to get you there unobserved."

"All right, I'll go tell my ladies. You'll probably want a bath, and a shave. Just do me a favour? In front of Aileen and Estelle, can we call this man a burglar? I don't want 'Stella to start thinking her mother's killer is back."

"So long as Dr Henning is aware that there could be danger."

"Oh, she knows. She definitely knows."

Holmes thought that even the young female Adler was plenty bright enough to see through an attempt at reassurance, but he nodded. "I shall take care what I say around the child. However, there is one thing."

"Oh God, what now?"

"One can do little about Estelle's distinctiveness, but in combination with Dr Henning, here in France, they make for an eye-catching pair. Aileen will need to dye her hair."

"Oh, she won't be happy about that."

"Yes. That is why I shall let you break the news."

CHAPTER TWELVE

HOLMES

Removing a woman, a child, and an artist from their hotel unseen by others was not a simple operation. The first hitch was when Holmes discovered the quantity of their luggage. Most of it belonging not to the woman, or even the child, but to Damian.

"I told you I intended to work," the artist protested.

"I did not anticipate your having brought the entire studio with you."

"I suppose I could park some of it here."

And have to come back for it? Holmes thought. "No, I will arrange alternative transport."

"While you are doing that," the doctor said, "I shall go and buy myself a wig."

Holmes raised his eyebrow at her. "When one wishes to leave a place unnoticed, it is generally best not to advertise the fact beforehand."

"I see. Then I shall have to send one of the maids out to purchase one."

Would dye not be simpler? "You have two hours."

He then looked at the child, but she at least had no objections to his plans. Or none that she voiced.

In the end, merely packing their bags took two hours. The delay in finding suitable transportation ate up three more, followed by the lunch that Aileen insisted they take, then another half hour before the hotel maid came back with a suitable wig.

Holmes spent much of the time standing behind the curtains, looking at the office building across the street. He was particularly interested in those windows with half-drawn curtains. As the day wore on and the sun hit the building, three of them shut completely, while those in a room on the second floor closed a few inches. Slightly later, they did so again. At neither time did Holmes glimpse the person in the room, either with his bare gaze or using the small monocular he had brought.

"What is that, *Grand-père*?" said a voice from his hip.

He immediately stepped away from the window so the child would follow and not be standing in full view, gazing up in a manner that made his own presence all too obvious.

"It's called a monocular. It helps me see things that are far away. Here, come sit in this chair and use it to look across the room."

She climbed up into the armchair, settling Kiki beside her and reaching for the slim brass tube. He helped her position it, first shifting it from where she'd rested it on the bridge of her nose and onto her right eye, then obscuring her left eye with his hand in lieu of the squint that her young muscles apparently had yet to master. He used his other hand to keep the device from swinging all across the room.

He wished that the lorry-load of equipment Damian had brought included a pair of strong binoculars. He wished his companions might assemble themselves more rapidly. He wished for a room without small and inquisitive children. More than anything, he wished he had Russell here.

However, the sight of the brilliant green rag-doll squashed against the side of the chair gave him an idea.

"Estelle, do you carry your doll wherever you go?"

"She likes to see everything I do." At this reminder, the child removed the viewer from her eye and placed it against Kiki's green-painted one.

He considered the problem. How does one manipulate a clever child? Does one employ the techniques one would use on a slow adult? Or was intelligence a universal, no matter the age and experience?

"There must be some places you can't take, er, Kiki," he said.

"Some. But I always tell her about them after."

"Do you."

"Yes." She looked up at him, and confided, "Dolls don't really talk, you know."

"But you talk to her anyway."

She nodded, and raised the glass to the bridge of her nose again, then remembered and planted it over one eye.

"Do you ever think," he asked, "that Kiki might like to have an adventure of her own, that she could then tell you about?"

It was well into the afternoon when a delivery lorry pulled into the alley behind the hotel, one of a regular stream that kept the establishment well stocked with onions, beefsteaks, fresh flowers, and cleaning supplies. This one was slightly out of the ordinary, in that it seemed to be taking on goods rather than leaving them, but one would have had to stand directly in the entrance of the alleyway to see that.

In twenty minutes, the lorry's back doors slammed shut. A few minutes after that, two figures, remarkably slight for deliverymen but wearing the right clothing, came out of the kitchen door and climbed into the front. The smaller figure, in the passenger seat, seemed to disappear into the floor well. The other tugged down the brim of a large cap over a head of unruly black hair and started the engine, clashing the gears once or twice as they got under way.

While this was going on at the back of the hotel, upstairs in the Adlers' front-facing room, a doll sat in a window, meditating on the busy street below. Behind the doll, the room's curtains were drawn, as they were every afternoon while young Estelle had a nap. Usually, the doll napped with her, but today it seemed to have been overlooked.

Shortly after the curtains went shut, the distinctive tall, thin, bearded figure of Damian Adler appeared at the entrance of the hotel. He was hatless, though dressed in a summer suit and well-shined shoes, and he carried an ancient Gladstone bag. He chatted with the doorman for a few minutes, then set off south, in the direction of the railway station.

Ninety seconds later, about the time it would take to run headlong down two sets of stairs, a man in an ordinary summer suit and hat burst out of the office building across from the hotel. His pace slowed to a brisk walk as he turned in the direction of the train station, but as he did so, the sun touched very briefly under the brim of his hat.

Long enough for Sherlock Holmes, standing with the monocular pressed against the hotel's ground-floor window, to see the crescent moon scar on the man's face. A precise match for the drawing of the lascar Damian had made for him.

Holmes took his time going upstairs to the now-empty room— empty but for Kiki, her button nose still pressed against the window-glass. It had taken all his considerable negotiating skills before Estelle agreed to let the thing have an adventure of its own. He dutifully retrieved the beloved object, but rather than adding it to the valise, he tucked it into the back of his belt, then followed after his son.

Damian was waiting among the arches of the station. Holmes saw no sign of the man with the scar; but then, he had not expected to. The man had skills that were more than adequate for the purpose of trailing Damian Adler. Whether his skills would match those of Damian's father remained to be seen.

"Did you see anyone?" Damian demanded.

"I saw your lascar, although in an ordinary suit. Do not look around for him," he ordered.

"Christ. I didn't think . . . Dear God. You're sure?"

"Damian, a man came out of the building across the way and half ran down the street in your wake. He had brown skin and the same scar as the man you saw in your house Sunday night."

"I was hoping it was all my imagination. How the *hell* did they find us?" Damian was having to work not to look around in search of the figure. Holmes touched his elbow to guide him towards the station.

"The how does not matter at the moment. First, we need to lose him."

"You're sure we can?"

"I trust my skills. So should you."

"I do. Just, let's not tell Aileen. She doesn't need to know—or not yet."

"Agreed."

"You didn't forget 'Stella's doll?"

"Damian."

"Sorry, yes."

"All right. You know what to do."

Inside the doors, the two men separated, Damian heading towards the WC while Holmes joined the queue at the ticket office. There he bought two return first-class tickets to Lyons, making no attempt to hide what he was doing. He carried the tickets over to the board displaying the track information, compared the two, then set off in the direction of his train.

The Lyons train was already sitting at the station, gently steaming. He boarded, tucking his valise into the overhead rack.

Passengers climbed on and found their seats. Two minutes before the train was scheduled to leave, Holmes stood, leaving his hat and valise behind, to make his way to the end of the car. Unlike the WCs in the other cars, those in first class were unlocked, despite the train being still in the station—first-class passengers were trusted not to pull the handle until the train was leaving town. He disappeared, the whistle blew, the outer doors shut. In moments, the train jerked into motion. As it moved, those near the windows could see a bent-over figure in an attendant's coat and hat, walking briskly back to the station.

"Well?" Damian demanded. He had been drawing in the sketch-book, his habit whenever he sat and looked at the world, but he now flipped it shut and shoved it into a pocket.

Holmes held his reply until the waiter, who had seen him come in, bustled through the crowded tables with a box. Holmes had left it here early that morning. He thanked the man with a bank note, and asked for another glass to go with Damian's bottle of wine. He pulled open the top of the box, which had been used to ship chipolata onions to the kitchens of the Petite Bohème, and found the contents just as he'd left them: clean shirts, a slim book on Wagner's politics, his shaving kit—and, he was relieved to see, the revolver. He then reached inside the back of his jacket to work the doll out of his belt, straightening the green dress as he laid her atop the shirts and closed the lid.

When he sat, he looked considerably less bulky than when he'd left the hotel.

"It went as planned," he answered.

Damian began to object, but was interrupted by the return of the waiter with Holmes' glass.

This café was not a place of polished brass and spotless crystal. No one here objected to Damian's rather exaggerated coat, tattered hat, and scuffed boots, which he had donned in the station restrooms, leaving his other clothes behind with the Gladstone bag. Holmes' suit was more dignified, though somewhat rumpled from having spent the afternoon compressed by two other layers of clothing: Damian's oldest suit-jacket on the outside, then the attendant's coat beneath it. Holmes, too, was currently hatless. And feeling somewhat exposed because of it.

Glass delivered, wine poured, and further requests not forthcoming, the server left.

"*And?*" Damian asked impatiently.

"The man with the scar got onto the train, two cars behind me. He may have seen the 'attendant' go by, but not in time to get off the train and follow."

For the first time in hours, Damian relaxed. He tossed back a hefty swallow of wine. "God. I haven't felt like that since you and I were running away from the madman last year. Can we not do that again, please?" Another swig, a refill of the glass, then a lesser swallow before he let out the tension in a laugh. "Though I am sorry Estelle couldn't have watched that little dance at the railway station. She adored your game of dressing up as a delivery boy. We may never get her out of that cloth cap."

Holmes smiled and ventured a sip of the rather acidic red wine. When he looked up, he found Damian studying him, head tipped to one side.

"I keep getting the impression that this is all reminding you of something."

The lad looks as if he wouldn't notice an elephant in front of him, thought Holmes, *and yet he manages to catch a tiny quirk of the lips.*

"Oddly enough," he said, "you are correct. I was thinking about Estelle in disguise. When I was a child, my mother used to have us practice for amateur dramatics, dressing Mycroft and me in clothing from the servants' children and taking us into the nearby town. She'd reward us if we managed to fool the shopkeepers. I was much better at it than Mycroft."

"I wish I'd known her. I never had a grandmother. Mother had loads of friends she would borrow for me, all my honorary aunts and grandmothers—you met Mme Longchamps that day you came to the gaol. She was one of the more respectable ones. Some of them were madly idiosyncratic, if not simply mad, which was great fun for a child. So, tell me about her, my real one."

"No." Holmes felt the tightness that had taken hold of him, and moved to lessen his body's betrayal. "That is to say, I will, but it is a complicated story. This is not the time."

Damian eyed him, then shook his head. He rose and fished some coins from his pocket, laying them on the table. "When we get wherever you're taking us, then. Shall we go?"

Holmes and Damian reached Montpellier at dusk, and went looking for the delivery lorry. Holmes had told Dr Henning to park in a side-street to the north of the Place de la Comédie. He'd been quite specific. When they rounded the corner and the lorry was not there, he felt a twinge of anxiety. *Where is Russell when I need her?* But two streets farther on, he spotted the familiar shape, parked with its tyres up on the pavement.

Aileen was in the passenger seat with a drowsing Estelle on her lap. Her cheap black wig was slightly askew, and her expression was more than a little desperate. She must have moved slightly when she saw them appear, because Estelle shot upright, then bounced up to lean out of the window.

"Hello, Papa! We drove so well! I helped Mama Aileen watch for signs. Hello, *Grand-père,* do you like my cap? I look like a working man, don't I?"

"It's very handsome," Holmes replied dutifully. "Shall we—"

"Do you have Kiki?"

"I do. Damian, would you—"

"Where is she? Papa, I'm *so* hungry! Mamá said we would eat dinner when you came, but you've been *forever.* My tummy is going to starve!"

"Well, we can't have that," Damian said, and stood upright to look at the street around them. It was quite lacking in bistros and cafés.

"Not here," Holmes snapped.

Damian turned to fix him with a hard look. "Estelle is hungry. And we've all been very patient with your demands. We need to eat."

"Very well. But not here. Away from the centre of town."

"Oh, for Christ—"

"No, that's fine." It was Aileen. "But not too far, we're all hungry and need a civilised meal before we get back into this machine. And," she added, with a doggedness that explained her look of desperation, "a toilet."

"Absolutely," Damian agreed. "Estelle and I will ride in the back. And here, 'Stella *ma fille,* let's get Kiki."

When packing the lorry, Holmes had taken care to put the softer valises on the top, just behind the front seats. Damian climbed up into this padded area, Estelle scrambled to join him, and Holmes handed them the chipolata box, then slid behind the wheel.

Estelle's chatter filled the silence, a recounting of her day's adventures to father and doll. Damian responded, Aileen added comments, the doll said nothing, and Holmes was relieved to find the brasserie that he'd remembered from all those years ago, looking exactly the same.

Aileen grabbed Estelle's hand and hurried inside. Damian followed, with Holmes after—once he felt certain that their progress had gone unremarked by stray Parisian artists or Indian gentlemen with facial scars. It might be a simple matter to shake off a follower on foot in London, but it was quite another to do so in a half-remembered city when any pursuing figures were rendered anonymous by night-fall.

It was late enough that the brasserie was half-empty, though fortunately the kitchen was happy to serve another party. Holmes chose a table well back from the windows and claimed a chair facing the door. Estelle came skipping back, followed by a tidy and less tense-looking Aileen.

"Thank you," she said. "My, something here smells delicious."

Holmes was dimly aware that the food set before him was good, but his attention was not on his plate. His preoccupation was with the door, the windows, and the street beyond. Eventually, he realised that his companions were silent, and looked around to find their plates empty. "Shall we go?"

There was no general response and movement towards the door.

This time it was Aileen who took on the obstinate look. She straightened the ill-fitting wig for the seventh time since they had come in, and sat back into her chair. "Where are you taking us, and why?"

So much for keeping secrets from Aileen, Holmes thought.

He shot a glance at Damian, willing him to step in, but his son clearly wanted no part of that. He, too, sat back, abandoning his father to Aileen's attentions.

Drat the lad, Holmes thought. In the normal course of events, Aileen Henning was about as easy-going as a bulldog, and things at present were far from normal—for her, he reflected. Though this would have been a fairly typical day for him and Russell. Then he noticed her arm, which was stretched across the table-cloth so that her fingers could touch the child's arm. His eyes went to little Estelle, and his thoughts.

Miss Estelle Adler had experienced more distress in her four years than most adults accumulated in a lifetime. Pulled from her home, her mother murdered, swept up and plane-crashed and stashed with strangers while her father was on the run. Damian had kept the details from her, but no small human with eyes that clear could be deceived for long. And one did not need to have experience with the rearing of children to know that if he got this wrong, Estelle's parent would be slow to forgive.

The question had come from Aileen, but he directed his explanation at the child.

"You know a man broke into your house the other night." Estelle nodded. The doll on her lap merely listened. "We don't yet know why he did that or what he was after." The small person nodded again. "Until we do know, none of us feel at ease with the idea of you three moving back into the house."

"That is why we packed our bags and got onto the train."

"Correct. However, someone needs to figure out who that was and what it means. And that kind of . . . figuring out is what I do. What I'm good at."

"And Mary."

He smiled. Yes, this child did understand a great deal of what was going on around her. "That, too, is correct. But I—she and I— cannot go and find out what is going on if we are trying to watch over you three. We need to make certain you're quite safe—from being disturbed—before we can . . ." *Start overturning a wide swath of France.* ". . . investigate. If you're at home, we will need guards to keep you . . . to keep strangers from bothering you. It would be much easier if you were simply to stay away from home. For a short time. Until we're sure you won't be, er, disturbed." He lifted his eyes to Aileen, making sure she heard the meaning behind his modu- lated choice of words: *We need to make certain you're quite safe from being murdered in your beds. We need to keep strangers from climbing in your windows with a machete.*

He was aware that the child nodded her acceptance of his logic and turned to her father with some question. But it was not the child he'd been talking to. He waited. Aileen looked fondly down at the little girl, running an affectionate finger through the glossy hair. She then lifted her head and transferred the affectionate smile onto Holmes. "You're telling us that we are a distraction."

It was boorish to reveal to others that you found their presence an interference, but this was not the first time he had done so. And, he feared, not the last.

"I would not have been so blunt, but yes."

"We are grit in a sensitive instrument."

"Sorry?" he asked. When she did not reply, but only let her smile deepen, he returned his attention, ostensibly at least, to the child. "The place I intend to take you is quite pleasant. And I shouldn't think you'll need to be there too many days.

"Now," he said, placing his hands on the table. "May we go?"

CHAPTER THIRTEEN

HOLMES

Dawn found them passing through autumn-ripe fields on roads that, as the heat grew, were sure to raise a column of dust. Cresting the higher spots gave the odd glimpse of pointed towers above the walls of a Medieval hilltop fortress city. Holmes felt eyes on him, and glanced sideways at a solemn, grey-eyed gaze. He nodded at the child, who had moved up from the lumpy bags in back to the welcoming arms in front at some point in the wee hours. She peered back to where Damian was snoring. Satisfied, she snuggled against Dr Henning and alternated between watching Holmes drive and following their surroundings as they skirted the town's edge into an area of fields and woodlands.

At last, he steered in through a gate and up a drive to a cluster of buildings, something between a hamlet and a large family's farm. Damian snorted awake, the doctor stretched hard with a squeak of enquiry, and Estelle sat upright to push her nose against the glass.

Holmes brought the lorry to a halt before the main farmhouse, pulled on the brake, and shut off the motor. He ached all over.

Damian cleared his throat. "What is this place?"

"Think of it as a holiday home for the deserving."

"It looks like a farm."

"It is that as well. One occasionally needs a bolt-hole outside of London, for others if not for oneself. And because some of the temporary residents are individuals who require a change of scenery to, shall we say, settle their nerves, the neighbours are well accustomed to strangers coming and going."

"You own this?"

"I have an interest in it. I cabled ahead to ask them to have one of the cottages ready for you."

"Where are we?" the doctor asked.

"Slightly over a mile from the fortified walls of Carcassonne. And yes, Damian, there is a space for you in which to paint. One thing, before we get out." He waited until Estelle had turned to look at him. "Some of those who stay here are brave men who were badly injured fighting for their country. We try not to stare at them. And if we have questions about how they look or act, we wait until they are out of hearing before asking."

"Like *Oncle* Pierre," she said.

"That's right," Damian said, adding to Holmes, "Mme LaRue's brother, who lives in the back. You've brought us to an asylum?"

"Call it a refuge. Ah, and here is Madame."

Madame was a short, muscular woman of sixty, with steel-rimmed glasses and close-cropped grey curls. She'd been a nun, then a front-line nurse during the War, and now oversaw this combination holiday home and psychiatric ward for soldiers whose injuries were only in part physical. Holmes had first met her during a case in the spring of 1914, then again a few years later on a more personal investigation.

He got out, trying to conceal the stiffness of his joints, and opened the door for Damian to clamber out.

Hair awry, clothing rumpled, shoes in the lorry somewhere, Damian helped his daughter climb down from the lorry, then straightened to look around him—and his face changed.

"Sister *Aubert?*"

"None other. My dear *Capitaine* Adler, it gives me joy to see you well."

"Good Lord. What on earth are you doing here? The last time I saw you, I was in gaol."

"I go where I am needed, and currently where I am needed is here. Which brings the added pleasure of a climate that makes my bones happy and the occasional chance at seeing new faces. And here is your daughter? Ah, what a beauty. Estelle, that is your name, child, *n'est ce pas?*"

"*Oui,* Madame."

"And the doctor-wife. I am pleased to make your acquaintance. Call me Marie, all of you."

"Aileen Henning," she said. "Doctor, yes, but not yet wife."

The one-time nun waved away the niceties of legal documents, and kissed all the cheeks in sight, including those of Sherlock Holmes.

"Leave your things, Théo and the boy will bring them in, once you've chosen where you want them. My friend here thought you would be staying for at least a few days."

Holmes cut in before Damian could object. "The young man needs a place to set up his canvases and work. I said there would be one here."

"But of course. And perhaps the ladies will enjoy seeing something of the town. They may even like to help with the garden. Do you like figs, young lady? Ah, your face tells me perhaps not. What about plums? The Mirabelles are still coming ripe."

"Oh yes, please, Madame Marie."

"Oh good! I have some set aside for your breakfast—come, all of you, the kettle should be hot, I shall make coffee. Or perhaps, Mlle Henning, you would prefer a pot of good strong *thé anglais?*"

The grey-haired woman was gathering her two female guests towards the house. Damian, watching in bemusement, said, "Where on earth did you find her?"

"Through a lawyer, oddly enough. Two or three times, I have

been presented the case of a soldier accused of criminal intent, when the only thing of which he was guilty was shell shock. I met Sister Aubert before you did, and after the War, found her too valuable a resource to waste. I helped her arrange for a retreat. She is generous about welcoming my guests as well. Even those who are not wounded soldiers. And yes, she knows about your . . . intruder. The compound is as well guarded as you could hope."

The two of them watched the women make their way inside, then Holmes laid a tentative hand on his son's shoulder. "Now come, put on your shoes, and prepare yourself for a proper French farm breakfast."

CHAPTER FOURTEEN

I was finding that grim thoughts about abducted children, past and present, had begun to undermine my enthusiasm for the already difficult task of translating the journal. Fortunately, the next morning provided a distraction both from code-breaking and from tales of exploitation.

Two distractions, in fact.

The first was generated when I saw a pair of heads passing by the kitchen door, and scrambled and hopped over to get the door open.

"Monsieur LaRue?" I called.

"*Oui, Madame?*"

He was holding a basket of new-laid eggs. The man with him took no great thought to identify. "And you must be Mme LaRue's brother."

"Ah, apologies, Madame—yes, this is Pierre, who has the cottage at the back. Anything you need, he is happy to be of assistance."

The siblings must have looked alike once. One could see vestiges of a pleasant face on the half of his that was not scar tissue.

"*Bonjour,* Pierre," I said easily. "I've been enjoying the garden, which I understand is largely your work?"

He dipped his head to acknowledge both introduction and praise, rather than meet my eyes. I imagine that was a habit any man in his condition would soon adopt, rather than see the horror in people's faces. I merely nodded and returned to his brother-in-law.

"M. LaRue, the photographer who reproduced Damian's sketch. Could you ask him to come and take some photos for me? At an hour when the sun is strong, with a camera and lens capable of doing very close-up work. I'd pay twice his usual rate if he can come today."

"If I may use the telephone?"

"Certainly."

He handed the basket to Pierre, who continued around the house while M. LaRue cleaned his tidy-looking boots on the mat and went through the kitchen into Dr Henning's surgery. His voice came for some time, with two long silences generated, I thought, by the call being not to the photographer himself, but to a nearby shopkeeper with a telephone.

He eventually returned, triumphant.

"Monsieur will come during his dinner break, and put a sign on his door. I did say we would feed him."

"Heaven forbid we should rob a Frenchman of his midday meal," I agreed.

"There is also a person coming who may have seen the man in the drawing."

"'May have'?"

"A girl of fifteen, who assists her mother in the small shop near the photographer. The mother says her daughter only wishes a reason to feel important. However, I said we would pay for her to take the bus here this morning, and add a few francs for her trouble. I trust that was correct?"

"Absolutely."

He nodded, pleased that he had judged my interest correctly. "I told the child where to come. I imagine she will be here in one hour, or perhaps two."

"Thank you, M. LaRue. And I should ask, your brother-in-law, Pierre: Does he speak? His injuries, that is . . ."

"His throat is fine, he simply doesn't have much to say."

I spent the time with a bath, then sorting out laundry, and finally hunting through Damian's study for the equipment I needed before the photographer came. Since that included crushing a charcoal stick into fine powder, I then had to scrub again and add another shirt to the laundry.

When those distractions had played themselves out, I reluctantly made my way to the dining room, where I had left the translation and notes. The night before, I had wrestled the long, polished table over to the wall, so the lead of a desk-lamp would reach the room's single outlet, but I saw now that the table had been returned to its place and an extension flex added to the arrangement.

The notes did not appear to have been touched.

But before I could settle to my efforts again, a welcome interruption arrived at the kitchen door.

"*Madame?*"

"*Oui,* Mme LaRue," I called, "I'm just coming."

The girl with Mme LaRue wore a clear expression of dismay as she examined the workaday kitchen. If she'd spoken aloud, it could not have been more obvious that she had expected more from the abode of a famous foreign artist and his exotic red-headed wife. She was herself barely into adolescence, although her hair showed the valiant attempt at a bob and traces of red around her mouth betrayed a hasty attempt to remove the Hollywood lipstick she'd come here wearing.

She perked up when she laid eyes on me, a young woman with cropped hair, a cane (that promised a tale to take home with her!), and actual, in-person trousers such as she'd only seen on the screen.

"*Voici* Dorothée Fontaine," said Mme LaRue. Her disapproving glance at the girl's mouth told me who had been responsible for the hasty *démaquillant*.

"*Cole me Daunt,*" the child purred.

I waited in vain for my ears to provide a translation, then decided to try fitting the syllables into English instead: Call me ... ah: Dot.

"Hullo, Dot," I said, and held out my hand. She looked at it with uncertainty, then remembered and stuck out her own hand, enormously pleased at this opportunity to participate in a glamorous ritual.

Normally, I would have taken her to the sitting room to ask my questions, but I was afraid that her excitement would drive all thoughts from her head. So instead, I thanked Mme LaRue and picked up the kettle myself, to fill it and set it on the hob, then sat down and gestured the child into the chair on the other side of the table.

Mme LaRue was shaking her head as she went out of the door, and little *Daunt* looked disappointed, but the familiar surroundings did their work and gave me a glimpse of the sensible French schoolgirl beneath the paint.

"Thank you for coming here so quickly." I started off in English, but seeing how intently she followed the movements of my lips, shifted into French. "I hope your mother is not too troubled by your absence from the shop. I imagine she depends on you a great deal."

She gave a pleased shrug, and did not try to assemble the English for her reply. "We have a girl who comes in some days, to help."

"I shall try not to keep you too long. So, Dot, M. LaRue told me that you saw the person in the drawing."

"Him? No, I don't think so." My heart sank and my irritation rose—but before I could express either, she explained. "I said that I saw two men who might be with that man, although they were dressed very differently."

"I see. Then perhaps you could tell me about the two men. Let's start with when you saw them. This was in Délieux, was it not?"

"Yes, in my town. It was the Wednesday—not yesterday, last week. I have the afternoon off, and because the new films come to the cinema on Thursday, if there is one I saw before but want to see again, I will sometimes go before it leaves. And there was—with Ronald Colman. Don't you love Ronald Colman? I dream of him. I saw *A Thief in Paradise* three times—once I hid behind the seat after it showed so I could watch it again! And *Her Sister from Paris*—so naughty, that one! I did not tell my mother *that* story!"

A year or so earlier, I had spent far too many days surrounded by a bevy of blonde, would-be starlets. They'd taught me how to keep a conversation on track: ignore all distractions and press on. "And one of the men looked like Ronald Colman?"

"No! Nothing like! No, it was because one of them made me think of the newsreel that had played during intermission, that showed the Queen of India going to church, and I had noticed that some of the young Indian men with her were very handsome, the ones without all the beards and turbans. There had been some handsome young men in another film about a young woman who sails to India and falls in love, although my friend Marianne and I had an argument about that because the man the girl falls in love with, he's a major from England who was once in love with her *mother*! And even though they decided they weren't really in love, and wanted to be just friends, that still would mean that he was her mother's age and that's really too old for a girl to fall in love with, don't you think?"

I was not about to touch that particular question. "So, the film's English major reminded you of these two men?"

"No no! Again, some of the handsome young Indian men—in the background, waiters and friends of passengers, you know?— they showed me what an Indian person looks like. And when I saw the two men leaving the train station in Délieux, after I had just seen the newsreel that reminded me of the *Innocent Danger* film from earlier in the summer, well, I thought that, although they were wearing ordinary clothes, they might be Indian."

"But not wearing turbans or *salwar*—or Indian clothes?" I thought I had grasped the key elements of her narrative.

"That's right. One man was very handsome, and dressed very well. Linen suit, with the kind of coat that has two rows of buttons. Shiny brown shoes, the kind with the stitching all over the toes. A red silk tie—dark, not bright. He wore a nice hat, a sort of straw fedora, tipped a little. I like that on men."

Double-breasted summer suit, Panama hat at a rakish tilt, maroon tie, brown Oxford brogues: as identifying marks, all of those could be shed in moments. "But what did he look like? Tall or short, fat or not? Anything distinctive about his face? Why did he seem Indian to you?"

"Taller than me. And a nice shape, not too thin. I didn't look at his face too much. I didn't want him to think I was being forward. He did have a thin moustache, I could see that. And his skin was a little darker than most people's. But to tell you the truth, I'm not sure I'd have immediately thought 'That man is from India' if it hadn't been for the other one. He was much darker, and heavier, and his moustache was thick, like in the movies and newsreel. His clothes weren't as nice, either. Ordinary."

I considered this for a minute. "Did they look like friends, or as if the one man worked for the other?"

"Not friends. Maybe . . . they might have been related? The darker one could have been old enough to be the other's father, but not old enough to have gone completely grey. Anyway, if they were related, the younger man had more money. As I said, the older one didn't dress as well. Though he did have a golden ring."

"What kind of ring?"

"It didn't have a jewel—it was one of those with a flat place on the top with a design cut into it. He was wearing it on his little finger."

"A signet ring. I don't suppose you were close enough to see the design?"

The childish features screwed up in thought. She shook her head. "No, not really. It had some curly shapes on it, but that's all I saw."

"How old were the two men, would you say?" I did not have much hope for accuracy here, since girls of her age could think of someone my age as being "old." But she made a try.

"The younger man was maybe my cousin's age, he's thirty. The other . . . I don't know. He was old."

"You said he wasn't completely grey. Was he a little grey?"

"Yes! He had mostly black hair, but I could see some bits of grey under the hat."

She'd given me more of a description than I'd hoped for. Although it did not sound as if either of these men was the one who had climbed in through Damian's window, four days later.

"Now, can you tell me what the two men did? Where did you first see them? Did you speak with them at all?"

"They came into the shop. I'd seen them perhaps an hour earlier, coming out of the train station—at half past eleven, so it was the Paris train. They stood for a minute looking around, then turned up the main street and went into the news-agent there. I had to go help a customer then, but I saw them a while later, talking with Old Mme Auclair, who was feeding the cats. She feeds the town cats every day at noon, but she doesn't talk to people, and she didn't talk to them. After a minute they moved on, to the hotel. Half an hour later, I saw them in conversation with *Père* André, who is happy to lean on his bicycle and talk to anyone. But I'd guess he didn't know the person they wanted, because they walked away while he was still talking.

"At any rate, a while later, they came into the shop. Mother was there, so they didn't talk to me at first, but they wanted to know if there was anyone in the area named either Adler or Vernet, or was

related to the Vernets who were painters—artists, not house painters. She said she'd never heard of any in Délieux, but I know who
M. Adler is. He comes from the train sometimes, a tall man with a
big beard and nice eyes. So I told them, and they asked—the
younger one, that is, the older one didn't say anything—he asked if
we thought the artist might live in Ste Chapelle. I suppose someone in the town had seen him there, and told the men, but neither
Mother nor I had ever been to Ste Chapelle. He asked us a few
more questions, as if he wasn't sure to believe us—he acted a little
irritated—and he and the older man were talking some foreign
gabble as they left. Mother was cross as well, since they didn't buy
anything or even say 'thank you.'"

Two days later, according to M. LaRue, a young "foreign" gentleman had motored into little Ste Chapelle during market day,
asking the close-mouthed villagers about their resident Vernet.

And two days after that, in the wee hours of Monday morning,
a "lascar"—though one without facial hair—broke in through the
window, in search of something more specific than the merely
valuable treasures in the sitting room.

I absently thanked the girl, handed over rather more francs than
she had been promised, and went back to my coded journal.

CHAPTER FIFTEEN

SECOND IMAGE

SAILS

The next picture my memory gives me is of sails. This one, too, includes odours, in this case a mix of sea air and coffee, unwashed clothing and fresh tar, meat beginning to turn and the bake of hot canvas. Unlike the first image, this one is less a framed rectangle than a painted dome overhead, stretching to the horizon in all directions.

Uncle Christian and I were sitting in a quiet corner of the deck. He was drinking a cup of coffee and reading a book. I was watching the men scamper up ropes and spread out along the masts. The deck beneath us shifted then, like a carriage going around a corner. Soon after, as if obeying some invisible impulse, the shape of the sails changed, growing full. A tiny increase of pressure on my spine told me we had gained speed.

"Uncle Christian, what are the men doing?"

"Bringing us into the wind. The wind across the ocean moves in a direction, and the more sail it pushes against, the faster we go."

"But we turned, too. Did the captain decide to go to a different place?"

"Clever child. It's like this. Hold up your hand and blow into it.

Now turn it to the side. Feel how much more of your breath you can feel when your palm is facing you?"

I experimented, and nodded.

"So, we can either sail in a straight line and go really slowly, because the wind is coming from the side direction, or we can zigzag—you know what 'zigzag' means?" I nodded. "We can zigzag and go this way for a while, then before we go too far out of the way, we turn back again. This back-and-forth is called tacking. Which, though it covers more distance, makes for faster speed in the end."

I sat watching the sails. He went back to his book. The men around us chattered as they worked. Some were browner than most of the people I knew in France. Others were not quite so brown, although one of them, a friendly man who always said hello to me, was nearly as dark as ink. The brown ones mostly wore long shirts and had cloths on their heads. The not-so-brown ones didn't use head-coverings unless it was a really hot day, and their clothes were different—more like the gardeners and working men wore at home. They talked differently, too; the brown men had one way of speaking, the lighter ones another, and though they could talk to each other—and the captain and mate could talk to them—they seemed to stick to their own skin colours.

"Uncle Christian, what language is that?" I had learned recently that people spoke using different words, one day when Papa had visitors I couldn't understand. But the words these men were using did not sound like the ones Papa's "Germans" had used.

"That's English, because this ship happens to be from England. English is a language you will need to learn eventually, although fortunately for you, my own family—your new family—speaks French most of the time."

"Do they also speak other languages?"

"Oh yes. Bengali, Hindi—English, too. A few other languages as well, some of us."

"Can you teach me other languages?"

"You want to make a start? Certainly." He closed the book around its ribbon and held it up. "*Livre?* Book."

"Is that the Bengal?"

"Bengali—no, this thing in Bengali is called a *bai*. 'Book' is the English word. In Hindi it's *kitaab*, in Latin it's *liber*, or *libro* in Spanish, *buch* in German— What is it?"

I had started to giggle, my mind tumbling over the idea of so many identities for the same thing. "So many names!"

"It is a wonder anyone makes sense of anyone else, I agree. Even names—proper names. You know me as 'Uncle Christian,' yes? Well, my family knows me as Krishna."

"Should I call you Krishna?"

"Not unless you're used to calling your papa by his first name. How about Pitaji?"

"Uncle Pitaji?"

He laughed. "We can drop the 'Uncle.' Just 'Pitaji' is fine."

"Can I have another name?"

"If you like. What about . . . let's see. Loukya? Or how about Lakshmi? She's a goddess, in India—one of the more amiable ones."

"What does 'amiable' mean?"

"Friendly. Or easy-going. Her name means worldly wise, which would be appropriate for you."

"Are there unfriendly goddesses?"

"Well, one wants to think carefully before naming a child for some of them."

"I like Lakshmi."

"So do I. Lakshmi it is."

The men had finished up in the sails and were coming back down, reminding me of a monkey one of Papa's friends had that stole a necklace and climbed up the curtains with it. The sails were filling with the wind. We had *tacked*.

"Pitaji, does the wind over the sea sometimes blow in the wrong direction? Can the ship still 'tack'?" I knew that wind blew from

different directions—one of the houses where *Maman* and I liked
to walk had a weathercock on top, and the man who lived there
had explained what it meant.

"It can sail completely against the wind, though it's slow and a
lot of work, so usually the captain bases his course on . . . You know,
Mademoiselle Curious, if I'm going to explain the idea of trade
winds and how the world's weather works, we'll need to ask the
captain if we can borrow his globe, and I wouldn't want to bring
that up on the deck, in case it rolls off the side. Shall we do that
another time, when it's not so nice out?"

I nodded. The captain had overheard, and called down a question. Pitaji replied, and the two talked for a bit, and laughed like
adults do over the heads of children.

"Pitaji, teach me some of that man's words."

"Who, Captain Lawson? Certainly." So he did.

And that was how lessons worked with Pitaji, on the voyage
and in the years that followed, lessons on language and technol-
ogy, social customs and comparative religion and the workings of
the world. By the time we reached Calcutta, I was chattering with
the crew in several languages—English to the officers and some
of the lighter-skinned crew, Hindi for most of the browner crew
members, and French with the majority of passengers.

I don't remember how old I was when I realised that Pitaji, the
name I used for him after that day on the deck, meant Father.

CHAPTER SIXTEEN

This considerably more cheering section of the image-journal— and I was glad to have at least a first name for its author—had been briefly interrupted by the arrival of the photographer from Délieux. Although, having paid his respects, he was then taken away by the LaRues to be properly fed. He returned nearly two hours later, red of face and with both LaRues and Dot in tow. When I explained what I needed, they were all so thrilled, I might have invited them to step into a cinema screen.

The raising of fingerprints was clearly the most exciting event to have taken place in Ste Chapelle's recent history. My audience of four gathered so ardently around the kitchen table that their own clothing was threatened by the ink I used to record the finger- prints of both LaRues, and then the charcoal dust I brushed on to the knife and torch with a soft, clean paintbrush from Damian's shelves.

When I gently blew away the residue, there was a collective gasp of appreciation at the prints that appeared out of nowhere.

To my relief, the photographer knew his business well enough that I did not have to elbow him aside. When we had finished,

M. LaRue pulled the cork on a new bottle of wine and we toasted the triumph of modern forensic science.

"Two prints of each negative," I reminded the photographic gentleman. One for us, the other in case there was any interest from the local or Parisian *policier.*

My photographer hurried out, eager to see the images locked into his camera's film, and necessarily taking the others with him. I dampened a cloth and wiped down all the peripheral surfaces, but before I returned the now-mottled torch and machete to their hiding place atop the cupboard—one never knew when something might go awry with film—I sat and turned the two objects around beneath the strong desk-lamp the photographer had used.

The torch was marked as one might expect of a metallic object kept relatively polished by being carried in pockets: a combination of sharp lines—a clear thumb-print over the switch, other crisp ovals where a right hand slightly larger than my own had grasped it—and indistinct blurs from the palm or where earlier prints had been rubbed away.

The black ovals on the long knife were less predictable. The grip, naturally, was a jumble of prints and palm-prints. The blade, less expectedly, also held prints: halfway up, along the blunt edge, he had grasped the steel with his thumb on one side and three fingers on the other. The angle made it clear: he had held the blade, manipulating the point of it between the two sides of the shutters, planting his index finger along the blunt spine as he probed upwards for the latch.

I also noticed a series of distinct marks, equally spaced, around the very end of the grip. It was an odd place to find fingerprints—in truth, only the rapt fascination of my audience had caused me to continue applying the charcoal dust past where I expected to find anything. Instead, there they were, five clear ovals, as if he'd dangled the knife for a moment, point deliberately downwards.

I frowned, wondering whether there had been any significance in that gesture. In the end, I returned the torch and knife to the cabinet top, checked the table and floor for stray charcoal dust, and went back—with less dread this time—to Lakshmi's coded journal.

CHAPTER SEVENTEEN

THIRD IMAGE

THE DANCING LANTERN

Next comes a picture captured during my earliest days in Chandernagore, perhaps even the night of our arrival. I had been told that this would be my new home, but I was in a turmoil of confusion and unhappiness. Clothing that I'd rarely worn on the voyage had grown tight and short in the weeks since we'd left, and itched in the heat. The floor seemed to sway underfoot, the air smelled wrong, and I was fighting against the weakness of tears. The only thing I could cling to—literally—was Pitaji.

He sent the women away, not only those in saris but also the angry-looking one in the rustling vastness of a European skirt. She objected loudly—in French, though she was hard to understand, either because the shape of the words in her mouth was different or because her anger made her speech tumble and twist—but then a stern, grey-haired woman in a sari tugged at the loud woman's arm, and we were left alone.

Pitaji sat down beside me on the bed. It was softer than the ship's bed I'd grown used to, but no larger, with a curtain of fabric so thin I could see through it gathered up onto the bed's high frame. He sat with me, and said nothing.

Looking back, it occurs to me how often he knew to say nothing.

The house was strange, like home but not. It was large, with very high ceilings, and around all the edges were long, narrow rooms—like hallways, except with shuttered windows on both sides, one side overlooking the garden, the other looking into rooms. The hallways had furniture, wicker chairs and carved wooden tables, as if people moved out of their dark rooms to sit closer to the light. When we came through the house, I had seen the courtyard at its centre, with a set of decorative metal stairs in one corner that went all the way to the roof. Everything smelled . . . warm. Like gardens on a hot, rainy day, mixed with the spices and the burning sandalwood that I had met first in Bombay, then in Pondichéry. The fishy smell of this house's oil lamps was the only thing like home, although I was glad that my room's light—my own room, right next to Pitaji's and with only a door between us—was from a candle, rather than the lamp hanging on the wall.

As I watched, a lizard appeared, creeping head-first down the wall. I had met these on our first night in Bombay, and been alarmed, until Pitaji explained them. His name was Tikatiki, or Chipkalee, from the sharp little ticking sounds he would make, and his job was to keep the room free of insects. He would never bite me, Pitaji promised. Never.

Still, I kept an eye on Tikatiki as I leaned into Pitaji, whose comforting arm went around me, as it always did.

"Everything is new, my darling," he murmured into my hair. "I know that. It will be difficult at first. But there will be things and people here you will come to love. I promise."

"*Tante* Sophie doesn't like me." *Tante* Sophie was the angry lady.

"She doesn't know you yet. Although it's true, my brother's wife is hard to please. However, Sophie is not as important in this house as your *grand-mère*, and your *grand-mère* likes you already."

The stern, grey-haired lady liked me? She had touched my head, lightly, when we first met. Only much, much later did it occur to me how extraordinary this was, to welcome the illegitimate child of one's elder son. Looking back, I can come close to sympathising with my aunt's fury and my uncle's scorn.

"Is she your mother?"

"She is. You can call her *Daadi-ma,* if you want."

"Is she Indian?" She wore a sari, went barefoot, and had a *tilak* mark on her forehead like the servants, and was a little browner than Pitaji. On the other hand, her sari was silk and her hands were smooth. And she had authority: even the angry lady had deferred to her.

"She's both Indian and French. Most of us in this family are both."

"But not *Tante* Sophie?" She was the one in the rustling French clothing, and she had no *tilak.*

"Oh, her, too, despite the dress."

There was some message there, some degree of tension in his throat—but I knew that when an adult spoke like that, they would not answer a question. Not even Pitaji, who tried to be mostly honest with me.

I set the thought away for future consideration. At any rate, I had another question.

"Pitaji, what is that?"

On the table beside the bed was a peculiar contrivance, a foot or so tall. It had a base like a lamp, but instead of a glass chimney or a silk shade, there was a wide metal hoop hanging from its top. Wasn't that going to block all the light, I wondered? Only a small amount would come through the narrow slots cut into the metal. I knelt on the bed to look at it more closely. Inside the hoop was a piece of candle in a glass cup. At the top of the device, above the candle, was a circle of thin, tilted paddles. Like a tiny windmill, only lying flat, instead of standing upright.

"That is a thing for when you're in bed. Do you want to get yourself ready, my Lakshmi? I'm afraid that starting tomorrow, you'll need to submit to the ministrations of your *ayah,* but for tonight, we'll pretend I'm still your nursemaid."

I hurried to change into my cotton shift and splash my face in the wash-basin, then came back and watched him transfer a flame from the candlestick, which he then blew out.

I was right about the poor light this odd lantern gave: almost none, and that in narrow beams against the plaster.

And then I noticed that the windmill had begun to turn. Slowly, slowly—and somehow it was pulling the slotted lamp-shade along with it, like the skirts of a spinning dancer. At first, that seemed the extent of it, but as the shade picked up speed, the dancing motion smoothed out, replaced by a flickering vision—when I bent down to the level of the lantern's shade, I saw a horse, galloping along inside the lantern!

I exclaimed and stretched out a hand, but Pitaji's ring flashed as he reached out to grab my wrist.

"My heart, you may touch it, but first you have to absolutely promise me that you'll never light this on your own."

I considered this verbal contract. "Never?"

He laughed. "All right, my little lawyer, not until you're, let's say, ten years old."

That was forever—but this was too compelling. I nodded.

"Say it aloud."

"I promise, I won't light the candle until I'm ten. Did you make this, for me?"

"I wish I could take credit, but no. It came from a country called China. One of *Daadi-ma*'s family was a trader there, her grandfather I think it was, and he brought it home. I spent many a feverish night watching it go when I was small."

"How does it work?"

So he showed me, starting with the mechanism. The heat from the little flame rose into the windmill, whose angled blades pushed it around—like miniature sails, only metal instead of canvas. As it turned, four wires pulled the slotted shade with it.

Then the horses. He reached for the shade, using his thumbs to work free a strip of paper that rested along its lower edge. When the paper was free, he handed it to me and bent down to a box on the floor, pulling out another strip. While he was working this one into place, I looked at the one he had given me.

It had a series of drawings—each one, I saw, a little bit different from that on either side. In the first, the horse's front foot was tucked up tight under its chest. In the next, the foot was going down. It continued to straighten, reaching for the ground, then touching down—and there the foot stayed while the horse's body moved, shifting until it was above the hoof, then slightly ahead, and further yet, stretching the leg back. It finally lifted off the ground, then pulled forward until, in the last image on the strip, it was prepared to tuck up tight under the chest once again.

I looked at the lamp, turning again with the new image-strip inside. This one had a bird—standing at the bottom, then sprouting wings, flying up, and flapping, nearly disappearing, and then descending with something in its beak, which it swallowed before it landed and stood, its wings tucked in, before it took off again.

"Let me see," I demanded.

Obediently, he slid out the paper and reached for a third one as I studied the two in my hands.

"The pictures go back to the beginning!"

"That's right, it ends where it began."

"But in the lamp, it's moving."

"The eyes think the figures are moving, yes. Each slot gives us a quick glimpse of a drawing, then we fill in what's missing. The human mind likes to see patterns."

"Are there more drawings?"

"You can have a new one tomorrow. But now, my Lakshmi, you need to get into your bed and I'll tuck in the net, so the mosquitos won't find you."

"Won't the lizard eat them?"

"Monsieur Tikatiki can't catch them all."

"He won't crawl on me, will he?"

"No, he can't get through the net."

"Why didn't we have mosquitos on the ship, Pitaji?"

He laughed. "Your eyes are drooping, child. We'll discuss the natural history of mosquitos tomorrow. And I need to go down to dinner, but if you give me your word that you won't touch the lamp, I'll leave it burning."

I promised. He kissed my forehead, tucked in the netting—arranging the folds to either side, so that only a single layer of the net would obscure my vision—and stood for a minute, watching this new form take over the image-lantern. It was a dancing lady with a long scarf, which she tossed and caught while at the same time circling round and round.

He left then, the light from the hallway causing my room to brighten, then dim. Tikatiki crept into the light, as if he, too, found it magical. In the darkness, I saw that the windmill created another dance on the ceiling, a flicker of light almost as magical as the figures inside the shade.

On subsequent nights, I would discover that the candle did not burn nearly long enough, and I would lie awake until I heard the sounds of the *chowkidar* making his rounds. But that night, I was asleep before the lady's flying skirts had gone dark.

CHAPTER EIGHTEEN

When Mme LaRue came over with a tray full of supper, she interrupted my re-reading of the translation, and noticed the expression on my face.

"You look like you're enjoying yourself," she said.

"I suppose I am. Certainly more than I was."

"Good. There's no reason to be gloomy just because your husband is away."

I started to protest, decided not to, then realised that in fact, she was right. I was uneasy, at what might be happening with the missing Adlers. But I had also been brooding over the opening chapter of this journal, at the idea that its author had been snatched from her mother, and somehow given away, even sold.

Instead, Lakshmi appeared to have been removed—after an affair by her married French mother?—and found herself in a magical land of automated zoetropes and mosquito-eating geckoes, with a father—whether actual or adoptive—whose love for her shone through the pages.

A part of that pleasure Mme LaRue had caught on my face was from my own memories.

A year and a half earlier, Holmes and I had been sent to India by Holmes' spymaster brother, Mycroft, in search of a missing agent. Holmes had been there long before, during his three-year absence from London—an absence that led up to Montpellier and Irene Adler. He had tutored me in the language and customs before we arrived, but nothing could have prepared me for a place as maddening and compelling and enigmatic and colourful as India, and I looked back on it as a time of considerable joy and adventure.

Lakshmi's description of the bedroom in Chandernagore had brought it all back: the spices and dust and dung-fire smoke; the ubiquitous *chipkalee* house geckoes on the wall, the women with *tilak* marks, and the *slap-slap* of the cook forming chapatis. The firm thump of the night-watchman's stick as he circled the house to frighten away intruders.

I was getting some clues as to the era of which she was writing. Sails could be anytime before 1900, although steamers took over most passenger runs long before that. Her aunt's "vast skirts" dominated the nineteenth century, but her reference to oil lamps pointed to a date before the 1860s—coal-derived paraffin had been invented in 1846, but lamps using it would have taken a long time to reach even the wealthier enclaves of India. I was less certain about the development of the zoetrope, but in my father's house in Boston I'd played with one that he'd had as a child, so it had been commercially manufactured by the 1870s.

"Did Damian show you the, er, I'm not sure of the French word. Zoetrope?"

She recognised the English, and broke into a smile. "A charming device, it reminds me of a simpler one I had as a child. Did you see the drawings M. Damian made?"

"The hatching egg is a delight."

"He loves the child so; it is good to see."

I agreed, a father who loved his daughter was a beautiful sight.

CHAPTER NINETEEN

HOLMES

Holmes had no intention of submitting to Damian's familial interrogation—not until this was all over. He did need to confirm the details of the lad's Paris trip, but that would not take long. Yes, when the urgency of the current situation was past, after he had identified and dealt with whatever threat had raised its head in Ste Chapelle, he would then make himself available to answer Damian's questions. It would be uncomfortable, and was as likely to increase the acrimony between them as it was to defuse it. Nevertheless, one could understand why Damian felt it necessary.

But not now. Not while Russell was alone, and in a compromised situation.

However, when he asked Mme Aubert about the train schedule, she had said that the next few hours offered nothing but slow local services, with dozens of stops along the way. If he waited for the midday Express, he would actually reach Paris somewhat earlier. So he had sat down to breakfast with the others, after which Mme Aubert dispatched him to an upper room, promising to wake him in two hours. Plenty of time for Théo, her *homme á tout faire,* to take him to the station for the faster trains to Toulouse and thence to Paris. Gratefully, Holmes stretched out his spine on a quiet bed.

He was wakened by the unlikely roar of an engine passing directly overhead. An aeroplane? Where was— But the moment his eyes came open, he knew Marie Aubert had lied to him. The slant of the shadows, the faint odours of cooking—the day was nearly gone. *Damn the woman! So much for gratitude and partnership.*

His stockinged feet hit the floor, but as he was tying his shoe-laces, his eye caught on the folded paper someone had slid under the door.

My old friend, your son tells me you and he agreed to have a conversation tonight, and I decided that this promise takes precedence over mine to you. In case I am wrong, I shall wake you in time to catch the last train north. In any event, you look exhausted.

—Marie

What is it about one's hair going grey? he muttered to himself. *People treat a man as if he were a child.*

He jerked his tie straight, splashed his face with water from the jug on the washstand, and shrugged into his jacket. Brisk steps across the floor, his hand seized the doorknob . . . then he paused, considering Mme Aubert's words.

He had *not* agreed to hold this damnable conversation, and definitely not the minute they reached this place of refuge. Damian might assume he had, but Damian was not a child, to sulk at deferred pleasures. At any rate, one delayed conversation was nothing, compared to Holmes' other failures as a father.

Plus that, he did not wish to be away from Ste Chapelle any

longer than necessary. Despite her claims of robust health and in-domitability, Russell was vulnerable, and surrounded by allies of unknown abilities. She would, without a doubt, be annoyed to think that he'd hurried back to save her, but compared to his other failures as a husband . . .

What is it about one's body being female? he could hear her say. *People treat a woman as if she were a child* . . .

Not that he was in the habit of so doing. He had shaken a great deal of his Victorian upbringing, and chivalry was never his stron-gest impulse even as a young man.

Still, he thought, *one might take a moment to weigh consequences.* Would Damian be surprised at having the conversation post-poned? He would not. He might even, Holmes knew, be braced for it, as yet another indication that he mattered for little in the life of Sherlock Holmes.

In 1919, Holmes had learned of the boy's existence, met him for the first time, freed him from a charge of murder, and parted under the final and deadly accusation that he of all people, the great Sherlock Holmes, ought to have realised that Irene Adler was with child.

"You should have known," Damian snarled at him, furious and proud and wronged.

And Holmes could only agree. Yes, he should have known.

For five years, Holmes lived with the memory of those angry grey eyes, until Damian had come to Sussex in desperation, all hostilities suspended under the pressing need of finding his miss-ing wife. Holmes had found her, albeit too late, and saved Damian and the child. They had parted, one year ago, in a state of neutral-ity, and had met twice since, brief encounters that had been polite, but reserved.

One did not have to be an expert in the human heart to know that this third encounter could well prove decisive. Damian was already feeling pushed about (*treated as if he were a child?*) and relegated to the side-lines. A grown man, a veteran of the trenches, sent to safety along with his woman and child. Patted on the head whilst his aging father took over the greater responsibilities.

The bonds between any father and son were inherently problematical. Some, however, were more fragile than others. The threads that tied Damian to his father were far from robust, and would not take much strain before they broke entirely.

No, Holmes decided. *Those consequences would be too great.*

His hand finished turning the metal knob. He listened to the sound of voices rising from below—was that Damian's easy laughter?—then passed through the doorway, moving more slowly than he'd approached it.

It was all so much easier, he thought, *when I only had Watson's sensibilities to consider.*

Very well: tonight he would do his duty by his son. But he would return to the north, and Russell, first thing in the morning.

Marie Aubert's cuisine was somewhat limited, but she had as good an idea of a proper meal as a French peasant woman. Ribs were meant for sticking, wine was there for drinking, and the day's main meal—in this case, unlike many farms, held in the evening rather than noontime—was meant for taking time over.

The eleven who sat down at the long table were only family in the broadest sense. All chimed in an obedient *Amen* after Mme Aubert's grace, and reached for the nearest bowl or platter. Easy conversation made it apparent that the Adler-Henning trio had been well integrated into the life of the refuge during the day, and there was no awkwardness when it came either to the resident wearing the painted tin mask over his wounded features or the one who twitched at any sharp noise and spoke not a word the whole time.

It was a pleasant meal. At first, conversation centred on the

minutiae of harvest, but then Aileen said something about the
aeroplane that had gone over, and the man with the mask—his
name was Jules Simon, and he seemed to have built an instant
friendship with all three Adlers—started talking about the bur-
geoning aviation industry in Toulouse, some forty miles away. He
had been a pilot during the War, burned in a crash, and was trying
to prove that he was fit to return to work. A company in Toulouse
was building a series of aerial postal routes, and needed experienced men. And who cared what a postal delivery pilot looked
like? Estelle was thrilled, Aileen appalled, and Damian more animated than Holmes had seen him before.

At last, Mme Aubert folded her table napkin onto the ancient
wood, and the others responded like a well-oiled machine, gathering plates and glasses and whisking them off to the scullery, wiping
away crumbs, fetching a broom to run across the spotless floor.

"You two," Mme Aubert said, gathering up Holmes and his son
with a firm gaze. "I've made up a fire in the study. Drinks are in the
corner cabinet. We'll bring you coffee."

I am, Holmes reflected with grim humour, *the victim of a con-
spiracy.*

Damian, too, despite being the one who had called this meeting,
seemed equally uncertain where to begin. The easy camaraderie he
had shown at the dining table had faded. He now fiddled with his
coffee, took out his ever-present sketchbook, opened it, realised
what he was doing, then clipped the pencil on the cover and set it
on the table between them before getting to his feet and walking
over to the drinks cabinet.

"*Digestif?*" he offered. "Mme Aubert has a nice Calvados."

"Brandy is fine, thank you."

Damian brought the glasses back, took a swallow, and cleared
his throat. "Aileen seems to feel safe here. I did tell her that you
thought you saw the lascar, back in Nîmes, though we're not going

to say anything to Estelle. Aileen agreed that we need to stay here until you get things sorted out."

"No telephone, telegraph, or posting letters?"

"We won't let anyone know where we are."

"If you need anything that Mme Aubert can't get you, have someone take the train into Toulouse or Narbonne. A cable or trunk call to the LaRues from there won't lead anyone to Carcassonne."

"That seems—"

"Please." It was not an easy word to say, when Holmes wanted nothing more than to shout at the lad. Fortunately, Damian heard the effort it took to implore rather than demand.

"Let's hope it doesn't go on too long."

Holmes decided not to press matters further. "Damian, you wish to talk about . . . matters, but perhaps I might first ask about your trip to Paris last month."

Damian looked surprised. "What about it?"

"It would be helpful to have details: where did you go, who did you see, when?"

"Why? Do you think my visit to the *Institut* has something to do with the man breaking into my house?"

"The men in Délieux knew that you are related to the Vernet family. Unless you have permitted that fact to become common knowledge?"

"Good God, no. Vernets are thick on the ground in Paris. The last thing I'd want is to get cornered at a party by some distant cousin wanting to know how I was a Vernet, forcing me either to lie or to admit that my father was Sherlock Holmes, who no, actually wasn't made up by that writer Doyle. Can you imagine? Well, I suppose you can. At any rate, we haven't told anyone but the LaRues and one or two close friends. And as you say, the man at the *Institut*, although I didn't go into precisely *how* I was related."

"But he believed you. Enough to send you some boxes left in the storage attics by Horace Vernet."

"Not just Horace. And evidently he did believe me—at least, enough to show me the rooms where Horace and later his nephew Émile had worked. The crates came later, when he remembered they were there and wrote to ask if I wanted them."

"He simply wrote to offer, with no proof that you were who you claimed?"

Damian shrugged. "There doesn't seem to be much of value there—I imagine they were happy enough to get rid of things that had been gathering dust for so long. And I suppose they thought that, if I'd been someone wanting to con them out of some old paintings and memorabilia, not only would I have been more as-sertive about it, but I'd have chosen an artist whose work was actu-ally worth something."

Holmes' chin dropped to his chest as he considered, then: "De-tails, please."

What Damian recounted was much the same as Gervais LaRue had told them: He had gone to Paris with Aileen and the child during the first week of August, to visit the Art Deco Exposition and see some friends who were about to leave for Antibes. On Wednesday the fifth, he had a luncheon appointment with his gal-lery owner, to decide which of his paintings should go into his upcoming one-man show and which should be sent to the Surre-alist exhibition in November. When they'd finished, he happened to find himself walking past the *Institut*. On a whim, he went in-side to ask if it were possible to see the rooms where Horace Vernet had worked during his residency. He was passed from one office to the next until one of the concierges—"an elf of a man named LeGrand, couldn't have been a hair over five feet"—took a shine to him, recognising the name Damian Adler from a show that had got quite a bit of press the previous winter. "The fellow had even gone to see it, and said my technique wasn't bad!" Damian said with a laugh. After a gentle inquisition to establish Damian's bona fides, LeGrand led this most modern of new artists to the formal,

light-filled rooms in which one of the *Institut*'s chosen favourites
had produced some of his more famous works. The two men had a
long and rambling chat, first about the Vernet family, but moving
on to all manner of topics, including Monet's cataracts, Duchamp's
absurdities, Picasso's morals, and the tendency towards inflexibility
in the *Académie des Beaux-Arts*. Damian slipped LeGrand a generous thank-you as he left, along with his card, in case the concierge
thought of anything else.

Then a letter arrived, the end of the following week, August
thirteenth or fourteenth, he thought. It offered to send him some
boxes that had been in storage since the 1890s. Amused, Damian
wrote back to thank his guide for his thoughtfulness and the *Institut* for its patronage, and more to the point, offering to pay the
shipping costs.

"After that I got busy again. As I said, I promised some new work
for the show—both shows. Frankly, I'd forgot about the things until
the railway station rang us last week."

"The day?"

"Wednesday? No, it was Tuesday, because Mme LaRue's girl
was there. So, Tuesday, September first. Gervais went to Délieux to
pick them up, and I had him and Pierre—did you meet him? Madame's brother, who lives in the back—I had them put the boxes in
my studio. When I'd finished for the day, I gave the contents a
quick look. The only thing of any interest was a little lamp that
Estelle liked, but since Aileen thought it was a bad idea to have her
playing with a burning candle, I packed that up, too. The rest of it
can wait until the show is out of the way."

Holmes rested his steepled fingers against his lips, considering
the sequence of events. "The fifth of August, you go to the *Institut*,
and leave your card with a concierge. The thirteenth or fourteenth,
you receive a letter about the boxes, which themselves arrive on
September first. The next day, two men appear in Délieux, men
described by the LaRues as 'foreign,' with black hair and dark skin.

They ask questions about the artist Adler and the family Vernet. Two days after that, on Friday, the younger of the two men comes to Ste Chapelle, where he asks specifically about you. And then on Sunday night, just after midnight, someone breaks into your house. Your 'lascar.'"

"Though as I said, that one did look Indian. The others, well, sounded as if people weren't so sure."

"Would anyone in the Children of Lights have known of the Vernet connexion?"

Damian's face closed in, but after a generous swallow from his glass, he replied, "I certainly never told Brothers."

"Did your wife know?"

"Yolanda? I don't think so. I tended not to tell her things like that. Matters that could be, shall we say, used."

Holmes let his eyebrow rise. "Information to drop in the right ear? Or perhaps," he said carefully, "in the wrong ear?"

Damian started to protest, then stopped, and gave a rueful shake of the head. "I'm pretty sure that if Yolanda knew I was related to the Vernets, she'd have made use of it. Just like I know that if she had any inkling that I was the son of the world's greatest detective, she'd have plastered your name across any review of my work. When we got to London, I knew she'd find out eventually, and I wasn't looking forward to the argument about it."

"I see."

"No, if those men found me through my visit to the *Institut*, then I don't see how they could have been related to that damned cult of hers."

"You may be right."

"So, have we finished with your questions about the men who ran me from my home? And if so, is it my turn now? Or is this the point at which you suddenly remember that you need to be else-where?"

Holmes stretched back into the chair, hands clasped across his belly and ankles crossed before the fire, giving an attitude of set-tling in for a long session. Internally, he was considerably less se-rene. This was a door he had agreed to open, but he was very aware of the need to brace himself for what lay within.

"I am yours," he said.

CHAPTER TWENTY

HOLMES

Despite the go-ahead, Damian began by walking across the room to fetch the Cognac. When he had topped up both their glasses, he left the decanter on the table between them. "Do you know, I think yesterday was the first time you ever mentioned your mother. Let's begin with her."

Holmes ruefully eyed the liquid in his glass. Well, that was one place to start. Although he needed a deep breath before the words would come.

"My mother committed suicide when I was eleven. She was being blackmailed."

Silence thudded down between them. Then: "Jesus. Do you know . . . ?"

"What the blackmail was over? Not in any detail. I was given to believe she'd had a . . . dalliance. Father never talked about it. Mycroft did not know much more than I did. And the letter she left did not go into detail, beyond her heartfelt regrets and her wish not to bring shame upon the family."

"I . . . I honestly don't know what to say."

"There's nothing to say. She was an interesting woman. Not . . . motherly. Love from her was not a soft emotion. She could comfort, when comfort was needed, but she was more likely to challenge and reward. However, one never doubted the sincerity of any praise that came from her. And one felt that was how she showed her love.

"I think you'd have liked her, once you got used to her. Estelle would have adored her. But she was an ill fit in a staid country house, married to one of the landed gentry. I cannot imagine why anyone thought a vigorous young woman who had grown up at the centre of the Paris art world would be happy hidden away in the English countryside. Looking back, one speculates about the reason she left Paris and never spoke about her family. None of the Vernets ever came to visit. Not even for her funeral. As a boy, of course I thought nothing of it. When one is young, whatever one's parents do and are seems natural.

"Still, whatever her past, with us she was undoubtedly happy—at least, while your uncle and I were growing up. She was a private person at the best of times, and though she had friends, she seemed to prefer our company to that of her peers. For one thing, she was far more physically active than women were then. She rode, she went mountain-climbing in Switzerland, she scandalised the neighbours by playing tennis. She loved to swim—actually swim, not just paddle in the shallows. She'd have fit well in the modern age.

"My father, although he could not bring himself to approve of her more vigorous activities, did look on them with a dose of amusement. He often rode with her. And they played golf. She always won," he added.

"Instead, Mycroft and I played the role of her friends—and, I think, her vocation. We had tutors, naturally, but many of her games were like lessons, intended to hone our wits and senses. We'd dress up, as I mentioned, and see how thoroughly we could convince people. She bought a microscope to see if we could identify things she'd put on slides. We took apart and re-assembled half a dozen clockwork automata. On a trip into town, she'd challenge us to recall the shoes on the last six people we'd gone past, or the contents of a shop window." He paused, then gave a wry laugh.

"It occurs to me that when Russell first dropped out of the skies on me and was in clear need of tutoring, I used those same methods of challenging her intellect under the guise of games."

"I do the same with Estelle," Damian said. "Although I hadn't thought to dress her up as a delivery boy until now. But it sounds like a happy enough life. For your mother, I mean."

"Whatever drove her to suicide, it was not a generalised depression. She was content, certainly while we were young. But then Mycroft went off, to school and then University, and I was soon to follow. My grandfather took ill, leaving more and more of the estate's management to my father. Mother started spending time away, in Town or visiting friends, which must have been her attempt to counteract the lack of stimulation in the country.

"And then one week—this would have been in the spring of 1872—she went to Town to assist a friend. The woman's eldest daughter was being presented at court, after which they were holding a ball.

"Father went down to join her for the ball itself. When they returned, something had happened. She had changed. She was . . . brittle, somehow. Distracted. Or rather, distracted at one moment and overly attentive the next.

"Twelve days later, she was dead. She kissed us good-bye one morning and took the carriage to the station, saying that she had some people to see in Town. And she only carried one small valise, which meant she intended to be home in a day or two.

"But a few hours after she left, one of the maids discovered a letter on her desk, with my father's name on the envelope. He took it into the library and shut the door. An hour or so later, he summoned his valet and sent him to fetch Mycroft.

"It made for a very long day, for a boy of eleven, with the library door shut and the servants knowing no more than I did. Mycroft didn't arrive until very late indeed, wearing his scholar's gown—he hadn't even stopped in his rooms before coming home.

"Father's valet brought Mycroft up to collect me. Despite the hour, the other servants were still awake. I could see their faces, peering around the doorways. We were ushered into Father's presence. He sat us down before the fire, told us that he was very sorry to give us bad news but that our mother had died. And then, while we were reeling from that, he read us the letter she had left.

"Portions of it are seared into my memory, although at the time, I was not altogether clear on her meaning. It said in essence that she loved us all, but that she had done something very stupid and could not live with the shame it would bring on the family, so she planned to go for a long and lovely swim, and simply not turn back to shore. That was her phrase, 'a long and lovely swim.' As if she wanted our last image of her to be of her swimming figure, headed towards the horizon.

"And then he burned it. Laid her letter on the fire and let her final words be consumed."

Holmes stared into the low-burned coals, seeing the shapes of burning pages. After a time, Damian leaned over to refill their glasses. Holmes rested the glass on his stomach. "Curious, isn't it, how certain images or events remain vivid in the memory? The next day, Father had the servants carry most of her other possessions out onto the back lawns, where he doused them with paraffin and set them alight, but it is the letter that remains with me. Wanting to dive after it, knowing I must not, merely watching the glowing line take hold of the paper.

"We were sent up to our beds a short time later, with cups of cocoa and biscuits that the cook imagined we might choke down. Mycroft, who was eighteen, understood better what the letter had been saying. He tried to explain the concept of blackmail, how a person might choose death over dishonour.

"I understood, eventually, although I clung to the thought that this all might turn out to be one of her games. But the next after-noon, attendants cleaning the bathing-machines at the place of our last seaside holiday found her clothes. A few days later, her body washed to shore. There was a funeral, since not to have had one would have invited the very questions she died to save us from. But our father never mentioned her again. He would leave the room if her name was brought up. He died not many years later."

"He loved her."

"He did. She was like an exotic bird that had chosen to trans-form his drab life. And I believe that she loved him. Although looking back, I cannot help wondering if, sooner or later, their es-sential differences might not have brought about a degree of . . . alienation between them."

The fire whispered. The old house creaked and shifted with the night. At last, Damian spoke.

"Your mother sounds remarkably like mine."

"Strong-willed women, the both of them. And unwilling to part with their secrets."

"I do remember that, about Mother. The harshest arguments she and I had were when I discovered things that she had been keep-ing from me. I found out one day—I was perhaps fourteen—that one of her close friends was the Délieux brothel-keeper."

Holmes laughed aloud, and Damian gave a reluctant grin. "You can imagine the fireworks when she told me who my father was. My eighteenth birthday, my first paintings in a gallery, life opening up in front of me, and I learn that I am sprung from the head of—well, if not Zeus, then some equally mythic creature."

"You and Russell could share stories."

"I imagine." Damian's smile went crooked, and the intent way he stared at his glass warned Holmes that matters were coming to a point. "I also imagine," Damian said, "that having had that kind of pain, that abandonment, from such a young age made it all the more . . . difficult when my mother sent you away."

Holmes drained his glass and leaned forward onto his elbows.

"You were right, Damian, that day on the steps of the Sainte Chapelle gaol. I *should* have known that your mother was with child. I, of all men, should have caught the signs, early as they were. I was too quick to believe that when a woman in her thirties did not have children, it meant that she *could* not have them. And having missed that, I compounded it by not questioning her reasons for sending me back to London. I was, I admit, hurt. That she did not . . . That my affection for her appeared to be greater than hers was for me. And since this seems to be a time of confession, I will concede that to some degree, her rejection was convenient. I *did* want to return to my work—I needed to. I had left things unfinished in London, increasingly urgent things that only I could do. Your mother's decision was unilateral, and deeply distressing, but it did serve to simplify my own. I sent her a letter, no doubt as pompous as anything I've written, to say that if she changed her mind, she had only to let me know. But as time went by and she did not write, I put those months in Montpellier away and went on with my life. Only six years ago, when I first learned of your existence, did I begin to understand just how deadly a combination of wounded male pride and a belief that one's work is imperative can be."

With deliberation, he reached out to set the empty glass on the table.

"Nonetheless, you are correct. Between my mother and yours, I have learned that trust does not come easily."

He rose and let himself out of the room, closing the door behind him.

CHAPTER TWENTY-ONE

FOURTH IMAGE

THE KICK

Violence fixes an image to memory like mercury vapours fix a scene to a daguerreotype plate. Before the camera's shutter is uncovered, the world is filled with motion; afterwards, life resumes, but the moment itself, caught and then fixed, remains indelibly.

I was seven or eight, and I had seen fistfights before. Ships, docks, crowded streets, even markets would have occasional outbursts of shouting and shoving and punches thrown. I'd seen a slap once, when I was looking out of my window on a moonlit night and a young servant pressed his attentions a little too assiduously on a housemaid. And one time, a knife had been drawn, its blade gleaming in the waning sun before the man's companions took it from him.

But this was different. Somehow I knew that this vicious act did not stem from the same impulses as the others. This was a kick, a gesture so full of contempt, it did not even require that the person delivering it so much as dirty his hands. A gesture more suited to a dog with mange than to a human being.

I was standing at the window of Pitaji's Calcutta office, looking down at the endless whirl of activity. In the background, the river was crowded with fishing canoes and thatch-roofed *ulaks* and

Western ships like the one we had come on, tall masts and sails waiting for the tide. The street below matched the bustle, with slow bullock carts and quick horse *tangas*, feathered hats and wide parasols and a hundred kinds of turbans, with bright parrots and langur monkeys on the roof-tops and bony dogs and pale, high-humped cattle below. Vendors of water and betel and naan called their wares; men with laden carrying poles threaded their nimble way between ladies in long skirts and men in brief *lunghis* and children wearing nothing at all. I had twice seen an elephant from this window; and once, a camel whose lofty gaze reminded me of my aunt.

This day, Pitaji and I had been following the uncertain progress of a hand-cart loaded with such a precarious mountain of straw, one could scarcely see the legs of the man pulling it. From around the corner came a European—English, I thought—in a silk hat and too-heavy suit. He was walking along the wharf past a line of our stevedores carrying bricks when the load on one man's head began to shift. Another worker, who was circling back to take on his next load, jumped forward to help. As he reached down to retrieve a fallen brick, the Englishman was forced to take a small step to the side—and as his other shiny shoe came up, he aimed it at the stooped man's head. The stevedore and his turban fell to the ground. The Englishman spat out a couple of words but continued on his way without a pause.

The kicked man staggered upright, swaying as he adjusted his turban. Moving cautiously, he leaned down again for the straying brick, set it atop the other man's load, and went on towards the start of the queue.

I had seen the entire brief, vicious act, and I turned to Pitaji in shock. "What did that man in the hat say?"

"It was a rude word," he told me. "Not in itself—if you simply mean that you've cut your finger, you may say it is 'bloody.' But in the way he used it, it is very bad manners."

"What about the other word?"

"Ah. 'Lascar' is what English people call sailors from India."

"Don't they like them?"

"No. You remember we've talked about the idea of 'caste'?"

We had talked about it, why the sweeper couldn't do the cook's job, why my tutor's daughter couldn't marry the shopkeeper's son even though they liked each other. I can't say that my young mind actually understood what "caste" meant. Still, I nodded.

"Most people of that Englishman's caste—or class—feel that even an English sailor is beneath them. Those from foreign countries are little more than dirty animals."

"But isn't he the foreigner here?"

"Remind me to talk to you about the word 'irony' when you get a little older."

The man whose load the other had rescued from falling had finished unloading it and was walking back along the boards. The rescuer was in the line of laden men now, one hand up to balance the board under his bricks.

They were both dark. Pitaji was lighter than they were, but nowhere near as light as the man in the silk hat. Skin colour had much to do with caste, but caste was also how people talked and the clothes they wore. Today Pitaji was wearing his European clothing, high collar and scratchy wool (which always smelled, no matter how thoroughly the *dhobi* tried to clean *them*). He moved differently in that suit than he did in *kurta-pajama*. I wondered if the Englishman would move like an Indian if you took away all those rigid layers and put him in Bengali dress. I doubted it. He was probably like his clothes all the way down. It reminded me of my life before Pitaji had taken me away, where everything was stiff, and dull, and bad-smelling.

I decided I would rather be considered an inferior caste than be forced to wear European clothing all the time.

"Pitaji, do English people call you a lascar?"

"No. They mostly call me a black devil." His voice suggested he was making one of those adult jokes I didn't understand even when he explained them.

"Am I a black devil?"

"You most certainly are not. Although if you don't keep your hat on like *Tante* Sophie said, she'll be angry at me for letting you go dark."

Going dark was a bad thing, I knew—although personally, I thought brown skin was far more beautiful than what they called white, which was often blotchy, uncomfortably pink, and in hot weather, dripping with sweat. My own skin was the lightest in the house, a fact that, while it should have earned the approval of *Tante* Sophie, instead seemed to cause her considerable irritation. Particularly when I took it for granted.

In any case, going dark meant the open disapproval of *Tante* Sophie, and I had long since learned that whenever I caused problems in the house, I might get the beating, but Pitaji would get the blame.

Pitaji was the older brother. In theory, he was the authority within the house, but in practice, the cost of exasperating my aunt and uncle could be disproportionate.

So, I tended to choose my enquiries and rebellions with care. I wore my hat when the sun was high, and my European clothing when I might be seen by Sophie's European friends or Ram's business partners. I saved my idiosyncratic questions for when I was alone with Pitaji, or his mother, *Daadi-ma,* or my ever-patient *ayah.*

I was even learning the finer points of needlework.

CHAPTER TWENTY-TWO

E ach of Lakshmi's four memory-images, I noticed, was linked
to a metaphorical frame: twice the image was inside a window,
and once a bed's frame with a mosquito net. Even when the image
was of the sky's painted dome, she mentioned the word *"cadre"*:
frame. And yet, like the lantern's paper strips, the images around
which each of her chapters was built seemed to flicker past, like
the zoetrope, rather than sit in static solitude within frames on a
wall. The chapters reduced her "seven or eight" years of existence to
four brief scenes, and yet I felt that I was seeing the continuity of
the child's development, from a near-infant weeping for her
mother, to a young mind wrestling with physics, natural science,
and linguistics, to a child becoming aware of the beauty, the wonder, and the cruelty of her adopted home.

Was this going to be the memoir of a woman fighting to lib-
erate the sub-continent, before Mr Gandhi had created his own
movement towards independence? And what did her experience
with India have to do with the three Indian men—*possibly* Indian
men—who had asked about Damian and then broken into his
house? My mistrust of coincidence was not as inflexible as Holmes',
but to have a "lascar" break in, probably searching for boxes that

happened to contain a journal about India? Simple common sense would say the two were related.

On the other hand, Damian's sketch could as easily be of a man from Isfahan, Istanbul, or Cairo. As for the testimony of Dot, the cinema devotee, I would not want to rest the path of an investigation on her identification. Lascars tended to work on British ships, not French ones, and even in Britain were seldom found very far inland from a port city.

If in fact the invader was from somewhere other than India, the "coincidence" took a large step back, and the reasons to mistrust it grew thin.

I could only hope that the rest of the journal contained clues that would set me on my way.

CHAPTER TWENTY-THREE

HOLMES

Friday's dawn found Sherlock Holmes on a train travelling west out of Carcassonne. Not as early as he might have chosen, but the slight delay was preferable to the risk of granting a pair of watching eyes the advantage of full darkness. And the faster train meant that no one could get to Toulouse ahead of him.

None of which internal discussion had he shared with Damian, for fear that he would regard his father's caution as further evidence of paranoia.

Once in Toulouse, he should be in time to catch one of the faster trains to Paris. If he failed, he would be forced to abandon his plans and instead make his way back to Ste Chapelle: there would be little point in presenting himself at the doors of the *Institut de France* after their closing times, when the Academicians had gone home to their *bifteck* and burgundy.

He'd picked up a two-day-old copy of *Le Temps* in Carcassonne, and used it to keep an eye on his fellow passengers above its pages and under the brim of the hat he'd borrowed from Damian. None looked remotely Indian, or even foreign. None had evinced the slightest interest in him.

A stir ran through the car as passengers familiar with the landmarks began to collect their things. The train puffed into the station only seven minutes late, having been delayed in a tiny village by a cart that had lost its wheel as it crossed the tracks, spilling melons in all directions. Many of the travellers currently rising to their feet had a cantaloupe melon tucked under their arm like a football.

Holmes slipped out ahead of the triumphant gleaners and onto the north-bound Express, taking a seat towards the back of the car. The seats were open-style rather than compartments, so he saw the man with the turban get on at the front end of the car. The man stood for a moment to survey the other passengers, showing no more interest in the thin, grey-haired man at the back than he did in any of the others. It was not the man of Damian's sketch, being both slimmer and shorter. Still, Holmes watched him, until the man disembarked in Limoges, having not spoken to another soul other than the ticket collector the whole time. Nor did he appear to make contact with any of the boarding passengers—although Holmes kept an eye on the late-boarders, most of whom were either young women or old men. None looked even faintly Indian; none paid him the least attention.

In Paris, he did take the precaution of giving a decoy destination as he entered the taxi at the ranks, changing his mind as soon as they entered the stream of traffic—but by that time it was merely a bow to protocol.

The *Institut de France* was not an entity that embraced the traveller and tourist. Its doors were firmly shut most of the time, other than the gilded cupola and the *Bibliothèque Mazarine*. With luck, the library would still be open, and save him from negotiating with the guards on the steps of the *Coupole*.

Fortunately, he was well armed with francs.

Patience, a stubborn refusal to be dismissed, a manner as aloof as any grandee, and a lavish distribution of *gratuités* eventually led him to the home of Damian's diminutive concierge with the paradoxical name. M. LeGrand peered curiously around the door at his intruder, a large checked table napkin under his collar. Damian's description of him as an elf was oddly apt, less for his height than for his delicate features, wind-tossed white hair, and vague air of mischief brewing.

"Monsieur LeGrand?" Holmes asked in his most Parisian of accents, and without waiting for confirmation, launched into profuse apologies for interrupting this faithful servant of the *République* at his dinner hour, lengthy explanations of the difficulties of needing assistance during the *fin de la semaine* (no crass "week-end" here), oblique mentions of the bribes already handed out to concierges, and sincere concerns over the well-being of a certain artist whom M. LeGrand might recall from a visit during the summer.

The man's expression had gone from irritation to impatience, though it dipped into interest at the mention of hard cash—but when he realised who the referred-to artist was (and perhaps remembered the artist's own *gratuité*) he snatched the napkin from under his chin and flung open the door, practically clicking his slippered heels in an eagerness to assist.

"Come," he urged. "I am pleased to meet any friend of M. Adler, a most charming young man, and so very talented. Myself, I am an avid devotee of the modern styles, and I believe M. Adler will be a force to be reckoned with. It was fortuitous, that meeting—I am partially retired now, so I am only at *l'Institut* three days a week. Come, sit. A glass of wine? Have you eaten? Perhaps a soupçon of this really quite adequate coq au vin?"

The man had not cooked his own dinner, which sat on the table in a dish along with potatoes and a mélange of carrots and haricots verts. Whether part of serviced accommodations, or a less formal arrangement with a neighbour, this was a meal for one, and although it had indeed been a long time since Holmes' last meal, he was not keen on receiving portions transferred from the man's own plate.

"No, thank you, I have eaten—please, you must finish your meal. Although I would welcome a glass of your wine."

Wine served, chair pulled out, and napkin reluctantly replaced, M. LeGrand shyly resumed his meal while Holmes narrated some pointless and half-invented story about Damian Adler that served primarily to make it unnecessary for the man to speak.

But when the bones had been stripped and the serving dishes were mostly empty, Holmes extended an invitation to perhaps venture down to a nearby establishment where he might be permitted to repay M. LeGrand's hospitality with a glass of wine?

Shoes instantly replaced slippers, neck-tie and suit-jacket were resumed, and LeGrand amiably led Holmes three streets away to a bistro several stages more expensive than the four they'd passed along the way.

As Holmes had anticipated, a liberal hand with a bottle of good wine opened the man up to an accounting of what LeGrand called, with an arch and slightly inebriated humour, *L'Affaire Vernet*.

Holmes sat patiently through the man's tale of how Damian came to the *Institut* last month, how LeGrand had been on duty, how he was busy, but when M. Adler revealed that he was related to the great Vernet family, LeGrand had decided he would show this eager young man where the great man had worked. "But you think to yourself, surely Vernet is a painter that LeGrand should scorn, *un artiste démodé*? But no! Horace Vernet was a man who turned his back on the Classical style, who experimented with the new, who disdained austerity and embraced the physicality of his subjects, from soldiers to horses. His work is out of fashion, but in it one can see the groundwork of what the avant-garde is aiming to do. Monsieur Adler, as I said to your young man—"

Holmes stirred, to correct him on the name, then decided not to interrupt the man's flow of words out or wine in.

Eventually, however, when most of the wine was gone and Holmes was halfway through his cassoulet (LeGrand, demurring that he'd already eaten, then capitulated and ordered two hors d'oeuvres and a dessert that cost more than Holmes' entire meal— "To keep you company, Monsieur Adler"), Holmes corrected him.

"I am sorry, Monsieur, my name is not Adler. It is Holmes."

The small man dropped his fork in astonishment. It was an extreme reaction to a minor correction, and Holmes kicked himself, that he hadn't moved the discussion on to business before LeGrand could reach this level of inebriation.

"*Holmes?*" the *Institut* man exclaimed.

"That is correct." He was not about to add the name Sherlock, which would surely confound the man completely.

"Adler *and* Holmes? Both of you?"

After a moment, Holmes lowered his own fork. "The names mean something to you?"

"The instructions! *Bon Dieu,* that I should meet you both!"

At that, the detective shoved his meal to the side and leaned forward over the table. "M. LeGrand, please explain yourself."

CHAPTER TWENTY-FOUR

FIFTH IMAGE

FRAMES WITHIN FRAMES

It is curious, how a vivid memory-picture may enshrine what seems the most mundane of events. One can understand why a young mind would preserve a mother's tears or a shocking act of casual brutality, but why should a row of leather spines on a shelf create such a persistent memory, or a brown hand lifting a gilt-edged tea-cup? And what is remarkable about a tableau of four people standing before a fireplace, holding a brief and nearly incomprehensible conversation?

I suspect that this particular image was carved into my mind because of all the emotional overtones—that what I was seeing was clearly important, yet also contradictory and perplexing. I had spied on Sophie and Ram before, often with one or another servant, fascinated by the change in their speech, attitude, even stance when they were alone. But in this case, I was spying by accident.

The frame around this image is low, dark, and uneven. I was looking through the legs of a long rococo sideboard, which I had feared was too narrow a space for me until I had actually forced myself beneath its carvings. My back throbbed where I had scraped it, and the dust prickled my nose, but I lay absolutely still. This was a room I was not permitted, which made it the place I was most tempted by.

Our house's formal drawing room was never used for mere domestic events, and only rarely for gatherings of non-European guests. The furniture, curtains, carpet, and chandelier—slightly too long for the height of the ceiling—were entirely French. The sculptures and vases were European, the art on the walls showed distant landscapes and unfamiliar events, but for one.

Over the fireplace, and the other reason I came here, was a painting of *Daadi-ma*. It fascinated me. In it, she was not much older than *Tante* Sophie, and dressed not in a sari, but a blue European gown with a million ruffles that bared a startling amount of chest. She wore glittering sapphires at her throat and ears, her hair was elaborately lifted, and her skin looked so pale, I suspected she used rice powder like Sophie. I did not believe it was the same woman until *Daadi-ma* herself confirmed it.

The expression on the painting, however, was one I knew well. I saw it most often during our family dinners, at which I was getting old enough to occasionally be included. Whenever *Tante* Sophie had a grievance, and would stab at her food while reciting every detail of her indignation, *Daadi-ma*'s face wore that expression: tolerant, serene, and not really listening.

The disregard only added to Sophie's anger, although she could not react openly.

This memory-image includes the lower portion of that painting, with the half smile and the sapphires, but it seemed appropriate, since one of the four people in front of the fireplace was *Tante* Sophie in a state of indignation, and having to hide it.

She wore a blue silk dress with vast sleeves, newly arrived from Paris. My uncle Ram was sweating in the many snug layers of his European evening suit. One of their two guests wore European clothing, although his was a day suit, and some years out of style.

It was the fourth man who held my attention. In part, it was the *kurta-pajama* he wore which, though silk, simply did not belong in this room. He was also bare-headed, which was rare for non-Europeans inside the house, and had a dramatic white streak in his hair, beginning at a scar along the top of his forehead. But mostly, it was his manner.

He was unmistakably the most important person there. No, it went beyond that, I decided: my aunt and uncle were afraid of him. They tried to hide it, Ram in his jovial manner and Sophie in her nervous laughs, but I could feel it from where I lay, and it kept me pressed motionless into the darkness.

Which was strange. The two of them, faced with the most aristocratic of Hindus or Muslims, would invariably cling to their sense of superiority. We were, after all, French.

Except we weren't, not really. Pitaji's French-speaking ancestors had come to India in the 1690s, but only the men. Early generations married local girls, or went to one of the other Franco-Indian colonies for a bride—the lighter-skinned, the better. Not until Pitaji's grandfather did one of the sons go to Paris for a bride-hunt. And yet, Sophie, Ram, and most of their friends violently denied the thought of being mixed heritage. *Nous Français* were not Indian—even though any actual French people who came to India openly disdained people like us with accented voices and tinted skins. It embarrassed Sophie to have her mother-in-law wear a sari and mark her forehead with the *tilak,* or have Pitaji change into *kurta-pajama* as soon as he got home. She tried to pretend we all ate French-style bread for breakfast and went to church every Sunday, ignoring the *slap-slap* of the cook making roti and the sprinkles of water on every threshold from *Daadi-ma's* morning *puja.* Ram kept his hubble-bubble private, and smoked cigars with his friends. Curry and roti were never served to guests. *Dhobi* and *mali* became "washerman" and "gardener" in conversation with their friends.

Sophie tried to behave as if the family was merely enjoying a brief time here in India before we returned to our home in Paris. She had never been to France, not even for her honeymoon. It made her face twist in bitterness to be reminded that I was actually from there, just as it infuriated her that my skin colour was lighter than hers, despite her using rice powder.

Even without this man with the white streak in his hair, I would have taken care to keep my silence. Were I noticed, Ram would drag me out, Sophie would beat me—the marks would not show— and both of them would then go and harangue Pitaji about my ill behaviour.

I was already, I knew, on the uncomfortable edge of a change. Restrictions were coming—no cause to hurry them along. Lie still, don't sneeze, think about other things, instead of why Sophie and Ram were frightened of a man who had darker skin than they did and spoke poorer French.

Think about being twelve years old.

I had turned twelve a few weeks before. I knew, even then, that this would be my last year of untrammelled freedom, a bittersweet time of joy and exploration of my place in the world—my several places, for my several worlds.

First there was the home around me, a stuccoed brick Franco-Indian palace in the French colony of Chandernagore, some twenty miles upriver from Calcutta, which—although once Chandernagore's poorer neighbour—was now the capital of the British East India Company, and therefore of British India as a whole.

Over the years, my own family's business turned exclusively to indigo, primarily as brokers. The indigo was grown, fermented, and processed up in the Bengali hinterland, with the dried cubes of dye packed into crates or barrels, then arranged in mango-wood boxes and marked with the identity of each factory.

Our name was known to Paris *couturières,* famous for the dependability of our dyes and the richness of the blues they produced. When Pitaji met my mother—my married, French mother—he had been in Paris representing the business to the court of Louis Philippe. *Tante* Sophie's dresses, cut in whatever latest fashion had reached this faraway place, were almost invariably some shade of blue. She was a walking advertisement for our wares.

The house was on a rise well back from the River Hooghly, in an area exclusively French—or at any rate, "French." In the mornings, we woke to the odours from a nearby bakery, which would later deliver the dull and tasteless version of bread rolls that my aunt Sophie ate every day, while the rest of us enjoyed our roti and fruit. In the afternoons, the *mali* and his boy would try to keep Sophie's bed of cut flowers alive by hauling buckets of green water from the pond created when the building's bricks were made, nearly a hundred years before. In the evening, a breeze would rise, rattling the palm fronds and banana leaves and trying its best to push through the mosquito nets over our sweating bodies.

Chandernagore was an active port. The family godowns, wharves, and docks were prominent on the waterfront, and the place where Pitaji and his brother, Ram—who called himself Richard—spent most of their working days. Once a week, leaving sometimes before dawn, Pitaji would take the family carriage down to Calcutta for a day of meetings. If Ram wasn't going, and if I could talk my way out of the day's sessions with my tutors, I might be allowed to go along.

Because a day in Calcutta was a glorious thing.

Not only was the city filled with all the heat, colour, smells, noise, and motion imaginable, it gave me an entire day without the constraints of *Tante* Sophie and *Oncle* Ram. Best of all, now that I had turned twelve, once our carriage reached the company godowns, a place of colossal bales and mountains of wooden crates and the bustle of clerks and the chants of stevedores, I could disappear.

Before that year, Pitaji had judged me too young to be off in the city without him. And at thirteen, I would be considered a young woman, with all the complications thereof—my future was already the topic of heated discussions. But for that one year, every two or three weeks for twelve precious months, he permitted me to roam.

Not unsupervised, by no means. But I see that I have yet to mention Arjun.

Arjun was my co-conspirator, my friend, my uncle in all but blood. To *Tante* Sophie, he was a servant with ideas above his place, shown by his occasional appearance in a European suit. To *Oncle* Ram, he was the aggravating voice that turned his brother against any business plans Ram might propose. To Pitaji, Arjun was his right hand, the assistant who knew every secret, his partner in all but name. The brother that Ram refused to be.

Arjun was the one Pitaji could trust with me.

Looking back, I suspect that my relative freedom that year was a hard-fought compromise: I would be permitted a degree of autonomy, with Arjun setting aside his other responsibilities to keep me from harm.

In truth, I was more than happy to put myself under the care of this de facto uncle. Arjun was a little younger than Pitaji, in his middle thirties when he joined our ship in Pondichéry, travelling with us the last thousand miles up the coast of India to Chandernagore. He and Pitaji had known each other for more than fifteen years, Arjun as the company's representative in the southern colony. His wife had died in childbirth just two years before, and he had decided to turn their two sons over to his sister and join Pitaji in Chandernagore.

I doubt the decision cost him a lot of time. His sister's family was large and amiable, while he and Pitaji fit together, as I say, like brothers. Infinitely capable, darkly handsome, Arjun managed to combine an enormous decency and grace with a most unexpected taste for devilry. And his eyes never missed a thing when it came to the trouble I was about to take us both into, whether it was jumping near-naked into the river or setting off into parts of the town no European girl would ever be seen in.

We would return to the godowns filthy, exhausted, and pleased with the day's mischief. If we had the time, we would scrub ourselves and change our clothes—Arjun only donned a suit if he had to participate in a meeting. As the carriage trotted us back to Chandernagore, I would invariably fall asleep to the voices of the two men, Arjun's reporting on what I'd seen, done, and learned during the day—the bounce of Pitaji's chest as he laughed sometimes rousing me from sleep—followed by the calm drone of Pitaji bringing Arjun up to date on the day's business.

We always returned home at the appointed time. If I was clean, Pitaji and I would both go in the front door, all demure, taking care not to meet each other's eyes. If I had been too rushed to change, I would scurry around the back, so Sophie would not witness my ragamuffin ways.

That night in the drawing room would have been after a Calcutta day. I rarely wore *kurta-pajama* when *Tante* Sophie was at home, and almost never those of a boy. However, as I lay beneath the sideboard, praying that my stomach didn't growl or my nose succumb to the dust, I was not merely worried about what Sophie and Ram would do if they discovered me. There was some threat in the room far greater than the risk of Sophie's beating and Ram's more subtle punishments.

I could not understand what was going on in front of me. The conversation was about a shipment and a bribe and the need to keep the British away—so far as I could understand, the usual things. But the degree of tension in the voices kept me motionless. Ram and Sophie were afraid of this man with the white streak, and yet they were also plotting something with him. And the man, he seemed to be toying with them, holding it over them that, despite the big house and the family name and the crystal chandelier over his head, he was the one in power. The one whose favour was being sought. It was a negotiation, I knew that, but using the kind of adult talk—business talk, not flirtation talk—that had layers of meaning even a bright child could not interpret.

Whatever it was, they eventually reached an agreement. Ram and Sophie were relieved. The man with the white streak was satisfied. The fourth person, the man in the out-of-date suit, had said not a word the whole time. As Ram and the man with the white streak shook hands, I studied the cold look of contempt this voiceless man wore, and shrank even further into my skin.

I remained like a mouse in a snake's den until they left, and for some time after that. Only when I heard the front door close did I fling myself at the narrow gap under the sideboard and fight my way out, ripping the back of my *kurta* before I scrambled for the stairs.

I needed to ask Pitaji what it meant. He would explain those adult overtones to me. But I knew Pitaji would go to Ram, which would make Sophie even more furious with me, and both of them would find some way to make Pitaji pay for my many wickednesses—the hiding, and the wearing boys' *kurta-pajama*, and the being in the drawing room in the first place, and my adventures in Calcutta would come out, and . . .

And Ram might decide to tell the man with the white streak that I had spied on their conversation. The thought of the man and his silent, contemptuous partner showing up in my house was enough to bring nightmares.

I never did talk to Pitaji about it, but a long time later, I asked Arjun about that night. When I described the man with the white streak, he looked startled, and said a word that a young lady was not supposed to know. The man was the head of a criminal organisation, a band of *Thuggees* that specialised in crimes to order—robbery and murder, yes, but also smuggling. This last not only fit with what my young ears had heard, but with rumours that had come to Arjun. By the end of that discussion, neither of us would have been shocked by the idea of Ram dabbling in criminal enterprise.

But that was later, and in another place, when India and its beauties and enchantments and dangers were far behind us.

CHAPTER TWENTY-FIVE

At least I was assembling a few clues, out of the painstaking labour of translation. Chandernagore was not a large city, and any family of indigo merchants important enough to own godowns—warehouses—on the riverfront would surely have left its stamp on the city's history. Should I send a telegram to the city hall, or the police department? Where in India were public records kept?

Perhaps I should start at this end of things. No doubt the indigo industry collapsed into nearly nothing once synthetic dyes came along in the 1890s, but any French research library would have some degree of information about the large import firms in their colonies. And with a name, I might be fortunate enough to track down Lakshmi's descendants through the telephone directories. Who knows, there might be a granddaughter who could tell me how the journal had got into the Vernet boxes.

Then again, Lakshmi might shed the coyness and give me her surname before the end of her story. Someone this extraordinary must have left her mark on the world—even if she was a woman, thus kept from the important realms of politics and scientific advancement. She had lived long enough to write this journal. Perhaps, given a birth date and the few facts she had let drop, I could find more about who she had been. French girl, lived in India, indigo exporters in a small enclave such as the French colony north of Calcutta—yes, I was certain that would be enough to get me started.

I began to review the names of people I'd met in India who might help me, wondered if it wouldn't be simpler to summon help, realised that this meant asking Mycroft to act as go-between with his counterparts in French Intelligence, and finally decided that I really did not want to bring either Mycroft or the *Deuxième Bureau* into matters. Simpler to wire directly the city hall and the office of the colonial governor in Pondichéry. I was writing a note to remind myself when a sort of scratching noise came from the kitchen.

I listened, then got up to see whether Damian had rats.

Not rats, but a face at the door's window: Mme LaRue's brother, Pierre.

He saw me and held up both hands, one with a bucket, the other with the basket I'd seen the previous morning with eggs in it. I opened the door and greeted him, but he merely nodded and edged in around me with his burdens: coal for the cookstove, and eggs, which he laid, one by one, along the narrow ledge on the back of the counter-space. I thanked him as he left and reached out to close the door, but he held up a hand to stop me, went down the two steps, and turned back with a perfect little bouquet of summer flowers.

I thanked him profusely. He touched his hat and left. I found a vase in a cupboard, and took the flowers with me to the paper-strewn dining table.

Following that light-hearted interval, the author's next lines came as a shock.

CHAPTER TWENTY-SIX

Sixth Image

The *Tilak*

When it comes to death in India, there is no room for lingering doubts. Nothing to soften the blow. A person dies, and within hours, their body is gone. For the traditional Hindu, this means being washed, wrapped in a white cloth, and taken to the burning ghats by the side of the river. Dry wood is laid, a torch is lowered, and the loved one is consumed in eager flames and a cloud of smoke that smells like nothing else in the world and coats the back of the throat for days. When the fire has cooled, the priests sweep the bones and ashes into the river to complete life's cycle.

For a Christian, there is not even the elemental spectacle. A hole is dug, the body is hidden away. Where the Hindu is dispersed to the waters in a city's midst, the European is hedged around by lead and covered over by stone.

But no matter the faith or heritage, in a hot climate there is no delay.

I had just turned fourteen when Pitaji died and my life ended.

No more laughter. No more adventures, no more lessons in peculiar activities—peculiar for girls, certainly. No more days in Calcutta, no more speaking in Hindi, no more word games or dressing up as a native or lying out at night tracking the stars.

Pitaji died on a Tuesday morning in a Calcutta alleyway, alone.

I was not with him that day. Even though I was officially a "young lady," I still went with him into the city as often as I could, but not that day.

I had proposed that morning to abandon my breakfast and throw on my clothes, but he shook his head. "I need Arjun today, there's been some difficulties he needs to look at. I can't do it myself—I am to meet with a textile manufacturer from Lyons, who saw that silk we sent the Princess Hélène two years ago. He wants an exclusive contract for that colour."

"Well, make him pay heavily."

"I intend to."

"You should take Arjun, after he's finished with his difficulties." Arjun had a knack for judging when a negotiation could be pushed a bit farther.

"I think he'd prefer to stay at the godown. We don't know this man." Meaning, he did not know how this Frenchman would look upon sitting down to negotiate in the company of a man with brown skin.

"Well, Arjun will be happier anyway if you don't make him climb into a suit. That's a handsome one, by the way."

Pitaji made a perfect picture as he stood framed by the library doorway: a good-looking man with traces of grey in his hair and humour in his eyes, dressed in a cream-coloured silk suit that would be well creased by the time he returned home.

"I thought new clothes might bring me luck."

"I could go with you. I'd distract him while you quietly upped the price."

He laughed at my offer of coquetry. "Tempting, but your history tutor is coming."

"The man is only interested in Europe."

"Which you will need to know before you go back."

"Whyever would I want to return to Europe?" I asked.

"To see your mother?"

I was surprised that he would raise that delicate subject. Not that I was completely alienated from her—she wrote several times a year, letters that I read and re-read in search of meaning behind the mundane details of her life. My writing to her was more difficult, and had to be done through one or another of her friends. My half brother—my legitimate half brother—was only two years older than I, and reminding the man I had called Papa that I, the by-blow of his wife's infidelity, was still out there and writing affectionate letters would have consequences for which I did not want to be responsible.

Besides, *Maman* was another world.

"So I can lecture her about the Hundred Years' War? No thank you."

"Well, today is not a good day. Perhaps next week."

"With luck, it'll be a little cooler. You're going to be damp through by the time you get home."

"I'm afraid so."

"Too bad you can't wear that nice *kurta* the *durzi* made you last month," I said.

He looked down at the form-fitting tailored suit and shook his head sadly. "It will be a long time, I fear, before a European recognises the *kurta-pajama* as business attire. We speak the language of those in power, and at present that language is French or English, along with uncomfortable clothes and the Hundred Years' War. So perhaps you ought to get on with it."

"Well, you look very impressive," I told him, and ate my egg as the carriage left.

In the afternoon, I retreated to the relative cool of the library with a book, to be wakened by the sounds of the cook answering the back door. After a moment of vague pity for the poor soul who had been forced to do a delivery in the heat of the day, I retrieved the book and propped it open on my stomach—only to have it bang to the floor as an unearthly wail rose up through the house. I dashed out of the room and went in search of the noise, following voices to the sitting room where *Tante* Sophie awkwardly patted at the hunched-over shoulders of my *grand-mère*.

"*Daadi-ma,*" I cried, "what is it? What happened?"

She raised her tear-soaked face and told me.

He was gone. My life, my friend, my companion at arms, my father: Robbed. Stabbed. *Dead?*

My world went still—and yet, all around me, everything began to move so very fast. Before sunset, Arjun had come with Pitaji's body. I had a glimpse of cream-coloured silk stained with dried blood, but when I tried to follow, *Daadi-ma* stopped me, saying I was too young. She and Meera, the old *ayah* who had been with the family her whole life, would take care of cleansing and anointing and wrapping what was now an empty body.

I was permitted to see him when they were finished. The casket was lined with the finest silk, the pale blue of a dawn sky. The marks of his assault were hidden from view, with a length of his cotton wrapping-cloth around his head to conceal the damage. All that showed was his face, framed by silk and cotton, bruised but peaceful. On his brow was the first *tilak* I had seen him wear. *Daadi-ma* had painted it on. *Tante* Sophie frowned at it, and turned away.

Pitaji was buried in the afternoon, in the family's portion of the Chandernagore cemetery.

And when we got home, *Oncle* Ram was wearing the signet ring. He was now the head of the family.

The arguments began at once. And they centred primarily on me.

I was not a child, despite my father having treated me as such. In the future, I was to dress and behave as my station required. No more native clothing; I would wear proper skirts from here on, at home as well as outside. Enough of the tutors as well—and surely it wasn't too soon to begin looking for appropriate marriage partners?

Under different circumstances, I might have been outraged. As it was, I was so stunned by grief, I barely registered what was being said over my head.

Daadi-ma broke it up, getting to her feet to pronounce to all that this was not the time or place for such decisions. And such was her natural authority, neither Ram nor Sophie argued further. She ushered me out of the room, helped Meera put me to bed, and sat with me until I fell, exhausted, into sleep.

Hours later, in the still of the night, her hands woke me—one on my shoulder, the other gently touching my mouth. "Shush," she whispered, "shush, child, but you need to wake up now."

"Wha—"

"Quiet! For the love of your father, you must be silent."

The room's only illumination was a beam of moonlight through the window, but she moved as surely as if she'd brought in a large oil lamp. Drawers were pulled open and left that way, as she gave me clothing to put on—*kurta-pajama*, not a dress. Other garments she folded rapidly into the valise she'd placed on the floor. On top went my hair-brush and little inlaid jewellery-box; a small, much-loved watercolour portrait of Pitaji and me, done by a friend; three books kept always on the shelf near my bed. She knew what I loved, she put them into the valise, and then she took off the shawl she was wearing—the one I loved best of all her garments, solid with embroidery, the silken threads all the possible shades of the family indigo.

She folded it, gave it a kiss, and put it on the top of the other things. She fastened the buckle.

"Come," she whispered.

But I paused, looking down at the first thing Pitaji had ever given me, the image-lantern. He'd never actually said it was mine, but . . .

She hesitated, then gave a quick nod. "Quickly," she urged, and helped me take it apart and pack it into its silk-lined case.

She carrying the valise and I the lamp, we went silently through the sleeping house to the kitchen, out of the door, and through the garden.

In the moonlight, I could see a figure, holding the reins of the pony.

Arjun.

He kept his hand over the pony's nostrils as I climbed into the buggy, to keep the creature silent, then walked back to lift my two bags into the dog-cart. There seemed to be a number of trunks and bags there already, held securely by rope.

He walked up to *Daadi-ma* and took her hand, bending down to press his face against it. She laid her other hand on his turbaned head, and as he straightened, just before she stood back, I thought I saw her push something into his hands, wrapped in a faded dish-cloth I recognised from the kitchen. But when he turned back to me, he held nothing.

She took my hand then, and when I bent down to kiss hers as Arjun had done, she laid her old hands against my face and kissed me.

"Do not write," she whispered. "I will know you are happy and well, but do not write to tell me."

Arjun slapped the pony into a trot, and we were gone.

CHAPTER TWENTY-SEVEN

HOLMES

Holmes thought for a moment that M. LeGrand was going to lay claim to his half-eaten meal, and prepared to drive his fork through the man's hand to keep him on track. Fortunately, the man's profiteroles arrived, and the coffee he'd ordered with it, and at last, he seemed to be ready.

"People give things to *l'Institut*," Damian's elfin friend began. "All of the time. Some of it is of value, or at least of interest, but most of what comes is of little importance to anyone outside the family who has donated it. Those things we either sell or, if the donation has come with a large amount of cash, put in storage for a few years and then sell it.

"I have worked at the *Institut* since I turned sixteen, in 1881, starting with the *Poste* and working my way up into positions of more authority. I happened to be present when the boxes were transferred into the attics. One trunk," he corrected himself, "and three boxes. I was given the task of recording where the boxes were stored, and of attaching in plain view a letter—properly sealed, with red wax—that I was told contained instructions for the person who came to claim the boxes. I was to have a rope tied around the boxes, that the four might remain together, and attach the envelope to the largest one.

"On the front of the envelope, someone had written: 'Possessions of the Vernet family: hold until claimed by Adler or Holmes.'"

"Nothing else?"

"Not on the outside. There was a letter inside, but I did not read that."

"When was this?"

"In 1897. Or perhaps the following year? Towards the end of autumn, I remember, since there was some discussion as to whether the contents, whatever they were, might suffer from the cold. I even made a note to myself to check them in the spring, to be certain they had not begun to leak or smell. They had not, so there they stayed."

"For three decades."

"Monsieur, there are things in distant corners of the buildings that have been gathering dust since the *ancien régime*. Every few years, we go through with the ledgers and check off that everything is still there, and not being damaged by roof leaks or mice."

"And things don't disappear?"

Any trace of humour in his manner was gone in an instant. "Monsieur, we are *l'Institut de France*. Our *académies* are responsible for the nation's arts, the study of her history, and our scientific development. We are trusted to preserve the very language we speak. We at *l'Institut* do not allow the things for which we are responsible to 'disappear.'"

"Certainly not these four boxes—or trunk and boxes."

LeGrand allowed his affront to subside, helped by a little more of the wine. "They had become like old friends," he admitted. "I dusted them from time to time, and made sure not only that they were not irretrievably hidden beneath the other stored goods, but that the envelope remained secure on its nail. I had begun to fear that I would never learn what they meant. Until M. Adler came and asked to see the rooms where Horace Vernet once painted. A relative of the young man's, I believe?"

"So I understand," Holmes said vaguely. "But you didn't give him the boxes, then and there."

"Oh no, Monsieur. For one thing, it was not my place to do so. But also, I am aware that there are many varieties of thief, and I am certain that some are more clever than I. No, I merely took his card so we would know where to find him, then turned the problem over to my superior the next morning."

"And what did he do?"

"He spoke to *le Directeur*, and then both men came to look at the boxes. *Le Directeur* pulled off the envelope and read the inscription—but I was greatly disturbed to see that the red seal had been broken away. I told them, however, that the flap had been sealed down again before the letter was returned to its nail. He tore it open—and out fell an old five-hundred-franc note! He read the letters—two pages of letter, both different kinds of paper. Then he folded everything up and took it away. He did not tell me what the letters said."

"Interesting."

"It was indeed. I understand that they later opened the boxes, in order to judge the value of their contents. But whatever they found, the prospect of losing them did not raise any alarm."

"You did not see?"

"It was a day I was not at work. When I returned, it was clear that the tops had been removed and then nailed down again. And then the following week when I came in, the boxes were missing entirely. I was told that they had been sent by train for M. Adler to retrieve, in a small town to the south called Délieux. But I assume you know that. I hope the boxes did reach him, in the end?"

"They did."

"Do you ... perhaps you could tell me, in general terms of course, what they contained?"

"I can't, I'm sorry."

"I understand, that was indiscreet of me."

"Not at all. I cannot say what is in them because I have not myself seen. Shall I let M. Adler know you are interested?"

"He will think me meddlesome."

"He will think you concerned. And I imagine he will want to thank you for your long years of diligent attention to these four 'old friends.'"

LeGrand came near to blushing with pleasure. "I am sufficiently paid. Only my curiosity stands unrewarded."

"I will see what I can do to assist. But surely others must have been curious. Did no one learn what the letters contained?" In Holmes' experience, one had to work to keep information from the clerks who ran such an organisation as the *Institut de France*.

"Oh, there was certainly discussion—even among the Members! I heard one say there had been nothing at all in the envelope, another that there was a stack of thousand-franc notes. There was also much interest that M. Adler himself had not 'claimed' the boxes, as the writing on the envelope had clearly specified, nor was there a sign of the Holmes person. Others were of the opinion that the note on the envelope, in absence of further details, was in fact the entirety of the instructions. That when someone named Adler or Holmes claimed the Vernets as family, it was the same as claiming the Vernet boxes."

"An appropriately academic dispute," Holmes commented. "I'm astonished they're not still arguing."

LeGrand gave him a grin containing all the mischief that Holmes had suspected at first meeting. "They might be, were their energies not taken up with constructing their critiques of the Art Deco Exposition. Who cares about the ownership of a few unimportant paintings when the *Académie* is faced with the abomination of requiring 'art' to be 'decorative'?"

Holmes gave an obliging laugh, then asked, "What happened to the letter—or letters—in the end? Were they sent to M. Adler with the boxes?"

"I imagine they have been filed away somewhere with the other forms and letters of bequest. One never knows when a donated piece of art will suddenly become the centre of a family dispute, and the *Institut* must stand prepared to defend its endowments."

A final pour from the bottle, a few more oblique questions, and Holmes had prised out not only the name of the Director, who had opened the letter, but the inside intelligence that he and one of the other *Immortels* were in the habit, in rain, shine, or whirling snow, of a long stroll from their homes in the Fifth arrondissement and along the river to the *Pont d'Iéna,* then back along the Rive Droite, pausing in the Tuileries before continuing to the Île Saint-Louis and home.

Holmes fished out his pocket watch, and sighed.

Too late even to send a telegram, to let Russell know where he was. He'd have to do it in the morning.

CHAPTER TWENTY-EIGHT

The abrupt and violent death of Pitaji came as a shock. I felt I had known this man—Krishna, also called Christian, who had nurtured an extraordinary little girl to maturity. It was ludicrous to grieve for a man who would in any event have died long before I'd found his daughter's book. Nonetheless, what I felt was grief. And suspicion. The murder of a man who was not only head of his family, but director of its business, raised all my instincts. Had I been there, I'd have begun by questioning the brother, Ram, as to his whereabouts, and his relationship with the local cult of *Thuggee* . . . but Ram, too, was long in his lead-lined coffin in Chandernagore's Christian cemetery, and the gold signet ring would have long since passed to another man.

I wondered if the town's constabulary—assuming it had one at the time—had even investigated the matter.

Still, I was relieved that Lakshmi had made her escape and been freed to survive long enough to compose the enigma of the image-journal.

I rose from my cramped seat and stretched, hard. Twisted ankle or no, my legs needed a brief walk if they were not to forget entirely how to function. I strapped up the foot, decided that the house would be safe from lascars or other burglars while the sun shone, and went for a circuit of the village.

I had seen it six years before, and thought it a charming place. It still was, with a cobbled main street, a handful of shops, a *boulangerie*—closed at this hour—and a small bar/bistro that was giving out some promising odours. The gaol where Damian had been held was now a shop selling cheeses, pâtés, and biscuits from all over—an unexpected touch of sophistication. A cat sat on a window ledge at the beginning of my walk, another occupied a wall at the end, with an elderly lady peering out of the lace-obscured window behind it. I gave her a wave; she instantly retreated, lest she be thought a busybody.

I could see why Damian and Aileen would choose to live here— why, indeed, Irene Adler had chosen it herself, as a place to raise a child. The distance to the end of the village and back to the cottage proved just the right amount of exercise for my ankle, and the front walk that had so challenged my crutches was simple with the cane. I admired the garden as I went through it.

I then remembered that I had intended to take a closer look at the marks on the ground under the window. I found a lesser path, circling towards the side of the house, and found I was not alone. Someone's back was half-concealed by an exuberant, currently un-flowering shrub.

"*Bonjour,*" I called.

The shrub leapt about wildly, and a head emerged: Pierre, a clump of weeds trailing from one hand. I apologised for interrupt-ing him and wished him a good afternoon, but then I thought of something he might be able to help me with.

"Er, Pierre, may I ask you about something? It's over here, against the house. I was wondering, were you here the morning after M. Adler surprised the intruder?" He made a sound I took as the affirmative. "This window here," I continued, the two of us having reached that side of the house. "It's where the intruder climbed in. Now, your sister and her husband said that the man had dropped his big knife in the garden bed. Can you show me where?" He took a step into the garden bed and pulled back a branch of the hydrangea that grew there, using his free hand to point to the ground. As I'd thought, the disturbance there that looked as if someone had been about to plant a bulb was where the machete ended up. Now for the key question.

"It was stuck upright in the ground, wasn't it? Not lying flat?" He nodded. "Do you remember which way the sharp side was pointed?"

He thought for a moment, then startled me by abandoning gesture and breaking into speech that had a minor slur from his injuries but was perfectly comprehensible. "Its sharp side was towards the house. The spine was facing the garden. I thought at the time it was an odd way for the man to have dropped it."

I thanked him. He nodded, and returned to his weeding.

I went back in through the kitchen and across the hallway to the sitting room, leaning out of the window again to study the patch of disturbed soil.

It was indeed an odd way for a dropped knife to fall. Not impossible—I'd once nearly pinned my foot to the floor with a dropped kitchen knife, and still remembered the taut quiver of the thing sticking out of the boards beside my toe.

But ten inches from the wall, immediately below the window's centre, at a near-perfect right angle? From a knife with a circle of fingerprints around the very end of the handle?

"It wasn't a weapon," I decided aloud.

Damian's lascar had brought the knife to open the window. He had taken it into the house with him, yes—but once inside, he'd leaned out, dangled the thing over the soil, and let it drop, point-down.

Intruder, yes; assassin, no.

Well, that was something of a relief.

I left the windows standing open and went back to my translation.

CHAPTER TWENTY-NINE

SEVENTH IMAGE

THE DAGUERREOTYPE

Arjun and I had already worn two different identities by the time we stepped away from the sea. For the first leg of the journey, we had been a wealthy zamindar and his shy young boy servant, keeping mostly to our cabin. Then in Bombay, we shed those roles and changed our names to become—with careful face paint, hats to cover my initial clumsiness with putting up my hair, and a number of garments I recognised from my aunt Sophie's wardrobe—an English Miss on her way home from a successful hunt for a husband in India, travelling under the protection of her fiancé's trusted batman on the steam-packet service to Alexandria.

This was not the way Pitaji and I had come from France. The first leg of the journey did bring us wind in the sails; but after Bombay, Arjun and I breathed in the coal-stink of a noisy little steamer, across the Arabian Sea and up the Red Sea to Suez. There we changed smoke for dust, perched amidst the bags of mail on horse-drawn wagons as far as Cairo, where we planned to adopt a third set of identities before boarding an even smaller paddle-steamer for the trip down the Nile to Alexandria and a ship across the Mediterranean to France.

We had checked in to our first Alexandria hotel, as the mademoiselle and her fiancé's long-suffering servant, without any problem. We were in the process of re-arranging our things for a third transformation—three trunks converted to seven assorted cases and valises, the affianced young lady turned into a grieving young widow, the batman into a fussy Bengali *babu* earning his way to Paris by escorting her—when the unexpected happened.

Arjun and I had an argument.

I was fourteen years old, and the room was unbearably stuffy and stank of camels and the too-sweet flowers I'd tossed out of the window. The desert heat and the little-washed clothing had inflicted the kind of maddening prickly-heat I'd never had in the baking humidity of Bengal. I was thoroughly sick of my aunt's clothing, and the pinch of the shoes, and the constant struggle to get my hair to come near to approximating that of the other female passengers. I mourned for Pitaji, but the thought of binding myself into the high-necked, long-sleeved, tight-waisted black dress Arjun had drawn from one of the trunks filled me with loathing. I both wished to see my mother again after all these years and dreaded returning to my family in Paris. I knew I could not go back to Chandernagore, but that was the only home I had.

Thus, we argued.

It hardly matters what it was about—my grumpy proposal that I be the *babu*'s nephew escalated into a half-humourous threat to scissor off my hair entirely, then a plea that we think about cutting all ties with both sides and set up our own establishment in Greece or Tangier, culminating in a furious adolescent protest that *he* wasn't my father and could not make decisions for me.

Even as I said it, I knew that last was a terrible thing to say to him, this man who had advised and trusted and loved Pitaji for longer than I had been alive. He nodded, picked up his hat, said he would return before evening, and left.

I did not cut off my hair while he was out.

He was late returning. I spent an hour of increasingly fraught indecision—go down to dinner on my own, since he was going to punish me by not coming back, or panic and go in search of him? I had arranged my hair four times, changed my clothing twice, and alternated between pacing the floors and staring out of the window at the street when finally his knock came at the door. I hurried over and flung it open.

"Arjun! Thank goodness, I'm so sorry, I was—"

"Good, you are dressed. Come—but bring with you the *kurta-pajama* you wore before Bombay. Not the silk ones."

"What is going on? Oh no—have they found us? We were so careful!" Why my uncle Ram might want me back so badly, I could not think, but *Daadi-ma's* parting words and Arjun's weeks of extreme caution made it abundantly clear that both of them believed he would.

However, Arjun did not look alarmed.

"Have who . . . ?" His face cleared. If anything, he looked pleased with himself. "No, there is no problem, not with your uncle Ram. This is another matter entirely, one that I think may be to our benefit. Come, hurry."

While he was out, Arjun had encountered one of those random coincidences that can cause a person to believe in the Fates, or the gods. He had gone down to the port offices and was waiting to book our passage to Alexandria when his eye happened to snag on a trunk's label, which bore a familiar surname. A few discreet questions directed him to the man himself.

An hour later I was sitting across from three French gentlemen in a private dining room, wearing the least travel-worn of *Tante* Sophie's indigo dresses, slightly too large and years out of style. Arjun sat beside me, which I took as an indication of the strangers' goodwill: any Europeans willing to break bread with a man from India could not be all bad.

They were an odd trio. The eldest, a man I would come to call, simply, Monsieur, was a well-known artist in his middle years, elegantly thin, avuncular in manner, and endlessly curious about the world. His assistant was a slightly myopic boy of twenty-one or -two, wide-eyed and worshipful towards his employer, with all-encompassing passion for a brand-new invention that allowed a person to set images—actual images of what was before him—onto metal plates. The daguerreotype had been revealed to the world just three months before and turned out to be the cause of the small mountain of boxed-up paraphernalia in the office that had caught Arjun's eye. The third man was Monsieur's nephew by marriage, a young army officer who had travelled with his uncle before.

All three were bearded, though recently shaven about the head. All three were dressed as if about to set off for a fancy-dress party, in Arab robes too new to have known a day's dust. I was not sure if Monsieur and his friends were indeed artists, or amateur explorers for whom art was an excuse, or if art was merely a camouflage for some government espionage that even I could see was fairly inexpert, but I did not suppose it mattered, for my purposes.

Shortly after soup, Arjun caught my eye and tipped his head at the door. I left, and returned a few minutes later wearing the *kurta-pajama,* my hair caught under the kind of loose turban worn here in North Africa. The waiter, who had cleared the soup and was serving the fish course, made to evict this urchin in the doorway, but I ducked beneath his arm, whining in complaint and thrusting out my hand, palm up, at Monsieur. He recoiled. His assistant spilled his wine. The army man stood to throw me out on my ear.

I then straightened, and addressed them in the voice they'd heard earlier.

In the interest of brevity, I will say merely that by the end of the evening, their wariness at the idea of taking me on had given way to amusement, or perhaps simply bemusement. Arjun and I between us convinced all three men that, once I had donned the proper local clothing, I could not only slip without remark into their assemblage of artists, guides, camel-wranglers, cooks, bearers, and general factotums, but that I might actually be of some use therein. As it turned out, the gentleman with the passion for daguerreotypes had very little skill to back up his enthusiasm, and although at first I knew even less than he did, my hands were clever enough and my eyes sufficiently sharp that I helped keep his expensive mistakes to a minimum.

Naturally, it all rested on my simply *being* a man, even after we returned to France. There was to be no scandal, no acknowledgment ever, that a young woman had spent some weeks in their midst. The local help hired over subsequent weeks thought merely that I was a young boy whom the Frenchmen had taken under their collective wings. But in the end, Monsieur didn't actually care, so long as I helped make it possible for him to work, and the others fell into line with his wishes.

The image that evokes this time of my life, then, is of a daguerreotype—but not the finished product. Rather, it is a picture of the camera itself, its brass lens pointing in our direction, the wooden box of it teetering on the tripod where our team daguerreotypist had left it before trotting around to join us. For nearly a quarter hour, we stared into the eye that was slowly imprinting our shapes on the plate inside, holding absolutely still despite the antics of the locals in the background, the occasional need to chase away a dog intent on marking the tripod, and the restiveness of the donkey whose reins I was holding.

CHAPTER THIRTY

laughed aloud in delight.

A daguerreotype. Taken in Egypt. With a donkey restless enough to blur on the plate.

I practically tripped over my cane getting to the sitting room, where I snatched up the mottled picture of the Sphinx that Damian had put on the mantelpiece, then carried the precious image to the brightest window in the house.

There she was. Lakshmi, my clever diarist, dressed as a local boy in *abayya* and loose turban, trying to hold a donkey still for long enough that it didn't spoil the picture.

And . . . wait. I now knew *when* this was.

M. Daguerre had introduced his photographic device to the world in 1839. Unless Lakshmi was creating a false lead for me, this was a few months later. Which meant . . .

Back I went to the studio, where I grabbed the long screw-driver to prise up the top of the large crate, pulling out paintings until I found the one I remembered.

Three proud men on camelback, dressed in colourful robes, two of them looking a trace dubious as they perched on their high saddles. Two of the men wore caps resembling soft fezzes with tassels, the other wore a distinctly Arab *kaffiyeh* and *agahl*. All had rifles draped about them, although only one of them had his in a position where he might be able to reach it without dropping it to the ground, or putting a bullet through the camel behind him. This was the man in the *kaffiyeh*, who also looked as if he'd sat on a camel before.

But it was the boy at the back of the trio who made me smile. The same "boy" who had held the donkey while the daguerreotype plate was being exposed. A boy whose secret mischief the painter had captured, with no mistake.

Lakshmi, in local dress. Painted by her unlikely employer, Horace Vernet.

This bright young Franco-Indian girl had managed, with the help of her father's best friend and right-hand man, to worm her way into the service of the famous Horace Vernet on one of his painting tours of North Africa. This went some way to explain why the journal that recounted her history found its way into his things in the *Institut de France*—although it was not at all clear *how* it came to be there. I could hope that explanation was in future chapters.

I had always been fond of the tales of women who claim the freedom of men by a simple change of clothing. The pirate Mary Read, stagecoach driver Charley Parkhurst, soldiers in every era up to the modern. Nine months before, I'd had an amusing conversation with Morocco's Resident-General, Hubert Lyautey, about women in trousers. He told me the story of Isabelle Eberhardt, a Swiss woman who had converted to Islam (or her interpretation of Islam) and dressed as a man in her adopted home of Algeria. There she had offended the locals, but outraged the French, who accused her of spying and expelled her. She eventually made her way back to North Africa, where Lyautey had met her, and talked her into becoming an informant on the local Arab peoples. His spy—*for* the French.

I did not know if Lakshmi's fellow travellers had anything to do with espionage, although I thought her original suspicions were not unfounded. Governments everywhere often took advantage of any citizen with a good cover story, whether a young officer accompanying his famous artist uncle around the desert or, like Mata Hari, a courtesan who moved among rich and powerful men.

Still, spy or not, this young woman had me wanting to hug her, or at least shake the hands of her descendants. If nothing else, she'd changed my picture of Horace Vernet from a dry, conventional painter of seascapes and battles to a man not only amused by the antics of a young girl, but willing to overlook the inconvenient details of her sex and simply make use of her skills.

I wondered if she'd met any of Holmes' other distant French relations, a thought that made me grin with pleasure. I vowed to find Lakshmi No-Last-Name's grave and pile it with flowers, by way of thanks.

Perhaps the next chapter of her image-memoir would tell me more about the Vernets.

CHAPTER THIRTY-ONE

HOLMES

Holmes had always had mixed feelings about Paris. To be sure, it was in many ways vastly superior to London. Were an Englishman not to have its riches—the music, the restaurants, the art—a mere day's journey from home, life would be much the poorer. But to live here?

It was late at night. Any later, and there would not be much point in wheedling his way into an hotel. But when he had left M. LeGrand, safely delivering him back to his own front door, Holmes had not immediately turned for his home-from-home in the City of Light. Instead, he had followed the river for a time, watching the reflections in the water, listening to the boats, passing two moored pleasure-boats whose hulls pulsated with the beat of the music inside. He passed over the pedestrian bridge off the prow of the *Île de la Cité*, and circled the front off the *Institut de France*, making his way to the *École des Beaux-Arts*.

Art in the blood, he thought. *My grandfather, my great-uncle, my great- and great-great-grandfathers . . . and now Damian. Perhaps*, he mused—although it felt close to a prayer—*perhaps Damian will find the satisfaction and security of art that those stolid*

Vernets found. Perhaps the unstable minds and grim depressions that seem to plague other artists, the Van Goghs and Goyas and Michelangelos, will pass him by. It is indeed liable to take the strangest forms. Perhaps it may even take the mysterious form known as happiness.

CHAPTER THIRTY-TWO

EIGHTH IMAGE

THE TICKET

For the next dozen years, travel with Monsieur was a large part of my life. I did return to France with him, and I did see *Maman*—in Paris, since she'd given up the house with the eyebrow window—but it was not a successful reunion, even without the realities of her husband in the background. She reminded me of *Tante* Sophie, to the extent of often wearing blue, although paradoxically, *Maman* clung to me more than I found comfortable.

I was, at fifteen, too young to be permitted an adult degree of freedom. However, I had succeeded in making myself indispensable to Monsieur, who would don the role of uncle as we travelled across all the Western world, seeking inspiration and employment. Our paths took us to Russia and Jerusalem, London and Morocco—occasionally with Arjun, more often without.

Arjun had left me in Cairo when Monsieur and the others set off into the desert, and was waiting in Paris when we arrived. It was Arjun who made it possible for me to ease into independence even before I turned eighteen. And Arjun who laid the groundwork for an identity—a life—that my family in India would not find: everything from visiting cards to a bank account, all in a new name. He arranged for one of my impoverished distant aunts to act as chaperone. And then he located a suitable house for this eccentric establishment in the outskirts of Paris: a house with a window the shape of an arched eyebrow set into its roof.

Nanterre was a rural district one bridge and a few miles away from the centre of Paris. The house had a strong personal history for me, so that when Monsieur and I returned home from a triumphant and hugely profitable tour of Czarist Russia and I discovered what Arjun had done, I wept in his arms, thoroughly embarrassing us both.

The small house had belonged to a friend of my mother, who let *Maman* use it whenever the turmoil of Paris and the irritability of her husband grew too much for her nerves. It was the house where she could entertain her foreign-born lover. The house whose eyebrow window and pink roses I had last seen through the carriage window the day Pitaji carried me away. A house that took Arjun months of haggling and a rather absurd final price before the woman would part with it.

When I was twenty, Monsieur's beloved daughter died. Around the same time, France underwent another paroxysm of revolutionary fervour. Monsieur was among those condemned for royalist leanings, his paintings burned by mobs—and although he was later claimed by Napoleon III and rendered acceptable again, he retreated for a time, both emotionally and professionally. He sold the home in which he had been so happy, moving what possessions remained into a small apartment.

His daughter, one of whose Christian names I shared, had been older than I, and nothing alike in looks or deeds. However, his wife was both ill and alienated, and his other child was too thoroughly immersed in the life of motherhood to spare him much attention. So—deliberately, in an attempt to repay a small portion of the countless good he had done me—I set out to fill the role of "daughter" for Monsieur.

One of his patrons wanted a painting—a large commission, set in Rome. I urged him to accept it, I offered to go with him to Italy, until half-heartedly he did.

Once on the road again, life began to return. His time in Rome charged up his energies, the paintings began to flow from his studio.

But things had changed. He was getting old, and less keen on exploring the edges of things. His politics, his tastes, his expectations shifted to the conservative.

Still, it came as a shock when he walked in one day as I was packing my bags for a trip, and he eyed with disapproval the boy's trousers I was folding, and asked if I wasn't getting too old for that sort of game. Why couldn't I assist him in the skirts of a proper French woman? I replied tartly that it might be difficult to control a camel while dressed in crinoline and feathered hat, but when he grumbled that he was afraid he wouldn't be doing that kind of arduous travel anymore, and that it might be time to find me a suitable husband, I could only stand and stare. Because he'd said it in the kind of manner that is only jocular on the surface. He was, in fact, more than half serious.

All of which would have been bearable had not the same malaise begun to infect Arjun.

With Arjun, however, the gift of hindsight serves to fill in the missing features: my dear friend was often alone when I went off with Monsieur. He was far from his home, a stranger in a strange land, who could not become French by a mere change of clothes. He hesitated to venture much into Paris, lest someone from the family business be there and see him. He was five thousand miles away from the place where he was born. His younger son, whose birth nearly forty years before had taken the wife Arjun loved, now had growing sons and daughters of his own.

After eleven years, it was time for Arjun to go home—not to Chandernagore, where my uncle might still hold a grudge, but to his birth-place in Pondichéry. Back to the warmth and the smells and the food he'd grown up with. Back to his family—his actual family. He'd done enough, loving and protecting this peculiar daughter of the man who'd been his brother in all but blood.

Arjun was sitting before the fire when I came in, frowning at a book. He let it close over his finger with some relief—a Dickens novel, I saw, in English, which he still found hard going.

I laid the folder in the centre of the small, polished table beside his chair.

"What is this?" he asked.

"Those are yours," I told him, speaking in Bengali, rather than French.

He opened the envelope. *Certificate for Passage,* said the form inside, filled out with his details. First class, an English ship, all costs included. "Your ticket home."

"Lakshmi, this is my home."

"Arjun, I love you like a father, but France is a place of exile for you. You need to go and see if Pondichéry still holds your heart. You can come back if there is nothing there for you. I will always want you near, and the thought of living without you fills me with pain. But I think you need to go and see."

My little house was distressingly empty after he had left.

CHAPTER THIRTY-THREE

Night had fallen long ago. I forced myself to put away my papers. What point was there in working another night through? Instead, I would leave Lakshmi to her empty house while I took myself to bed in an equally empty one. There appeared to be only four of her image-chapters left, but some were long, and they promised to be difficult—both technically, in translating, and emotionally. Something about that last scene felt as if Arjun's departure was an omen of sorrows to come. Better to close the journal now than to feel the cold close in during the night.

Despite my changing thoughts regarding potential night-time assassins, I nonetheless made sure that the doors and shutters were locked. I closed down the lights, took a long soak in the bathtub, cleaned my teeth, and stood looking at the empty bed.

Holmes, where the hell are you?

I required mindless reading matter, so I crossed the corridor to Aileen's surgery, intending to claim a racy novel from her shelves. Instead, my hand pulled out the Victorian book on women explorers. It was, as I suspected, a book that Irene Adler had owned—given to *ma chérie Irène, avec amitié*, according to a frontispiece inscription, by *"Grand-mère 'Elle.'"* I carried it back to my solitary bed and lay turning the pages, trying to fall asleep with the march of words before my eyes.

Instead, my thoughts spun around everything but the challenges of three Dutch lady explorers, clad no doubt in bombazine and bustles. I thought of the hands that had opened this before me. And the unlikeliness of a grandmother—"Elle"—giving even a granddaughter like Irene Adler this particular volume. And then, when I discovered that the story began in Alexandria and Cairo, my mind went straight back into the pages that awaited me.

I should exchange this for the racy novel, I thought. But in the end, I wrapped my dressing gown around me and went back to the dining room, finishing my translation shortly before the sun rose over Ste Chapelle.

CHAPTER THIRTY-FOUR

Ninth Image

Blue Eyes

I had money enough, thanks to Pitaji and *Daadi-ma* and Arjun. I had servants who freed me to come and go at will. I had interesting travels, whether with Monsieur or on my own. I had friends, thanks to my wide-spread life—and if I tended to follow Arjun's lead in avoiding Paris itself, that still left an entire continent at my feet.

And yet.

I was twenty-six years old. Monsieur's jests about finding me a match were not as easy to ignore. Not that I had any wish to become the subservient wife of any man, but . . . companionship? Surely that was not an unreasonable hope?

That summer, Monsieur's travel took him to London. It happened to be the Season, that time of year when young British women were polished and primped and set on display, in hopes of attracting the interest of eligible young men. This year, it was more feverish than usual, as there was an exhibition in the city that attracted visitors from all over—many of whom were young, wealthy, and male. Fortunately, I was safe from the ordeal inflicted on the girls, being both foreign and too old. But as a student of human behaviour, it was a rare opportunity—and I did in fact enjoy a certain amount of dancing, riding, dining, and theatre. I even took pleasure in the clothing, so long as I would not have to wear it all day, every day, forever.

A similar caveat applied to the ceaseless interaction at the balls and parties: it was entertaining, but taxing. As the evening went on, I tended to gravitate towards the edges of things rather more than most girls, particularly those who were actively on the marriage market. One night at an especially sumptuous ball, I had retreated to the palm trees on the upper balcony, a spinster of twenty-six years slightly mesmerised by the whirl of black suits and colourful silk below. The scene had reminded me of my childhood image-lantern, and I was wondering if it might be possible to capture the colour and motion of a waltz on a flickering strip of paper when a voice interrupted my musings.

"Sore feet?"

I peered around the palm, then adjusted my gaze upwards.

Framed by the branches was a tall young man, well over six feet, slim inside his handsomely tailored evening wear. His hair, slightly unruly, was the light brown one often saw on English people, along with the cornflower-blue eyes. They looked amused.

"My feet are fine," I replied. "My social stamina is somewhat challenged, by this end of the evening."

He offered an elbow. "If a single companion nearby would not prove more of a burden than a crowd at a distance, I know a corner inhabited primarily by marble people. I've found them pleasantly undemanding when it comes to social obligations."

After a moment's thought, I took his elbow.

Six months later, we were wed.

CHAPTER THIRTY-FIVE

TENTH IMAGE

THE BATHING-MACHINE

He was the elder of two sons, from a family that had lived for many generations in the English Midlands. A family not quite wealthy enough, or concerned enough with power, to maintain a house in London year-round.

I was struck, even at the time, with the unconventional streak that ran through this blue-eyed young gentleman. Without a doubt, it was one of the things that most attracted me—that he would laugh not merely at my jokes, but at my antics as well. That he would dismiss any concern over my unfashionably tanned skin, that he seemed to take an interest in my unladylike hobbies— mechanical tinkering instead of needlework—and even my shocking preference for riding astride. My mind was made up when, for a Venetian masquerade ball held at the end of that Season by some friends of his, he was delighted by my suggestion that we attend in reverse: I in the trousers, he strapped into a tight-bodiced, too-short silk dress.

How was I to know that the London Season was a world away from the year-round Midlands, or that a young man's Bohemian attitudes would succumb to the expectations of family and class once he was home? Oh, he loved me, of that I was never in doubt.

He admired me and was amused by me and encouraged a certain number of my hobbies, but ...

But it did not take long before my husband's wild oats had been overgrown by the domesticated variety. By the birth of our first child, the year before I turned thirty, I rarely appeared in trousers out of doors. In a touch of irony, it was during my occasional trips to London, three or four times a year, that I tasted freedom, and felt that I could breathe again. Even the trips when my husband went as well could be joyous, reminders that I had married this man, not only his house, his lands, his family name.

However, there could be no doubt: I had also married into the house and family. Indeed, I had contributed to it, with the next generation of heirs from my own body. Although, as these grew and explored and learned, I began to take an interest, and ended up finding them a more fascinating project than many of my travels with Monsieur.

They were a challenge, and a joy, and a source of endless variety. Every hour, an infant makes fresh discoveries, claims new lands, invents new things. A child's mind can be shaped, a challenge that I relished, making sure their tutors were up to the task of polishing gifted minds. It was a particular satisfaction, as each grew mature enough that I did not have to worry about their poisoning themselves or blowing us all up (or not worry much, although we did ruin a lot of clothing with nitrate stains).

We even discovered the pleasures of the family holiday at the seaside, when my husband would guide the young ones on a grand architectural castle-building project while I retreated to the row of brightly painted bathing-machines to trade my vast expanse of dress, petticoat, undergarments, and bustle (the crinoline, that short-lived monstrosity, was no longer popular even among the stylish) for a bathing costume, a garment oddly akin to the *kurta-pajama*. Once transformed and trundled down to the water, I would leave behind the splashing, shrieking ladies to swim along the shore-line until the weight of the sodden wool had exhausted me.

But satisfaction or not, maternal affection or not, I will admit that what made those years bearable was the railway, which could take me to London in time for luncheon. Once in Town, I could disappear—and being by then considered a responsible middle-aged woman, I was free of the need for chaperones and maidservants.

Seven years into marriage, four years after achieving maternity, I escaped for an overnight trip to London, and found myself in a part of the city popular with actors working in the nearby theatres. As I walked past one cheerfully painted doorway, I saw a note in the window: "Room to Let."

Under an impulse I could not have explained, I knocked at the door, and found it was a boarding house filled with actors. The room, on the top floor, was clean and relatively quiet. When I followed the landlady down the stairs again, I found that I had agreed to a year's rent on the room. For less than the cost of a ball gown, I had a refuge. My own room, with neither family nor demands, awaiting my whims, whatever those might be.

My mother had used her hidden house for a lover. I filled mine first with inexpensive but comfortable furniture, the makings for simple meals, and books. I would read, sprawled on a settee if I wanted, and feel safe from importuning children or enquiring husbands. After a few visits, I realised that I did not actually have to wear corsets and multiple petticoats in the privacy of that room, so I went into one of the local costume shops and asked if they had such a thing as an Indian or Arab costume—for my son's fancy-dress party, I explained, my son being approximately my own height and build.

It proved ideal clothing for lounging about reading. But it also got me thinking: if I could wear this here, why not wear a version of it out there? Perhaps, I thought, I could even return to my former life and don male clothing—not that of India or North Africa, but that of the natives here, allowing me to enter a restaurant without scandalising the patrons and forcing the maître d' to turn me away. I tried, and succeeded, and from there I built out, assembling the tools for creating other identities. Garments, for men and women of various classes and backgrounds. Makeup, again for both sexes. All the things one might need to change one's identity and move amongst the various neighbourhoods of an enormously diverse city.

To some extent, it felt silly. Like one of those childish parlour games indulged in by people with too much time on their hands. Then one afternoon on crowded Oxford Street, I came face to face with my mother-in-law . . . and she did not recognise me. I was as invisible to her as any of the hundreds of other strangers she passed. In a flash, I knew that this game of mine, while straight out of my own childhood, was anything but childish.

Those brief visits to London came to act as a balance to the flat, silent air of the country house. I would return to my familial duties not with regret, but refreshed by the change. And if I boarded the train to London rather more as the years went on than I had before, well, women have always done what they need to to preserve their sanity.

CHAPTER THIRTY-SIX

ELEVENTH IMAGE

DANCING FIGURES

And then, without warning, my happy life ended.

Change had been coming, I knew. Tutors and a well-educated mother could only take a young mind so far, and many of my contemporaries' sons had long since gone off to school. The time was coming for my youngest to join his fellows—"fellows" in age alone, not in ability—and I was faced with the question all mothers eventually confront: what do I do when the house is empty? Would life in the country with a man whose chief concerns with the land around the house be sufficient challenge for me? He was not interested in changing; I was not interested in stagnating.

And I had no wish to become a wife whose boredom made her husband miserable and soured his affections. It was not fair, to one who had been nothing but kind.

All of which meant that, unless I wished to inflict the devastation of divorce or separation on those I loved, I would have to take full advantage of the freedoms permitted a woman who had done her job as a producer of heirs for the family estate and accept the lesser shame of being thought idiosyncratic.

It was not without precedent. Throughout history, one finds a scattering of women who do the unexpected. So long as they had the means to pay their way, society's disapproval could be ignored. Botanist Jeanne Baret—dressed as a man—was the first woman to circumnavigate the globe, with the Bougainville expedition of 1766. I'd come across the memoirs of Lady Hester Stanhope on the library shelves, a woman who'd travelled all over the Mediter-ranean and Middle East (albeit with a company of maids, a per-sonal physician, a lover, and enough possessions to require two dozen camels) before settling down on the coast of Lebanon in a series of abandoned monasteries. And there was explorer Alexine Tinne, who set off from the Netherlands to photograph the White Nile and spent ten years happily outliving her companions, only to be murdered by Tuaregs just three years ago.

I will admit that, when I read the newspaper story of Miss Tinne's demise, I felt a wistful thrill at the idea of being murdered by Tuaregs. However, for a woman with funds, skills, and a willing-ness to be judged mad, there were options between murderous as-sault and terminal weariness. I had no wish to cut my ties entirely, with either husband or children—but I did long to loosen them, from time to time.

Thus, in my forty-sixth year, I began quietly to plan for a de-gree of independence. Not immediately, but once the house had emptied of its younger generation. And not permanently: Surely I could shape a compromise? One that allowed me to wander, yet permitted me to return for such things as school holidays?

There was no need to tell anyone yet. My rooms in London gained a steamer trunk, a few more male garments, an assortment of aids to disguise. In a well-concealed space behind one wall, I left a growing number of rolled-up bank notes. Long ago, Arjun had helped me set up a financial arrangement with a man in Paris— what amounted to a private bank for women, who naturally could not hold their own accounts. I had somehow neglected to mention this account to my husband. If I wished to travel beyond England (and oh, I did) my financial gentleman would supply me with funds in any number of currencies.

The future looked promising. Not without obstacles, but I did not foresee any troubles so devastating as to threaten the peace and security of those I loved.

Until troubles came, and it all collapsed.

I confess, I had never taken Arjun's warnings altogether seriously. We fled India when I was fourteen. On the steamer from Bombay to Suez, stifled by uncomfortable clothing, frustrated by my impossible hair, I had protested the need for the charade.

"In any event," I told him, "I'll be out in the open as soon as we get to Paris."

"We will not remain in Paris."

"Whyever not? I thought the point was to return me to my mother." I suspect that my voice was somewhat bitter.

"The point is to keep you safe," he said.

"What—from *Oncle* Ram? You can't imagine he's going to come hunting for me?"

"Your uncle Ram has some dangerous friends. And a long memory."

"You make Ram sound like some kind of *Thuggee* leader." I laughed—and then remembered lying beneath the sideboard, and the man with the white in his hair.

Oh ...

"What have you thought of?" he demanded.

I had never asked Pitaji about it, before he died. I had all but forgotten my fear at the inexplicable authority of the white-streak man and the contempt radiating from his silent companion. At the age of twelve, I'd had little understanding of what I was seeing.

At the age of fourteen, it all came back. And with it, a glimmer of what the conversation had meant, and how wrong it had been in that house.

So I told Arjun: Our day's outing in Calcutta, my mischievous visit to the forbidden sitting room, having to dive beneath the sideboard. The odd deference paid by Ram and Sophie towards this man in the silk *kurta-pajama*, and their discussion of bribery and shipments. I had never seen Arjun react as he did to my description of the white streak in the man's hair. In anyone but Arjun, I might have thought it was fear.

We sat, listening to the engines throb us across the sea towards Suez. I waited for Arjun to tell me that it had been nothing, that Ram was merely making a business agreement with a local industrialist.

He did not tell me that.

Instead, he went to his cabin, along the corridor from mine, and came back with a small bundle the size of two fists, wrapped in an old dish-cloth. It was the object I thought *Daadi-ma* had pressed into his hands the night we left, and dismissed as some kind of a snack for the road.

He undid the knots and folded away the cloth. I sat back with a gasp.

"Your father and grandmother wanted you to have a *stridhana*," he said.

In India, as in most parts of the world, a woman is expected to go from her father's care to that of her husband. The actual laws of inheritance were a hotchpotch of traditions and expectations, particularly in those years before the British crown took over from the East India Company, but the essence was: the only things a woman actually owned—her *stridhana*—were the gifts given directly to her by family or on her marriage.

That night after Pitaji died, Arjun explained, *Daadi-ma* judged what her son would have freely given his daughter, and put both the jewellery and the daughter into the hands of the man her son would trust. Some of the pieces were her own *stridhana*, thus arguably hers to give away. Others belonged to the family—which, remember, I was not legally a part of. According to the law, I was the daughter of a French man and his wedded wife. I had no legal claims to what this Indian family owned.

Sitting there in the chugging steamer, staring down at the glittering wealth, I heard Arjun say that a message had reached him in Pondichéry, that my uncle Ram was denouncing us as thieves.

My head came up. "*Daadi-ma?* Will she—"

"She is safe. I told her not to reveal her part in the matter. The servants know differently, but they will not talk."

I nodded. The old woman knew her younger son, knew that if he discovered that she had betrayed his inheritance, she would be out on the street.

What *Daadi-ma* had given me was no less than the family jewels.

They ranged from a Moghul woman's red-gold and pearl *maang tikka*—the broad pendant worn across the forehead—to a brooch with a cluster of diamonds as large as my thumb-nail. I reached out a finger and touched a spill of sapphires that I recognised from the portrait of *Daadi-ma* over the sitting-room fireplace, the young *Daadi-ma* in European dress and no *tilak*.

When Arjun spoke, his voice was soft, almost sad. "Lakshmi, you play games, acting and dressing up. But the games need to become real. Someday, perhaps, you can put it aside, but until then, you need to take on concealment as a habit so ingrained, so bone deep, that you never slip out of it. Only when I see that in you will I be certain that you are safe."

My protests died away. Arjun had not been unreasonable in his haste to flee, or with the need for disguise. The jewels in the dishcloth would mortgage half the family's house and land, business included. My uncle would not let this go without a fight.

However, my uncle was in India. We'd changed names, appearances, and methods of travel before reaching France. Once there, I had agreed to take on a new surname, and to avoid the salons and social life of the city. With the jewels safely placed with my private banker—oh, the relief I felt when I received word that Arjun had got rid of that immense burden—we had a greater degree of protection.

As the years went by, my sense of threat faded. We sold a few pieces—for expenses, to buy the cottage, to travel where I wanted. I had made Arjun take a generous portion when I sent him back to India. But it was surprising how many bricks, frocks, and deliveries from the grocer can be bought by a shiny bauble the size of one's thumb-nail.

Arjun had returned to India eleven years after we fled the country. The following year, he wrote to tell me that Ram had died, and Ram's son Rajiv, a child of five when I had left, was in training to run the company. The year after that, Arjun wrote again to say that *Daadi-ma* had died peacefully in her sleep.

Her passing seemed to end things in my mind. With her loss, a chapter of my life had closed, and I knew that by now the family's memory of a wayward French child who disrupted the house, flirted with shame, and finally tricked their matriarch into giving her their treasures would be fading into legend. Ram's son would remember the story, but when he had a son, it might even begin to seem an unlikely bit of family lore.

Shortly after that, I met my husband, and I had a decision to make. *Someday, perhaps, you can put it aside.* I longed for Arjun then, for his wisdom and his advice. Was this the time? How much of myself should I give this good man?

In the end, I decided to say nothing of India. When Arjun left, he had taken the last remnants of Pitaji with him. The surname on the wedding register was the one I had been born with, but it was not a remarkable one, and I invited no relatives. I did tell my new family, those safely English gentry, some vague stories concerning my French family, but it was of little import. For good English folk, France was another country, and with that distance, why should anyone care?

The answer came at a ball in London, at the end of May.

The dance was held by a cousin of my husband's, in a Town house rented for the Season to introduce a daughter to Society. My husband and I were invited, two responsible adults to help restrain the high spirits of the younger people. (She'd extended an invitation to our son, who had just turned eighteen, but as we all anticipated, the misanthropic lad did not even acknowledge the receipt.)

All was going well. The music was good, the food perfectly adequate, and enough of Society's darlings had accepted that the next-lowest tier had followed, filling the ballroom with a whirl of colourful skirts and black-clad legs. The room was hot, but kept from stifling by the many doors thrown open to the garden. A close eye was kept on both the garden and on the bowl of punch, that it might be quickly diluted whenever one of the lads emptied his flask therein. Spirits were high but not uncontrolled, and the daughter's dance-card was gratifyingly full. My guard was down, watching my husband guide his cousin around the floor, when a man's voice said my name, inches from my ear.

I took a startled half step away. "Yes?"

"Or perhaps you still go by the name Lakshmi?"

The whirl stuttered and slowed, drifting to a halt like the strips on an image-lamp. I took another step back, my thoughts making a rapid assessment of what nearby object I might use as a weapon. In truth, I need only raise my voice, and act the proper English lady receiving offense from a man who was clearly not English and possibly not a gentleman. The entire room would come to my aid and toss the impudent cad out onto the street—but something warned me that this reaction might have unforeseen consequences.

"You have the advantage of me, sir," I said, as cool as any affronted dowager.

"We have met, but long ago. I am your cousin Rajiv. From Chandernagore."

Ram's son was now a man in his late thirties, slightly chubby but well dressed. He was a little taller than his father, and a few shades lighter in colour—in the winter, he might pass for Mediterranean. The resemblance was in his gaze: imperious, self-absorbed, and quick to anger. I'd once seen Ram swat a housemaid to the floor after she'd dropped a cup in his presence; this man would not hesitate to do the same.

"I was not aware that I had a cousin in Chandernagore, met or otherwise. That is a town in India, am I correct?"

He switched to French, in which his accent was less marked. "You know very well where Chandernagore is, Cousin Lakshmi. And you and I need to have a conversation."

"I think not. Good night, Monsieur."

"So, you would prefer that I have a conversation with your husband?"

And there it was.

"About what, Monsieur?"

"About the man you called Father. My uncle Krishna, who lay with a married French whore from a good family and conceived a bastard girl with her."

"My, that's quite a story."

"One that I should like to tell to your husband. Do you think he will strangle you, or merely throw you out? And what about your children? What will they think, when they discover they are of mixed blood?"

I thought they personally might be more interested than offended. Still, that was not the consideration.

"I imagine you have an alternative to propose." I made my voice polite, but bored.

And now I could see the rage coming to the surface. "You will return to my family what you stole."

"That being?"

"The jewels. A fortune in gold and gems, stolen to fund your escape from the family that extended a hand of welcome and gave you shelter. The jewels that could restore the house and build up the business and return my family to the position it once held." His eyes, cold and furious, looked so like those of my uncle Ram that I had to force my spine straight and my chin up before them.

"My goodness, I did all that? How bloodthirsty of me—and I couldn't have been much more than a child. It sounds like a version of the Wilkie Collins story."

"Do you think your husband will be amused by it? What about his friends?" He flung out an arm to encompass the room.

As he did so, I noticed my husband watching the exchange from across the ballroom floor. He parked his cousin and began to make his way around the perimeter. Time to end this.

"Sir, it is best if we continue this conversation at another time and place."

"With the jewels," he ordered.

I gave him a polite laugh, taking care that my husband could see me. "I do have a few nice pieces in my jewel-box, apart from those that are around my neck at the moment, but none of them have ever been to India. I would be foolish, were I to own any illicit goods, not to leave them elsewhere. Perhaps in another country." I held his gaze, that he might get the message.

"The jewels are in Paris?"

"Two weeks, Monsieur. I will be in Green Park two weeks from tomorrow, around three in the afternoon. There is a place near the western end of the park where two benches face in opposite directions. I shall speak with you then."

"You will bring my family's jewels."

"*À bientôt*, Monsieur. You should go now, before my husband trounces you."

His eyes flicked sideways, then came back to me. "Two weeks from tomorrow, and you will bring the jewels," he repeated. I thought for an instant that he was going to seize my arm and leave bruises through the silk, but instead, his hand came up, one finger raised in threat. "Do not try to avoid me."

He turned away, and I was dimly aware of nearby sounds of protest at the force of his exit—but I did not watch. I was only slightly aware when my husband reached me and asked if I was well, then steered my oblivious body to a nearby chair.

I felt as if I'd been struck down by a lightning bolt. By Rajiv's hand, raised into my face. By the flash of gold, on a finger inches from my eyes.

A ring. A signet ring. The design so worn down as to be indecipherable. But I knew it.

Pitaji had worn that ring, as had his father and grandfather before him. The night Pitaji died, it had appeared on *Oncle* Ram's finger. I saw it, I noted it, I read its message: that the family authority had literally changed hands.

In my youth, my shock, and in my enduring distress that caused my mind to recoil whenever I thought of that day, I had entirely failed to read its other message. In thirty-three years, I had never felt enough distance from that awful night to ask the one key question.

Pitaji was robbed and left for dead in a Calcutta alley.

So why had his killers overlooked the ring on his finger?

CHAPTER THIRTY-SEVEN

As I read, I laughed aloud as I translated Lakshmi's romantic yearning for death by Tuareg. I mourned Arjun's absence. I paused at the image of a heap of Indian gemstones.

And I slapped the table in triumph when she finally saw the meaning of the ring on Ram's finger. My own suspicions had been roused when first I read of Pitaji's convenient murder—although admittedly, it was the death I noticed, and not the enigma of the ring. But then, she'd never said that her father wore it all the time, and signet rings are often locked away until a seal is required on a deed or contract.

I also had to wonder just how long it was after Arjun returned to India that Ram had died. I wondered, too, if the police reports or newspaper clippings might hold mention of an indigo exporter's mysterious death . . .

I found myself pleased, that this extraordinary woman had not chosen to disappear into motherhood and life as a country wife, and instead had arranged for a degree of life outside of those strictures.

But—jewels from India? If they turned out to bear a curse, or if I started to see a trio of Indian jugglers performing outside the window, I was going to rouse the ghost of Wilkie Collins and have a word with him.

CHAPTER THIRTY-EIGHT

TWELFTH IMAGE
THE LETTER

My "turn" at the ball was blamed on one of those women's issues that instantly deflect all masculine interest. I was swept into a quiet room, my hostess plying me with damp cloths and cool drink. I assured her I was fine, and all but thrust her and her servants out of the door.

The silence provided time to think—but in the end, what thought was there? Ram had died long ago. Rajiv was a child when Pitaji died, and would have no idea of the sordid history behind the family ring he wore. It was a shock, but was there a thing to be done? There was not.

I was, suddenly and unexpectedly, out of time, all my pretty plans come to naught. The compromise I had mapped out, the pattern that might allow me to keep my self-respect as an individual yet remain wife and mother to those who loved me, was ... no longer possible.

That night, before the band had ceased to play and the carriages arrived, I knew that my options were four.

First, I could simply permit Rajiv to tell my husband exactly whom he had married. Not that the dear man would mind my mixed heritage—but that I had neglected to tell him, that I had brazenly lied to him since the day we met: that would devastate him. Similarly, our children: I would not watch them spend the rest of their days—school, University, their every interaction—touched by society's scorn for someone such as I. Fistfights over schoolboy insults would give way to adult glances and remarks, more destructive than a bloody nose or blackened eye.

Or I could go to Paris and retrieve what remained of the hoard, and risk that Rajiv would not take out his resentment at the diminished treasure by shouting the secret aloud.

Third, I could contrive to murder the man. Was he here on his own? His repeated use of "my family" suggested that he was here to represent them all. Were he to die suddenly in London, they would know who was responsible. My back—my own family—would never be safe.

Or lastly, I could take a blade to this Gordian knot, and have done with it. Life had given me so many gifts in the four decades since Pitaji had bundled me into a carriage. Payment was due.

The twelve days that followed were bittersweet indeed. A portion of it was a school holiday, so all the family was together. I made it as happy a time as I possibly could, that they might retain a sweetness in their memories. I took care to revisit happy times as well, and planted the idea—in the form of one of Mama's slightly shocking jests—that someday women were going to claim the right to swim unencumbered by heavy woollen bathing costumes.

That last night, with the house sleeping around me, I rose and went to my desk to compose two letters. Both were short, and unequivocal.

The first was to my husband of twenty blessed years. In it, I told him the truth—parts of it, at least. I told him that he had married a woman who was not only illegitimate, but of mixed blood, and she was being blackmailed over it. I also urged him to keep this entirely to himself. Instead, let it be thought by the world at large that one of his wife's silly stunts had gone awry, and she had died. Only those close to us—the children, his parents, his dearest friends—need be told that I had done a thing that would bring shame on the family. That when someone found out and threatened me with blackmail, I had taken the way out that would preserve the good name of my husband and children. Let them think me a woman who, in a moment of weakness, had betrayed her husband's trust, but tried to redeem herself at the end.

I then wrote a message specifically for the children. I wanted them to know how sorry I was, for being a weak woman, and how much I loved them. I wanted them to think of me in the freedom of the sea, going into the waves for a swim . . . only instead of following the shore-line, I would swim out, and out.

I wanted who I was not to touch them any more than it had to.

Last, I resumed my letter to my husband and asked him to burn it before anyone else could see what it said. I told him that I was not ashamed of my father. I welcomed who he had been, I took pride in his heritage and would happily proclaim it my own—if only we lived in another world. If only our boys did not have a world of bigotry around them. I told my husband again that I loved him, that I regretted withholding the truth from him, and that I was grateful for twenty years of his affection and his patience and his good cheer.

I signed it with love, sealed it with wax, and left it in a place the maid would not discover until the following afternoon.

I took a small valise with me to the train station, and was at my favourite bathing-machines on the coast by mid-afternoon. This time, I shed all my clothing down to my camise and pantaloons, and slipped into the water too rapidly for my fellow bathers to react.

And then I set my face to the horizon, and swam out, and out, and out again.

CHAPTER THIRTY-NINE

akshmi's tale ended as abruptly as if the final pages had been torn away. They had not. I turned those that remained, but all were blank. Unless this impish and intriguing woman had suddenly loaded her pen with invisible ink—which, indeed, I would have to investigate—then the dratted creature had allowed fiction to cap off a story that I had thought was fact.

One does not write in a journal whilst in the process of swimming out to sea.

I re-read the final page, making sure my translation had not gone astray.

Perhaps she employed the past tense in order to offer a sense of completion to her future reader? Or was I to infer that the author has been fished out of the water, somewhere off the coast of England—in which case, why leave off there?

Perhaps this was just an elaborate piece of fiction after all. A modern Voynich manuscript, another long, drawn-out puzzle whose raison d'être was buried by time.

And I still had no idea when and how it went into the crate of Vernets.

I thought that the latest painting in the collection was the two women with the infant, done by Émile Vernet-Lecomte in 1895. He had died—if my memory served me—the year of my own birth, 1900. If he had owned those fourteen paintings, and they had been stored away with his death, the journal could have been sitting there for twenty-five years.

Of course, if someone had prised open the crate and shoved it inside, it could have been at any time before last week.

Perhaps I could narrow down when the thing was written? I pulled over a scrap of paper and a pencil, to make notes.

Her fountain pen—the text showed none of the characteristic fading-then-dark-again pattern of the dipped quill—could have been manufactured anytime in the past seventy-five years. The paper's watermark might help—both with the date, and to tell me where she'd bought the journal. The quality suggested it might be one of those noble old firms that kept a record of every customer since their establishment.

Not that I could count on it. Still, I wondered if Délieux was a large enough town for a stationer who sold high-quality papers? If not, a Paris stationer would surely recognise it.

The better evidence came from Lakshmi's own words. The Red Sea route she and Arjun had taken—by steamer from Bombay, then cross-country to Cairo—put it after 1830 and before the canal opened in 1869. Which would match her years of travel with "Monsieur," starting in the late 1830s. If that was, as I thought, Horace Vernet, the artist had gone to London more than once, on one of which trips she had met a man who sounded remarkably sympathetic.

I was struck by a thought, and paged back to her entry about going to London: *an exhibition in the city that attracted visitors from all over* sounded like the Great Exhibition, bringing in millions of people from May to October 1851. She'd been *too old* for the competition of the Season, at twenty-six. (Odd, I reflected, that I, too, would be regarded as over the matrimonial hill.) This put her birth in 1825, which agreed with her other information.

I was glad that she'd made a happy marriage, unlikely as that might have been, raising the children (no indication of how many, other than the two sons, a "youngest" and his misanthropic elder) to school age before she began to plot her move to independence in her forty-sixth year. That took us to around 1870, when her Indian cousin pounced and destroyed everything.

For an event half a century past, the rage I felt over this wanton destruction of a family was remarkably fresh and alive. I resented Rajiv's interference. I craved for the tale to have a different ending. I liked this woman, despite her unambiguous attempt to drive me mad. I liked her as a child swimming in the Hooghly River (upstream from the burning ghats, one hoped) and the way she'd stepped into Monsieur's team as a boy. I liked her standing behind a palm tree to watch the dancers, when the tall blue-eyed English stranger asked her if she had sore feet. I . . .

Wait.

What year was this?

I snatched up the scrap on which I'd written dates.

Can I have another name? she'd asked her father. *Lakshmi,* he'd offered, after *Loukya.* Born in 1825. Spent much of her life around Vernets. One son—the *misanthropic lad*—was eighteen the year she was blackmailed and driven to suicide. A marriage six months after the Great Exhibition of 1851—and wait, she had dropped one clear reference there, hadn't she? For those who had eyes . . .

. . . *explorer Alexine Tinne, who set off from the Netherlands to photograph the White Nile and spent ten years happily outliving her companions, only to be murdered by Tuaregs just three years ago.*

I scrambled from my chair and hopped my way into the bedroom, for the book I'd been trying to put myself to sleep with.

One of the books from Dr Henning's shelves, pushed aside and probably doomed to end up in a second-hand stall, bore the title, *Geographical Notes of an Expedition in Central Africa by Three Dutch Ladies*. Written by John A. Tinne, the explorer's son. I ran my eyes down the pages until I found: she had died in 1869.

I sat down with a thump, finding it difficult to breathe.

Unless this was one of Lakshmi's mis-directions—no names, no dates, an uncertain number of children throughout her journal—it put her death in 1872.

Meaning that her misanthropic, eighteen-year-old son was born in 1854.

The same year as Mycroft Holmes.

Mycroft's younger brother, Sherlock, had turned eleven in 1872.

The same year their mother committed suicide.

Lakshmi was not simply an employee of Horace Vernet, she was his niece. Not just a friend of the Vernet family, but Camille Vernet-Lecomte's daughter.

Lakshmi, also known as Louise Estelle Holmes, the woman who brought "art in the blood" into the Holmes line.

CHAPTER FORTY

HOLMES

Holmes watched the two men approaching along the Seine embankment, hands tucked behind their backs and heads bent in earnest conversation. The two could only be Academicians. Or possibly Oxford dons, kidnapped mid-debate and dropped down at a different river, but for the sake of argument, Holmes would go with the hypothesis of Academy rather than college.

He thought for a moment the men would walk straight into him, so absorbed were they, but fortunately the younger drew back with a snort and the elder drifted to a stop before he actually made contact with Holmes' chest.

The younger—a relative term, since he was a good ten years older than Holmes himself—looked offended, but here a scrap of luck condescended to visit a hard-working detective, and Holmes recognised him. Or at any rate, recognised who he had been before twenty years of soft academic life.

"Monsieur Dampierre, isn't that you? I do not know if you remember me, but we met towards the end of the Dreyfus Affair, when I was here to—"

"*Bien sûr*, M. Holmes, you look no older than you did then.

Albert, this is the famous Sherlock Holmes, English detective. M. Holmes, I follow your exploits with great pleasure."

"You are too kind, I will tell Sir Arthur he has an admirer."

Inevitably, the next minutes were more literary than useful, with Dampierre probing for details of cases about which Holmes knew nothing, or could only faintly identify from his own actual investigations, and then proceeding to tell the older man all about the stories, weaving in some elements that seemed implausible even for a Conan Doyle fiction.

Holmes waited until he paused for breath, following the climactic ending of a story in which a mad professor injected himself with monkey glands in an attempt at winning a young woman. Seeing the older Academician's frown, and hoping to stave off the ensuing discussion of whether or not such injections would manifest in either appearance or behaviour of that sort, Holmes interrupted.

"In fact, Monsieur, I am here in the course of an investigation, although one that does not concern langurs or men climbing in the windows of young ladies. You recently sent four boxes from your storage attics to an artist by the name of Damian Adler."

"Three boxes and a trunk, yes indeed. An odd affair, that. Do you know—but wait. Are you the 'Holmes' mentioned in the letter?"

"I may be, that is why I am asking. Do you know where that letter is?"

"Two letters, although both in the same envelope. They will no doubt have been filed, our clerks are usually fairly efficient."

"I need to see them."

"Oh, is this part of a case? How exciting!"

"Now?"

The two Academicians looked at each other, considering. The disapproval on the older one's face made it clear what he thought of this disruption to their plans, but to Dampierre, the thrill of involvement superseded the unbroken ritual of years. "Would you rather take your coffee now," he asked his companion, "or set off and I'll catch you up? This shouldn't take more than half an hour."

Grumbling at this untoward act of hastiness on the part of these younger generations, the ancient permitted them to settle him in a pleasant café with a newspaper, and Holmes and Dampierre set off.

It took more than half an hour, but not much more, before Holmes was holding the envelope that had spent its life nailed to a crate of artists' memorabilia.

Thick, cream-coloured paper. The remnants of sealing wax on the back, too broken up to discern an image. The writing on the front was a woman's hand, educated and slightly archaic—rather like that of his mother, another woman educated in nineteenth-century France. It declared, as LeGrand had told him, that the boxes were the possessions of the Vernet family, and should be retained until *claimed by Adler or Holmes,* no titles or honorifics.

One of the inside documents was on paper that matched the envelope, with the same handwriting. It said simply:

One box, two tea crates, and a steamer trunk are left in the cus-
tody of the Institut de France and the Académie des Beaux-Arts
until such time as a member of the Vernet family with the surname either of Adler or of Holmes should come to claim them.
If no such claimant should appear by the year 1950, the contents
will enter the possession of the Académie, who can do with
them as they wish.

There was no signature.

"Do you know when the boxes—and trunk—were deposited here?"

"Only very approximately. I was made aware of them in the first year of the War, although they have been here longer. They are in the audit our people conducted in 1901, although they could have been placed there anytime in the previous decade. There must be a record, and I have ordered a search, but since both Horace Vernet and his nephew Émile Lecomte worked and lived here, it is possible that no arrival was recorded because the boxes were already here, and were simply shifted from the studios to the attics. You understand?"

Holmes nodded, and picked up the other note.

This was on an uneven scrap of paper, written by a man with a mediocre pen and a careless hand. The contents made his eyebrows climb:

Enclosed please find 500 francs to cover the cost of sending a telegram to the residents of Hooghly House, Convent Road, Chandernagore, India, at such a time that a Holmes or Adler appears. The message is to read: The boxes have been claimed.

"Was the cable sent?" he asked.

M. Dampierre nodded. "It was, and I assume it arrived there, since we were not notified to the contrary."

Holmes knew India well enough to suspect that if a telegram arrived and proved undeliverable, it might simply have been tossed out. Telegraphists were generally scrupulous; delivery boys less so.

The handwriting was curious. French, but not classically so. As if the writer was from Chandernagore himself.

Interesting.

CHAPTER FORTY-ONE

I stared down at the journal, fascinated, and horrified.

Lakshmi, the half-Indian girl who'd written this, was Holmes'...
mother?

Did he know?

No. He'd have said. I was sure he would have told me.

Wouldn't he?

(Did *Mycroft* know? Worse, did Mycroft know and not tell his
brother? If that proved to be true, then my already murderous feelings towards my brother-in-law would—)

No. Not that an Indian heritage wouldn't explain a few things:
Holmes' choice of India as a refuge in the Nineties. His habit of
curling up in a lotus position to meditate on a difficult case. His
taste for curry—

Oh, that was ridiculous. Lakshmi's—*Louise's*—habit of concealment had indeed become, as Arjun commanded, *so ingrained, so
bone deep, that you never slip out of it.* So complete, not even her
brilliant, all-seeing sons had suspected.

Unless, as I'd wondered since the start, this was all some idiotic joke. Some idiotic, convoluted, unbelievably painstaking and
coincidence-dependent joke.

But that was improbable. And if one eliminated the highly improbable, what remained must be some form of the truth.

What evidence was there that I had spent the past few days in the company of my mother-in-law?

Holmes' mother had been named . . . Louise. Which, to continue the family's penchant for repeated forenames, was also the name of her uncle Horace's wife. Interestingly, her journal recorded that Pitaji's initial thought of an Indian name his child could wear was not Lakshmi, but the near homonym, Loukya.

What about their appearance? I had been picturing Lakshmi as, well, half-Bengali. Holmes' mother, on the other hand, had been painted as a small, slim, grey-eyed woman with brown hair and an aquiline nose. His grandmother, Camille Vernet-Lecomte, had those same grey eyes, both in the brooch of my miniature and in the portrait I had pulled from the crate in Damian's studio. Camille's reddish-blonde hair was similar to mine, considerably fairer in colour than Louise's.

Was Camille's skin also lighter?

I realised that I had been picturing a black-haired, dark-eyed child with skin, as she'd said, somewhat lighter than her father's, but darker than the usual Vernet. In fact, along with dates and names, she had taken care not to describe her own appearance, and there'd been considerable European colouring in her father's family for her to inherit. Hadn't she described the portrait of her grandmother as having—not *pale* skin, but at least *paler*? Camille's husband had begun to suspect that the child was not his, but there could have been any number of reasons for that besides the colour of the child's hair and skin.

It was by no means impossible, that a daughter of Krishna and Camille could have brown hair and grey eyes.

The sharp intelligence and the touch of humour that Horace Vernet had caught, in painting those eyes, was certainly akin to the personality I had spent the past few days with.

There was no disagreement when it came to dates, either.

Both women had married into a family of English country squires. Both had drowned (taking, for the moment, Lakshmi's statement as other than fiction) in 1872, in response to blackmail. Holmes had told me that his mother's body washed ashore many days later, and was identified by her husband. She had been buried, in a closed casket, nearly a month after her death. Her widower then burned most of her possessions, and rarely spoke of her after that.

None of them did. The memory was painful to both Holmes and his brother. Any mention of her was invariably brief and followed by a change of topic. I knew that she had travelled as a child, that she spoke several languages, that she was unusually energetic for a Victorian lady, and that she had an unexpected taste for mischief.

Unless Holmes was hiding not his grief, but the truth? Hiding his mother's true past? Why would he do that?

No. His mother might have deceived her husband, but mine had not done the same to me. That was a possibility I refused to consider.

Nothing he had ever said about her directly contradicted what she herself had said in the journal. Louise left France and became Lakshmi, then returned to Louise again when she met a young man with blue eyes. Holmes' mother was the author of the journal.

However, that left the conundrum of her final line: *I set my face to the horizon, and swam out, and out, and out again.*

One does not have to be a Sherlock Holmes, when hearing evidence of a voice from beyond the grave, to suspect a staged suicide.

If her death was faked, either her husband had been a party to the deception, or he was among the deceived. He had died before I met Holmes, and I had always assumed that burning her possessions and not speaking about her had pointed to a grief that was both authentic and profound.

If that was the case, then she had done him great wrong. But perhaps it was simply anger that drove him to throw her things onto the fire? And perhaps, once that faded, it was not heartache that stilled his tongue, but an unwillingness to admit to his sons, who had loved their mother, that he felt a degree of relief, that this eccentric, too-lively wife of his had removed herself from the scene.

I set my face to the horizon.

By writing it into the past, she had been easing herself into the idea of death. Writing it as a fait accompli made it harder to back away from the act.

Or was it part of her game, wishing to plant the idea of her survival in the minds of whoever found the journal? Did she intend to send it, at some future time, to her sons?

Not that she had done so. Had she died before she could carry out her intention? Drowning in fact, not merely in intent? Had she first sent her journal to the Vernets, to keep safe or to hide away? Or did she live another thirty years and place it in the box herself?

And if she had not died on that day, why had she failed to reach out to her sons from beyond the counterfeit grave?

I sighed. This was going to be one of the thornier conversations I'd ever had with Holmes.

Assuming he ever returned. How long did it take to stash a son and his family somewhere a lascar wouldn't find them?

With that reminder, the anxiety that my translation efforts had been keeping at bay stirred. I cast around for something to take my mind off it. Ah—the possibility of invisible ink. I'd look a bit of a fool if the rest of the pages held a sequel to the puzzle.

I had looked at those final, blank pages, and found no betraying scuffs or indentations from a pressing nib. Nonetheless, I took the journal to the kitchen and tried the more obvious methods of bringing invisible ink to light, but fumes, acidity, and heat did nothing other than threaten the paper.

What about the watermark's provenance? Perhaps the paper's maker had something to offer. Maybe even lead to a noble old Parisian firm with a hundred-year-old ledger containing all their customers' names.

I noticed, to my surprise, that early sunlight was coming through the cracks in the shutters. Good—that meant there would be a window bright enough for my purpose. I opened up an east-facing shutter and held a journal page against the glass, making a sketch of the manufacturer's mark. As I was carrying my drawing back to the table, I realised that I hadn't thought to use the cane. My ankle still twinged, a warning against abuse, but it was a relief to feel that I might be able to keep up with Holmes again, a man more than twice my age.

I should have gone with him. Even now, he could be battling for his son's life while I sat here dreaming over empty pages and expensive-looking watermarks.

To be fair, I'd not been entirely dreaming. I had the journal translated and with a clean copy to give him. And if it turned out to have fallen into the crate by accident, or if he laughed it off as some classic Victorian parlour game that I'd never heard of—well, at least I could walk on my own two legs to the train station and leave him here to deal with lascars and film-world Indians.

In fact, why not do just that?

Not abandon him, no—but instead of settling onto a garden chair with a book and cool drink, awaiting his return, I could finish the project I'd started on. My foot would take me as far as a stationers. And if it meant travelling into Paris to satisfy my curiosity, the city was only a short train ride from Délieux. I would be back by evening.

There was really no alternative. Any attempt to curl up with a book was sure to end with me pacing and chewing my nails over Holmes. Never my option of choice.

I heard the key in the kitchen door, and walked in to find Mme LaRue, unpacking my breakfast.

"Madame," I said for the fourth morning in a row, "there is no need to bring me a meal, I am more than happy to break my fast on coffee and toast."

She gave me the same French sniff she'd given me on previous

days, then shot a glance at my leg, and said she was glad to see it
was feeling better.

I accepted a cup of coffee, and told her that I needed to go to the
station, to catch the train into Paris.

"*Bien sûr,* Madame. When?"

"Now," I said. When she did not reply, I glanced up and saw her
looking pointedly at the clock on the wall, which informed me
that even the slowest of trains would deliver me to Paris long before any of the shops had opened their shutters.

"In an hour, perhaps. Oh, and while I'm away, could we make
sure that the crates in Damian's studio are closely guarded? I don't
know if we'll have another intruder, but I suspect we're not finished with the matter."

She made an exclamation of alarm, and agreed that Pierre
would watch with extra care, and that M. LaRue would keep his
shotgun to hand. I told her that I wouldn't want him to shoot anyone, that whatever the boxes held weren't worth a life—or a prison
sentence—but she just shook her head and went out, her key turning in the lock with an extra degree of emphasis.

That gave me plenty of time to dress, eat the breakfast she'd
brought, and choose a place to conceal the journal and notes.
Holmes was quite capable of coming back, looking through the
work I had done, pouncing on some clue I had either failed to
notice or failed to possess some essential piece of complementary
information, and haring off again into the wilds of France. I was
not having that.

It took less than five minutes to open the drugs safe in Dr Henning's surgery, which I judged a place where the translation would
be found sooner or later, but not inconveniently soon. I folded the
two sketches—mine of the watermark, and Damian's showing the
lascar—into a pocket, along with all the franc notes I possessed
and a Baedeker's Paris guide I spotted on the shelf.

M. LaRue took me into Délieux just as the shops were opening,
and I had him drop me outside the town's stationer. However, as

I'd feared, neither the owner nor the girl at the register recognised the watermark, so I continued down the street to the train station. The ticket agent looked at Damian's sketch, told me that he'd seen it the other day when M. LaRue had been showing it around, and shook his head. But he did not return it to me immediately. Instead, he frowned at it, and wondered aloud if it might be connected to those other men.

"Which men were those?"

Two, it seemed. Yes, that's right, they might have been Indian gentlemen. A little over a week ago—Thursday? No, Wednesday, it was. The second of September. Though they did not have a picture, and were not asking about a man with a turban. An artist of some kind, that's who they wanted. He'd sent them into town, with a suggestion that they ask at the postal office.

It was essentially what I knew already, but I gave him a tip and let him show me onto the Paris train. He even gave me a first-class seat—hardly necessary for the brief ride, but it provided greater comfort. Which I used to promptly fall asleep.

It had been a long night.

CHAPTER FORTY-TWO

I came snorting awake as the train slowed into a station—not, fortunately, the end of the line at Quai d'Orsay, but the penultimate
stop, Austerlitz. I hastily rose, fished Damian's sketch out of my
pocket, and went to speak with any uniformed employees I could
find.

Had they seen this man, or a pair of men like him? Foreign,
moustaches, older and younger, in more conventional clothing?
When one after another said no, I checked to see what trains he
had worked on two Wednesdays ago, and moved on to the next,
distributing francs as I went.

Inevitably, it was in the final compartment, with the train emp-
tying out onto the Quai d'Orsay platform, that one of the attendants finally nodded in recognition.

Yes, the Wednesday, ten days past, in the late afternoon. No, perhaps not this man, but foreigners like him. Yes, first class, although
one of them did not look the sort, dressed in an old-fashioned and
not very well made suit. Both had good French, although the older,
shabbier one had a marked accent. From India, yes—the conductor had fought beside some men from Pondichéry during the War,
and though both these men were lighter-skinned than the soldiers

he'd known, and their accents less, they were still identifiable. Yes, both had worn suits—and hats, not turbans. No, they had not taken the train to its end, but had disembarked at the Quai d'Austerlitz. Yes, Madame was correct, that was the edge of the Thirteenth arrondissement rather than the Seventh, where we were now.

Did he perhaps overhear any of their conversation, or pick up any suggestions as to where they were from or where they were going? Not that a railway employee would intrude on the privacy of their passengers—of course not! But occasionally, a passenger will raise his voice or ask a revealing question, or . . .

Ah, Madame, but of course no self-respecting employee of the *Compagnie de chemin de fer de Paris à Orléans* would ever consider violating a passenger's right to privacy. Of course not. Although occasionally, as Madame said, a passenger will carry on a conversation in rather a louder voice than was expected in a first-class car, and although two such men as the ones Madame is asking about naturally converse in their own language, not French, there are often words that drop into an exchange from elsewhere, and the younger of these two men did employ a number of French words in his otherwise incomprehensible talk. Such as *tiare, bague,* and *la Comtesse.* As if he were not certain of these specialised words in the language they spoke. And it was he who led the other to disembark at their station, as if he knew the way.

Tiara, ring, and countess: interesting.

I thanked him with francs and disembarked at last, to track down the nearest café with strong French coffee, where I might sit and stare off into space without rousing concern amongst the passers-by.

Three *demitasses* later—one laden with sugar—my blood was buzzing and my mind seemed capable of sequential thought. So I stirred my cup and let the ideas rise to the surface.

It could not be an accident that the three men who had come

after Damian Adler were from India. Somehow, they knew of the link between Damian and those *Institut* boxes. Had they imagined that their family's long-lost jewels might be inside? Or were they hoping that any Vernet who was given the boxes might have also, at some point, been given the jewels?

None of these men could possibly be Rajiv, who'd been in his thirties when he blackmailed Louise Holmes in 1872. However, as she'd said in her introduction, *Memories are long when greed and resentments combine.* An oft-repeated tale of theft and deception could become ingrained in the family mythos, fuelling resentments for succeeding generations. And knowing how stories expanded, this one might even have grown, from a handful of baubles to baskets of diamonds and gold.

Paris was too large a city to count on stumbling across a particular individual in its streets. A methodical approach was required. And even then, a touch of luck would be welcome—although I would not make that admission to Holmes.

I did not have sufficient information to prove a theory, but I might have enough to start building one.

First, the men themselves. The two in suits, whether they were related or not, came from different worlds. The older one in his out-of-date clothing was more fluent in whichever non-French language they had been speaking—Bengali, if they were from Chandernagore, or Tamil if they came from Pondichéry. The younger man, who had depended on the French words for "tiara," "ring," and "countess," not only wore a suit that blended in here, but knew how to get where they were going.

Hypothesis: the younger man lived here, the older was a more recent arrival.

As for the third man, the one who had climbed in a window barefoot and in clothing from halfway around the world: He would appear to be an uneducated retainer brought along for his muscle and nerve. A thug, either hired or an amateur—although probably a lower-case thug, without the capital T of the now-suppressed Indian criminal organisation.

Second, the jewellery in the overheard conversation. There had been at least one ring among the things given to Arjun, but what to make of "tiara"? They weren't a particularly Indian ornament—and how would Arjun have fit it into a hidden pocket? As for the "countess," who on earth could that be?

Their conversation seemed only loosely connected with Lakshmi's family jewels. Either they didn't know—that mythos-building at work—or they, too, were casting around for a lead.

"*La Comtesse*" was specific. Referring to a given person. It was possible for a French countess to be friends with a young man from India—the Jazz Age affected the aristocracy as much as any other social class—but it was somewhat more likely that any such relationship would be a professional one. Cook, couturier . . . jeweller.

Or he was a Lloyd's agent providing insurance for said tiara, or a policeman investigating its theft, but he was involved somehow with an aristocratic lady's gemstones.

Hypothesis: the younger man was in some way professionally involved with jewellery, whether selling, restoring, or retrieving.

That left me with two thin threads to grasp: the journal watermark, and an Indian man working in the jewellery world.

Until a more substantial clue came my way, it was all I had.

With a sigh, I laid some coins into the saucer and went in search of stationery stores and jewellery shops, whichever I came across first.

CHAPTER FORTY-THREE

The watermark results took me precisely seventeen minutes from the time I left the café. A cheerful *papeterie* called to passers-by with a display of pens, desk sets, and every kind of journal from cheap student note-book to Venetian leather. The woman at the desk did not recognise the mark, but her father, whose wispy white hair was bent over a hunched spine, took one look at the sketch I had done and told me the name of the manufacturer.

He also told me it was no longer in business, the last son having been killed in the War, and any records would have been lost long ago.

It had taken me longer to sketch the watermark than it did to solve the question.

I thanked him by making a purchase—although I would have bought the beautiful slim propelling pencil even if he'd had nothing to tell me—and went on to the *bijouterie* side of my search.

If I wanted a jeweller who might be selling tiaras to a countess, I needed to be on the other side of the river, most probably in the First or Second arrondissement. However, thinking that perhaps (oh, Holmes was going to have much to say about my clueless quest, strewn with guesses and baseless hypotheses) if these men did have a jewellery shop of their own, and if it was of sufficient quality to be in the First or Second, they would have taken the train all the way to the Quai d'Orsay. Unless, of course, they were headed home or to a restaurant or anything in the eastern sections, which given the hour had probably been the case. However, I thought I might have better ... yes, *luck* in duplicating their steps from the east and heading west. Would they be in the topmost tier, or among the slightly less elite but still prosperous shop-fronts of the Avenue de l'Opéra?

Knowing that I should have stayed in Ste Chapelle and read a book, I boarded a tram to cross the river, and began to walk. The paint on the shop woodwork grew fresher, the shop windows became broader and exquisitely clean, more streets had caped and capped policemen to control their traffic. I took advantage of a few shops along the way to trade Dr Henning's workaday cane for a shiny walking stick and my decidedly ordinary and noticeably sat-upon hat for a light straw number with a jaunty brim and a pretty blue ribbon that the salesman assured me was the same colour as my eyes, which cost five times what I anticipated. It did help to make the shopkeepers look more hopeful than critical when I stepped through their doors, and the conversations that ensued brought more information than if I'd been turned back onto the street straightaway.

I quickly learned not to show the sketch. Instead, I became a young lady in search of the exotic: Had they anything in an Indian style? No? Then could they perhaps recommend a place that did?

Eventually, a discussion between two shop-girls in their forties summoned their collective memory of a *bijouterie exotique* up in the ... was it the Eighth? Or Ninth? It was that very hot afternoon in July—no, June, I'm certain it was June—and we had walked all the way from the Pagoda and thought the *passage* might at least get us out of the sun, but it was so unpleasantly crowded—those *Americains*, remember?—that we ...

I thanked them and made my escape.

I thought the Ninth arrondissement marginally more likely, a district with grand *magasins,* a sprinkling of bijou little shops, and a number of the covered arcades the two women remembered. Not an arrondissement with the most fashionable, most exclusive, most French of shops, but one well suited to those with expensive foreign goods to offer. The sort of neighbourhood where a Jazz-Age countess might go in search of exotic jewels.

I dodged an elastic-suspender salesman and avoided getting flattened by a three-wheeled delivery bicycle carrying a bird-cage as large as I was, and elbowed my way onto a tram to continue my almost certainly pointless search.

I asked questions, paused for a very pleasant luncheon at a brasserie whose waiters wore clean, crisp white aprons, then went on and asked more questions. I bought a fountain pen I hadn't known I needed until I saw it, evaded a young gentleman inspired by the dancing couples in a small park, and managed not to step into any of the horse droppings, stand-pipe mud puddles, or wayward streams from a couple of ill-placed *pissoirs.* I paused for coffee, walked another mile of to-and-fro gauntlet, crossed forty-seven streets, and was nearly run down by three motorcars, six motor lorries, a tram, an omnibus, and a three-wheeled bicycle with a pair of small children in the back. After the last, I stopped for a glass of wine.

During the afternoon, I questioned twenty-three jewellers and countless shopkeepers of loosely related establishments, and not one of them had ever seen a man from India selling a tiara, or spoken with a man from India about a ring, or indeed knew anything about any Indian man at all.

At a quarter after five, I said, "Enough." This entire day had been a futile waste of time and energy, and soon I was going to be flattened by one of the scurrying motorcars that paid as little attention to a slow-footed pedestrian as they would to one of the city's pigeons. I would pay for my foolish quest tomorrow with a swollen ankle and Holmes' scorn.

I stood on the crowded pavement at the entrance to one of the many covered arcades in this district, planting the cane down to fend people off, and looked around. This end of the *passage couvert* held nothing but racing vehicles, but looking through to the far end, I saw a stationary taxi. I checked my pocket-book, decided there was enough to get me to the Gare d'Orsay, and limped off down the passageway of shops.

My arm ached from leaning on the cane all day, my ankle throbbed, I was hungry and thirsty and concentrating on the far street, praying the taxi had not been claimed by the time I reached it. I nearly walked past the shop.

One corner of the window's display held several old pieces of jewellery, a porcelain vase, and two small sculptures, all thematically linked: ornate, colourful, delicately worked, and sumptuous overall.

They could only be from India.

Reluctantly, dutifully, I turned away from the waiting taxi and went through the door.

The man behind the desk was no more Indian than I. And when I recited my query for what felt like the hundredth time—I was looking for a necklace from India, did he perhaps know anyone who sold such a thing?—I saw the same shake of the head I'd seen each time.

"*Non*, Madame, I regret I have nothing of the sort." I nodded and turned away, mumbling my half-hearted thanks. "Although if there is going to be a vogue for Indian jewellery, perhaps I will keep my eyes out for some."

I paused with my hand on the door's knob, then turned. "Have others been asking for such a thing?"

"Only one, Madame. And since he himself appeared to be from

India, I paid it no mind. However, you, Madame—you, perhaps, are not seeking a necklace from your native land." His smiling teeth were very white.

"He wanted a necklace?"

"He seemed willing to consider most anything. Although ... to be frank, I believe he may have been the victim of a theft, looking for a shop that was, shall we say, the willing receiver of stolen goods. I assure you, Madame, that is not this shop."

I limped back to the desk and took out the page with Damian's sketch. "Could it have been this man?"

"No," he said without hesitation. "This man looked, well, he looked like anyone on the streets. It was his accent, and I suppose his companion, that put me in mind of India."

"Nicely dressed, slim, with a thin moustache, while his companion was older, not as well dressed, and with darker skin and a heavier moustache?"

"Precisely! The one was perhaps thirty. The other fifty or thereabouts."

"What specifically were they looking for?"

"He said they—" But the salesman abruptly stopped, as it dawned on him that I was more than a potential customer making conversation. "What is your interest in this man, Madame?"

I folded away the sketch, then met his eyes. "Those two, and perhaps the one in the drawing, are threatening a friend of mine. For some reason, they imagine he might have those pieces they were asking about. He does not. What he does have is a wife and daughter, and all three have had to leave the area until we can be certain they are safe."

"Why do those men believe that your friend has the jewels?"

"That's what I'm trying to find out. In fact, my friend does not even know they exist. And none of us know exactly what the men are looking for, other than old Indian jewellery of gold and gemstones."

He glanced at my handbag, where I'd put the drawing, and made up his mind. "It sounded as if there were a number of pieces. Rings, bracelets, a sapphire necklace and earrings. One of those forehead decorations their brides wear." *Maang tikka,* I thought, but did not say it aloud. "He had two photographs, although I had already told him I had not seen any of the things he mentioned."

"Photographs?" I was startled. "Of which pieces?"

"Not the jewels themselves, but of a painting. The formal portrait of a woman wearing the sapphire necklace and earrings. She wore an evening gown, though she didn't look European."

Daadi-ma. "When were the men here?"

"A week past, I believe. Yes, also Saturday it was."

The day after the younger one had come alone to Ste Chapelle. M. LaRue had been positive that no one in the village would have given Damian away—but clearly someone did, before Sunday night. If not at Ste Chapelle's Friday market, then when, and who? Or if some villager had inadvertently given Damian away then and there, why wait until Sunday to break in? "I don't suppose they left you any information on how to get into touch with them?"

"No, the younger said he would come again, and that if I had any information, he would pay me for it. I assured him the chances of my hearing of stolen goods were small."

"Of course. Well, may I give you my telephone number, on the chance that he does show up again? Naturally," I hastened to add, "I would never let such a person know how I had found him."

Reluctantly, he let me write Damian's telephone number on a card and slide it across the desk. The instant I let it go he put his hand down and continued its slide, vanishing it into a drawer, which he firmly closed.

"Thank you, Monsieur." I would return, soon, with sufficient funds to buy something, but to say so now would taint our transaction, turning it from ethics to commerce.

However, it appeared that our conversation was not entirely finished. "Have you . . ." he began. "That is, I will notify you if he returns, but as you are concerned for your friend's safety, and may not wish to wait until these men come back here—although I would not wish to suggest that you, yourself—"

It was all I could do not to seize him by the cravat and choke it out of him. "Yes?"

"There are Indian families," he blurted, "up near the Gare du Nord. One or two shops and a small restaurant, you know? Not that the men who came have families—or who knows, they may— and it is not an area to which the younger of the two men would naturally gravitate, as his suit was not that of a working man. But I have travelled, myself, and sometimes a person who finds himself in a foreign country might wish to eat his own cuisine, and to listen to his own language, you know? And so you might—or, not you alone, since it is not a nice area for a solitary lady, not at all— but perhaps you have a friend—a male friend—" He stopped, and found a way to finish his thought. "You might wish to take your drawing and your questions there."

"Gare du Nord."

"With a friend," he repeated firmly.

"A gentleman friend," I said. Preferably tall and muscular, no doubt.

Had it been an hour earlier, or had my foot been a day or two more healed, I might have turned in the direction of this miniature community of immigrants and taken my chances against the resident *Thuggees, hashashin,* and restauranteurs. But this day, discretion ruled. I continued my interrupted way up the *passage,* found an actual taxi rank, and had one of them take me to the station.

The attendant woke me at Délieux, where I was fortunate to find a second taxi to take me to Ste Chapelle. The village was shuttered and dark for the week-end. Not so the Adler house.

With a sinking sense of inevitability, I saw that all hell had broken loose.

CHAPTER FORTY-FOUR

Looking out of the taxi window, I could see panic spreading in all directions: Madame LaRue on the front step, wringing her hands; Monsieur LaRue on the walk with his shotgun (fortunately broken open over his arm); Pierre disappearing briskly around the side of the house. Dread was instantly contagious: my heart rate doubled, I flung the last of my francs at the driver, and fought to get legs and walking stick out of the door in the proper order. Mme LaRue was already bustling down the walk, wringing her hands and exclaiming, followed rapidly by her husband.

And with them came Dot, for some reason. The cinema-loving shop-girl was dressed in what might be the shortest skirt Ste Chapelle had ever seen, with makeup to match and a look of avid interest and . . . was it pride?

And then Holmes appeared in the doorway. With all his limbs, no blood or bandages in sight. My pulse stuttered, then slowed down. I drew a breath. Then another.

He nodded at me, and vanished inside.

Dot and the LaRues met me halfway along the walk-way, all throwing words at me. Damian—the problem had to do with Damian. He had arrived—no, he had *not* arrived, although he had sent a telegram that morning to say that he was coming to the house—but only briefly, and he did not know when. Nor did he need anything, since he would only stay a short time. Madame was outraged: how could she provide him with a meal if she did not know when he was coming? Monsieur was irritated: how could they meet him at the station? Dot then verbally elbowed her way into the conversation, in a tumble of English and French.

"But he was there, at the *gare*, on the train from Paris! I would not have recognised him—*il s'était rasé, complètement*, except for a small moustache—*oh là là*, he is most handsome, M. Adler is, without his beard. But I noticed him because he stopped to talk with the man in the car. That man had been there for hours, we all noticed him and wondered who he could be waiting for, he just sat and read a book until passengers started coming out, then he would look up and watch, and when they had finished coming, he would go back to his book.

"But this time, when he saw M. Adler, he got out—and I recognised him! From the drawing!"

"The *lascar*?" I exclaimed.

"Yes! That man in the drawing, who has been posted in the town! The scar, *les taches*." She gestured at her face, indicating the smallpox marks Damian had noted. "And his skin, it was dark, a little. But he wore a suit, a normal suit, and shoes. Nice shoes."

"What did he do, when he recognised Damian?"

"He called. I could not hear, I was inside the shop, but I could see him raise his hand, and saw M. Adler look at him. M. Adler stopped walking, looked . . . *effrayé*?"

"Afraid."

"Or, no, perhaps more nervous? Maybe even angry—I could not see, really. But he did stand where he was, and the other man, the man from the drawing, walked towards him. Slowly, and talking, one hand out. The other hand was holding something, I thought at first it was a large book but then I saw colours and decided it was a small painting. He stopped maybe ten feet away from M. Adler,

and took something from his inner pocket"—she rubbed at where
a suit's breast-pocket would be—"and held it out. M. Adler walked
forward to take it, then moved away again to read it—it was a letter, two or three pages. I think he read it more than once. When he
had finished, the other man held out the painting. M. Adler walked
forward again, and this time, he did not go back.

"They stood talking for a few minutes, and then M. Adler gave
him back the painting and the two men walked over to the motor
and got in.

"They drove off in the direction of Paris."

I stared at her, unable to think of a single question. Which may
have been more a sign of my own astonishment than the com-
pleteness of her narrative, but I could only nod and walk through
the recommencing three-way conversation and into the house.

"Holmes?" I called.

"In here."

I followed his voice to the sitting room. I wanted nothing more
than to fling my arms around him, but the extremity of that response, following a mere four-day absence, would take some explanation. Instead, I closed the door and set my back against it, to
keep the LaRues out and him in.

"Where were you?" he demanded.

I noticed that the portrait of his grandmother Camille had been
moved—and with that, the thought of all the things I had to tell
him washed over me.

"In Paris, as I'm sure the LaRues told you. What happened? I
thought you were going to nail Damian's feet to the ground somewhere?"

"So did I!" He drew a breath and lowered his voice. "When I left
them yesterday in Carcassonne, he agreed to stay put. I took the
train to Paris. I needed to talk to various people at the *Institut*
about those crates the LaRues told us about. But the idiot boy
seems to have decided he absolutely had to have some sketchbooks
that he'd left behind. I'd already told him I would send them down

to him, but no, for some ungodly reason he dropped everything and came here. Walking right into a trap."

"You think the LaRues are lying? That they knew when he was coming?"

"No. It sounds like—"He broke off and went to fetch a cigarette. When it was going, he dropped onto the fuchsia settee and shook his head. "I imagine we'll discover that someone's been paying a telegraphist for news. It's even possible—unlikely, but possible—that they're being paid to change messages. In any event, the lascar discovered that Damian would be coming in, and lay in wait all day for his arrival. It sounds as though Damian did attempt something resembling a disguise—I doubt that he's been without a beard since the War."

My overworked brain had begun to absorb the facts that had been flung at it. I limped over to sit in the chair across from Holmes. "Mme LaRue said they received a telegram that he'd be setting off this morning. But he arrived this afternoon, because Dot saw him from the shop and it closes at five on Saturdays. How did he get here so fast?"

He gave me a grim smile. "Aeroplane."

"There's an *aeroplane* service from Carcassonne?" I exclaimed.

"Toulouse has an airfield and a growing industry in the accursed things. And, as ill luck would have it, one of the other residents in the place I took them is a pilot eager to get back on the job."

I thought about it. An artist, frustrated at the absence of his sketches and notes. A day spent chafing, in the knowledge that an aged father was on the front lines instead. A decision that, if care were taken, with disguise and a lack of solid information . . .

"It does sound like ill luck more than simple stupidity."

"The lad—"

"He's a man, Holmes. And you'd have done exactly the same thing, if there was some tool you needed that could be retrieved with a surreptitious flight."

His expression said that he did not agree, but neither did he argue.

"Have you any idea who that lascar might be?" I asked.

"No. But I do know that he has inside information about the doings of the Adler house. I saw him in Nîmes. Dressed in a proper suit."

"Oh dear."

"We lost him there, quite comprehensively."

"And he came back here to camp out on the doorstep of the Délieux station?" I said, doubtfully.

"He'd have returned to his base, most likely in Paris, after I shook him off on Wednesday afternoon. He no doubt got new orders that sent him here."

"Damian went with him willingly. He was suspicious of the man until he read a letter the man gave him and looked at something that Dot said was a painting, but after that he got into the car without hesitation."

"Yes, but if the letter was, for example, from Dr Henning, to say they were being held captive . . ."

Dot's cinema-fuelled imagination might have led her to a more optimistic interpretation of Damian's movements. And if the Carcassonne hideaway had been breached after Damian left, well, he was not the only one able to skip about the countryside faster than a train.

"Any thoughts on what we can do?" My voice, I noticed, was more than a little desperate.

He gave me a bleak look. "Wait for the telephone to ring with a ransom demand?"

"Or for Damian to motor up with an explanation."

He did not grace that with a reply, merely leaned forward to rub out his cigarette in a Deux Magots ash-tray. As he sat back, he glanced at the cane I'd leaned against the chair, then down at my foot.

"Your ankle put up with a day in Paris, I see. What took you there?"

And with that, four exceptionally full days swept over me. What, indeed? And which piece of information did he require most urgently? "Holmes, you and I have a lot of catching up to do. But first," I declared, "I require a cup of tea."

I supplemented the tea with scraps from the cool-box—heaven only knew when Holmes had last taken a meal—and we consumed it at the kitchen table. As we chewed, I divided up my various discoveries and put them in order.

The journal itself was first and foremost—however, I gave him only the briefest of descriptions: its code, the woman's hand, the period covered. I only had half his attention at first, since his mind was still fixed on Damian's whereabouts and well-being, but half would do. "Holmes, I'll need time to tell you about it properly, but the immediately relevant part is, there seems to be a Franco-Indian family that believes some relatives of the Vernets are in possession of their family jewels, worth a considerable amount. So today I—"

"Which relatives are those?" Perhaps three-quarters of his attention.

"Holmes, please trust me: at the moment, the answer to that question will be a massive distraction. There will be time, but not now."

He raised an eyebrow, but nodded.

"Now, before you left, the LaRues told us that there were two men, probably from India, asking questions in the area about Damian."

"First in Délieux," he agreed, "then two days later, here in Ste Chapelle—only the younger one, that time. And there was a third— the 'lascar'—who broke in and was interrupted by Damian."

"We thought at the time it might have something to do with Thomas Brothers' cult," I resumed, "but they're from India, not Shanghai. The older one reminded Dot—you met her, but it may not have come up that she's a great film devotee—he reminded her of the Indians she's seen on the silver screen. That judgment was more reliably confirmed by a conductor on the Paris train. The younger of the two probably lives in Paris, and has done so long enough to take on the accent. None of the persons who encountered the two Indians recognised the lascar in Damian's sketch.

"That suggested they had a rougher colleague available, the sort of man more comfortable in bare feet and native clothing, whom they could send to break in. And yet he later appears in Nîmes, as you say, wearing an ordinary suit, and later here at the wheel of a car, again in a suit and nice shoes.

"It is unlikely that two entirely unrelated parties from the subcontinent came after Damian at the same time, but I fail to see how any of them would have put Damian together with their missing jewels."

"I might be able to illuminate that question," he said. Inevitably. "Those crates, from the *Institut*."

"Three crates and a steamer trunk. I went through them, and as M. LaRue said, they seem to be mostly memorabilia. Definitely no jewels. A number of paintings and daguerreotypes linked to the Vernets. I found the journal in with those."

"The journal that you say would be a distraction."

"That one, yes."

"The crates were sent after Damian presented himself at the *Institut de France*," he told me, "and one of the concierges put his name together with an enigmatic envelope pinned to the crates. He consulted the Director, who did as instructed by the contents of the envelope, namely, he first arranged to ship the crates to Damian, and then he sent a telegram to an address in India, saying, 'The boxes have been claimed.'"

"Any idea where in India?"

"A place called Chandernagore, a tiny French colony north of Calcutta. I don't believe I've . . . You're smiling."

"I've heard of the place. When was the cable sent?"

"August the seventh."

"Three and a half weeks before the men showed up in Délieux asking about 'the artist Adler.' One of them may live here permanently, but even if the older one had to sail from India, that would still give him plenty of time."

I paused for a moment, thinking about two men, separated by thousands of miles—and the third man, the lascar-turned-chauffeur? Did he travel with the other from India, or was he a local ruffian? Were we about to get involved with a modern version of Ram's *Thuggees*? I shook off the thoughts as yet another distraction.

"Let me tell you about that knife."

I gave him a quick summary of my adventures with the cinema-loving Dot and the Délieux photographer, but I also took care to describe the odd arrangement of fingerprints around the very end of the knife's grip, and the way it had hit the ground outside of the window. He listened, but did not comment on any significance. I gave a mental shrug, and went on.

"At any rate, I decided the jewellery was the key. Not revenge, or some personal animosity, but valuables. And I figured that, unlike London, the Indian community in Paris would be very small, perhaps small enough that someone would recognise them. My ankle was feeling better, and I had another thing I was looking into, and I thought it might take my mind off whatever you and Damian were up to, and . . . Anyway, I took the train up this morning, thinking that I could ask in various shops about where to buy exotic jewellery, particularly vintage or second-hand pieces. It seemed to me that someone from India in search of stolen jewellery might go looking for a sort of high-class version of a pawnshop.

"But I also asked on the train, since those two men would have stood out amongst the usual passengers, and struck a bit of luck when one of the attendants had seen them on their return from the visit to Délieux on Wednesday. And what's more, he had eaves-dropped on their conversation—or tried to, although most of it was in a foreign language. But he thought they had used the words '*tiare*' and '*bague*,' as well as something about a '*comtesse*.'"

"So you knew you were looking for a tiara and a ring."

"I knew that *they* were, at any rate. And although I didn't find the men, I did find a shop where they'd made enquiries. A jeweller in a *passage couvert* in the Ninth arrondissement said they came in last Saturday with a story about a burglary, asking if he'd recently bought any gold-and-gemstone rings, bracelets, or necklaces. They had photographs, not of the actual pieces, but of a painting of a woman wearing some of them." I decided not to mention that the portrait would make an appearance in the journal—he'd see that soon enough.

"Did you get their contact information?"

"They took care not to leave him any, merely saying that they would come back."

"Meaning that they either intend a crime, or have already committed one. Did you get anything else?"

"It was late, and I wanted to return in case you'd showed up. But—"

"Very well, I suppose we can use your find for a starting place and move out from there, asking—"

"Holmes, wait. The jeweller made what sounded like an excellent suggestion. We know that the older of the two is less thoroughly adapted to France, and most likely only arrived from India a few weeks ago. The jeweller said that there's a small Indian community, with shops and restaurants and such like, up in the Tenth between the Gare du Nord and Gare de l'Est."

"And a man in a foreign land may wish to surround himself with even a modicum of home," he finished for me. "A sensible thought. Was there anything else I should know?"

He was poised to get to his feet and race off, and I was not having that. "You need to shave and change your shirt, so we're not arrested for vagrancy. I'll fetch the motorcar keys from M. LaRue. I have a city map—oh, and you might want to bring whatever francs you have. I've spent most of mine."

And I left the room, letting his protests die behind me.

CHAPTER FORTY-FIVE

was glad, as I steered us through the village half an hour later, to find the head-lamps on Damian's motor blessedly powerful. The wheel was on the French, rather than English side, and we did have an admittedly exciting few moments when I pulled on to the larger road and forgot briefly that the French not only steered but drove on the wrong side—but it was only for a moment, and not worth the fuss Holmes made over it. When we were settled firmly on the right-hand side of the road, I dug into my bag and pulled out the journal, the translation note-book, and the Baedeker's guide, dropping them all into Holmes' lap.

"There's a torch in the glove box," I told him. "You should read my translation before we get to Paris."

Ste Chapelle was a scant twenty miles from the city's outskirts. Not that it took him half of that time to read what I'd written, but the silence between us had no time to build before I needed to ask him for guidance from the map.

I did, however, need to ask him twice.

He folded the journal and notes into the compartment and thumbed through the guide-book maps, in the end merely ripping out the three segments that made up Paris and dropping the book on the floor.

"Between the Gare du Nord and the Gare de l'Est?"

"That's what the man said. I thought we might simply motor up and down that district, looking for restaurants. If they're run by Indians, they should be fairly obvious."

After a minute of wrestling with the thin, awkward sheets, he stretched down to retrieve the book and opened its index.

"I did look at the Baedeker's," I told him, "but they didn't list any restaurants that sounded particularly Indian."

"They wouldn't," he agreed. "But what about hotels? There's an 'Hôtel Indo' three-quarters of a mile from the Gare du Nord."

I was silent, then admitted, "I hadn't thought to be that obvious."

"I suspect the name refers to Indonesia, rather than India," he said generously, and directed me to take the next turning.

The Hôtel Indo was far from a first- or even second-class establishment, being a five-storey building on a narrow, perfectly straight street in the Tenth arrondissement. Still, if it made it into Baedeker's, its bed-sheets and table-cloths would not offend a tourist, and the front, as we went slowly past it, looked basic but clean. Electric lights shone at some of the windows.

"For someone whose family business was patronised by royalty," I mused, "this would be a bit of a come-down."

"I do not think they would be stopping here," Holmes said. "If the older man was on his own, perhaps, but it is more likely that he would be taken in by the younger. Particularly if the younger one is related."

"Is the older man Rajiv's son, do you think? Your . . ." I tried to work it out. "Your great-uncle's grandson—your second cousin, once removed?"

There was no response. When I looked over, I could see that Holmes was staring out of the windscreen, his jaw tight. "Holmes, I—"

"No. You were right, Russell. The time is not now. We need to find them first, and ensure that Damian is safe. After that, we can discuss . . . all the rest."

I nodded, and merged into the traffic on the next street.

We crossed the quarter, turning and weaving along the up-and-down streets, then the back-and-forth. Twice we fell into place behind men wearing what appeared to be turbans, only to have the next street-lamp reveal idiosyncratic but European headgear. Most of the shops were closed; though on a Saturday evening, the restaurants and cabarets were teeming with life.

The area around the two railway stations was filled with higgledy-piggledy roads and smaller, less affluent houses. I was steering cautiously down a *rue* that was more pot-hole than cobblestone when something orange caught at the corner of my eye. When I looked up, it was gone, but I managed to reverse without taking any corners off of Damian's machine and turned down that street.

There it was: Le Calcutta.

Perhaps we would be permitted a meal tonight after all.

I negotiated the wheels up onto the pavements—only a full-sized lorry would be forced to back out again, and there were few of those out this late. Holmes winced as Damian's fender had a noisy introduction to the French stonework, then he climbed over the gear-sticks to follow me out of the driver's-side door.

We paused to study the restaurant's colourful façade. It was small, with only one set of windows beside the door, but seemed to have a full complement of diners. As I watched, the woman whose orange sari had caught my eye moved across the room and through the kitchen door at the back.

Most of the customers were men, all were Indian. Several wore turbans, although a trio at one table wore Jinnah caps, meaning that the place was not regarded as exclusively Hindu. Holmes and I would not exactly fit in here, but we would probably not be refused service—or conversely, drive the other diners out.

Familiar odours wafted onto the street when Holmes pulled

open the door, bringing a smile to my face. The woman in the orange sari put her head around the corner, and looked doubtful, but
not offended. I found myself giving an automatic *namaste,* which
triggered her small bow and hand-clasp in return—again, hesitant.
She was probably wondering if we were lost.

Holmes quickly put that idea to rest, as he addressed her in a
Hindi that was smooth enough to be understood, but accented
with enough English to provide an identity: two English visitors
to Paris looking for a taste of their time with the Raj. Obviously,
we'd come by accident, but surely there could be no harm . . . ?

The woman glanced around the room and, seeing no dawning
outrage on the faces, ushered us towards a table at the back. We
were brought water to wash our hands—about half of the diners were traditional enough to eat with their fingers, rather than
cutlery—and glasses of water. Around us, talk started up again.

Holmes was at his most charming as he asked about the menu—
lapsing back into French—and reassured her that, yes indeed, we
were well familiar with Indian cuisine and its spices. He gave her
our order. When she had left, I leaned forward to ask in a voice too
low to be overheard, "Where do you want to start? I doubt we'd get
a sympathetic response by showing them Damian's sketch."

"Doing so would guarantee that the place closes early," he
agreed.

"So shall we start our questions with jewellery, or indigo?"

"I believe we should start," he said, eyeing the silver tray coming
out of the kitchen, "with our meal."

Our appreciation of the food went far to ingratiate us with the
pair who operated the small place, the man in the kitchen and the
woman out front. We made use of the forks, rather than our fingers, but in all other ways, we were merely two diners among the
roomful, tucking in with enthusiasm.

A few minutes into the meal, our waitress came to refresh our
glasses. Holmes asked a question about a spice in the prawn curry,
she identified it, he nodded and said it reminded him of Calcutta,

was that where the cook was from? She was sorry to say it was not, that despite the name of the restaurant, her husband was from Pondichéry, although in fact she herself had been born in a village not far from Calcutta.

Into that thin crack, Holmes inserted a conversational toe. Which village was that? Oh, he thought he had been there, but didn't know that area well. Did it grow indigo? He'd been taken on a tour of some indigo plantations, thought mostly further up into Bengal, though perhaps he'd been through her area.

A quick flick of his gaze told me it was my turn.

"Ooh," I exclaimed. "Indigo! I adore the colour of indigo, but you don't see it much in this country. Do you know anyone in Paris that sells the cloth?"

A woman whose sari embraced the full vividness of the synthetic dye industry might not be concerned with old-fashioned, plant-based colours, but she was polite enough not to say as much. "Perhaps a shop in *le Sentier*?" she suggested, and looked surprised when I shook my head to indicate my lack of familiarity. "Across the Bonne-Nouvelle from here? A district with many shops and workshops to do with garments."

"Of course," said I—a woman whose clothing was the polar opposite of orange saris, my present costume illustrating one who embraced the fashion industry at its most pragmatic.

I met Holmes' eyes, and could see we were both thinking the same thing: The shops would be shut tight until Monday morning. By which time Damian would have been in potentially hostile hands for nearly forty-eight hours.

"A ring," I blurted. The orange sari had been turning away, but now reversed. I looked up at the woman, actually seeing her for the first time: slim, lithe, a little older than I, with beautiful dark eyes and a vermilion mark on her forehead. I felt as if I was looking into the journal I'd spent the last week translating. "It would be lovely to have a ring as well. Sapphire, for that same blue. Do you know any good Indian jewellers?"

Her dark eyes rose to look across the room. I followed her gaze, and Holmes turned in his chair.

Neither of the men at that window-side table could be the pair we were after, both being round-bellied, in their seventies, and clean-shaven. They felt our eyes upon them and looked at us warily. I threw them a smile that I hoped was more reassuring than predatory, and pushed back my chair. "Would you introduce us?" I suggested.

They invited us to sit. We asked the waitress for coffee, and talked about sapphires. We talked about sapphires rather more than either Holmes or I really wanted to do. Carats and colour, shape and source, cabochon or faceted. At last, I wrenched the discussion onto a different track.

"As I was saying to the kind Madame, I would like some indigo fabric, to make a dress of the same colour. Doesn't India still produce indigo?"

The younger of the two shook his head—they were brothers, more or less retired, from Madras, not one of the French colonies. "There is some, yes, but nowhere near what there used to be. The artificial dyes came in . . ." He turned to his brother for a rapid-fire discussion in what I assumed was Tamil, then resumed. "Around the turn of the century. In twenty years, indigo has become an exotic thing."

"Just what I want," I said, putting enthusiasm into the statement.

"It's a filthy stuff," he said. "It stinks, brings in flies and diseases, the workers are in it up to their necks. The British made them grow it instead of rice. Until the revolt—I was nine when the farmers rose against the plantations, and though it was on the other side of the country, it was all that our father and uncles talked about. They said more of the planters should be hanged." He gave us a ferocious, if largely toothless smile. "My father would not have been a follower of Gandhi's peace-loving ideas concerning self-rule."

I nodded solemnly but, lest we get swept up in a discussion of sub-continental bolshevism, said, "I'd still like to talk to someone who has indigo fabric for sale. I can see if perhaps there are more enlightened plantations these days."

The older one said something—he understood French just fine, I could see—and the younger looked thoughtful. They went back and forth for a minute until the younger brother gave a shrug and told us, "There's a family that used to be indigo importers until the bottom fell out of the market, before the War. Dupont is the name. I thought they'd gone home, but my brother says he saw one of them a week or two ago, so it sounds as if they're still around."

Dupont, I thought. Did I have Lakshmi's Indian surname at last? Was Pitaji's name Christian Dupont?

"Where could we find them?" This from Holmes, his voice ever-so-slightly more urgent than a discussion of dyestuff should be. The tension about Damian's safety was wearing on him.

The younger brother gave him an odd look, but Holmes had corrected his demeanour, and there seemed no reason to withhold whatever information they had. So after a bit more discussion, it was determined that the older of these two brothers had been walking down the Rue de la Lune and turned onto the Rue Poissonnière when he saw an old face he'd once known, going through the door of a block of flats. Although it took him until that evening to remember from where he had once known the man.

"And where is Rue de la Lune?" Holmes enquired.

Just across the Bonne-Nouvelle. In the Sentier district.

CHAPTER FORTY-SIX

We stood in a dark doorway and looked across the Rue Poissonnière at the building our informant had marked on the torn-out Baedeker's map: a five-storey block of flats that had been nice when built but sporadically maintained since then. Its dimly-lit foyer showed a concierge desk, currently unmanned. If the building did still employ an attendant, he was only there during the day.

A light burned over the entrance, but it was late, and although the neon and nightclubs of Montmartre were just half a mile away, this street was quiet enough that Holmes could apply his lockpicks without interruption. I followed him inside, closing the door as he reached up to turn the single gas lamp down further.

Like its exterior, the building had seen better days. It had not been converted to electrical power. The tile floor was worn, patched in some places and needing patches in others. Even in the half light I could see that the floor could do with a mop and the woodwork with a scrub-brush. To my surprise, there was a lift, but either someone had carelessly failed to shut the outer door fully, or it was no longer working.

Five rows of wooden slots behind the concierge desk held the residents' mail. Irritatingly, each had a number instead of a name. Holmes started at one end, I at the other, nearly meeting at the middle before he grunted and held out an envelope. Dupont: 23. By the layout of the mail slots, this meant two floors up from the lobby, number three.

He slid the letter back into place and we headed for the door marked *L'escalier*—then leapt for it as we heard voices and a key rattling in the outer door. We eased the stairway door shut on the incoming resident's curses, that the *maudit* concierge had forgot to lock up yet again, and I took a step towards the stairway—only to have Holmes yank me back and into a noxious cupboard that smelled of mildew and mouse droppings.

Two figures went past, barely illuminated by the light over the stairs, and although we made haste to leave the broom cupboard as soon as they cleared the first floor, we waited for the voices to stop before venturing in their wake. Which took some time, since both were well inebriated and, following the sounds, one of them lived on the topmost floor. Good thing we hadn't tried to keep ahead of him, or we'd have had to take refuge on the roof.

When silence had fallen, we followed.

Room 3 on the second floor had lost its number. The people in room 21 were having an argument, and we could see a clear line of light under its door.

There was no light underneath numbers 22, 24, or 25.

I leaned forward to whisper in Holmes' ear, "Do we need to worry about their having a back way out?"

I felt him shake his head. "Short of climbing from a window on knotted sheets, I think not."

"What about weapons?"

We had brought the revolver, but the younger man—the Dupont whose flat this was—was of an age to have served during the War. And soldiers had a habit of retaining the weapons they were supposed to turn in, particularly when it came to sidearms.

To say nothing of machete-knives.

I looked down at the lock-picks in Holmes' hand. Did we really want to break into a flat that might hold three armed men? And what if they had Damian in there, with a knife at his throat?

I exhaled, and spoke again in Holmes' ear. "I don't know that we have a choice."

He knelt and slid the end of the tension wrench into the keyhole. I turned the flame down on the nearby gas light, set my handbag on the floor, and drew out the revolver.

The lock was as old as everything else in the building. This meant it was basic, but also meant that it had not been oiled since before I was born. It made a noise when the pick had found the pins and he worked the bolt back from the plate.

One's impulse, having made a noise that could raise an alarm, was to freeze and wait for a response. That was rarely the right impulse, and Holmes did not hesitate now. He pushed the door open and went through it, keeping low and holding the door's edge lest it slam into the wall. No shotgun roared, no machete flashed in the thin light. I took my first breath in what felt like minutes, and joined him. He eased the door shut, and we stood, letting our eyes adjust and our other senses roam.

The odour did not evoke India to me. No trace of spices in the air, no sandalwood, incense, or even marigold flowers. It had been a long time since anyone had cooked a curry here. I could smell cigarettes, and coffee, and one of the spirits, probably whiskey. And sweat—but with a rank undertone that suggested the inhabitants of this flat were meat-eaters.

And snorers. One, more distant and through a closed door, had continued unabated. A nearer offender, silent when we first entered, now began to give off a gentle rhythm of air being drawn in.

Two men, located and noted as non-threatening for the present. I pressed against Holmes, and when he'd lowered his head, breathed, "Have you ever heard Damian snore?"

I felt him shake his head. "Neither of those are he."

That reduced the possibility of an ambush down to the one Indian who was unaccounted for. I reached down for Holmes' hand and tried to press the gun into it. "When you can see, make your way to the sleeper and try to wake him without noise."

His hand refused the weapon. "I'll need both hands," he told me, and moved off into the darkness.

Not for the first time, I envied him his night vision. I stood, straining to pick out so much as a footfall on worn carpet. Only when his victim made a strangled snort did I move, switching on the little electric torch and sweeping it around the room.

There were only the two men: Holmes with both hands over the mouth of a man on a too-small sofa, and the man himself, kicking at his covers, hands attempting to peel away Holmes' fingers. He winced at the light, then subsided when Holmes spoke into his ear.

This was the younger one: dark eyes, tousled hair, bare feet sticking out from a tangle of blanket and striped European-style pajamas. I raised the revolver into the torchlight, and his eyes widened further, one hand going out as if to ward off a bullet.

"We don't want to harm you," I heard Holmes murmur, in French. "We only want to talk." After a moment, the man gave a small nod, and Holmes looked at me, tipping his head at the source of the other snores—but keeping his hands firmly in place.

I took the time to check the other rooms first: no one in the tiny kitchen, nor in the whatnot cupboard. Things were well ordered, and tidy enough to suggest that, reduced circumstances or no, the inhabitant was either handy with a broom or had a regular cleaner. Things were also, I noticed, strikingly European, from his shoes to his carpets. The only signs of India were a pair of Moghul prints near the door, and even those were the sorts of souvenir a traveller might own.

I shone the light on the sofa tableau again, wondering if I should have Holmes lift his hand long enough to check for a moustache, then decided no: if we had the wrong men, we would simply have to run for it, and vanish into the streets. Not the first time we'd done that—although I was not certain that I could make any speed with my stick.

I moved down to the bedroom door, where the snores continued. I transferred the small torch to my teeth just long enough to turn the doorknob, then eased the door open. The bedroom was small, with one bed and a single mound under the covers. That didn't mean someone else was not on the floor on its other side, but—

And suddenly, the room burst into motion, mid-snore. A choking noise, the bedclothes flew into the air and a very solid figure with greying hair and pajama bottoms launched himself out of bed and at the doorway—at me.

I was so startled I nearly shot him dead, but he wasn't armed and his middle-aged chest managed to look so unthreatening, I just shouted at him to *stop, I have a*—

His hand was out, and he was moving fast enough that he'd have bounced me hard against the wall, so I reacted by letting go of everything—gun, cane, and torch went flying—to seize his outstretched arm and throw myself backwards.

He was the one to get bounced, first against one wall and then against its opposite. He collapsed onto the floorboards while I leapt for the gun. The torch was still burning, and although it lay on the floor with its beam pointing in the opposite direction, it cast enough light for the man to see me as he sat shakily upright.

I recognised some of his curses—taught me by a trouble-making urchin in India—but I raised my voice over them to reassure Holmes that everything was all right, repeating the statement in French, for the benefit of our younger prisoner.

I spotted a dressing gown across the back of a chair, just inside the bedroom door, and tossed it in the direction of the man on the floor. He glared at me. I used the gun to invite him in the direction of the sitting room.

"M. Dupont," I said. "We need to talk."

CHAPTER FORTY-SEVEN

We sat the two of them on the settee, with Holmes on a chair and me planted in the doorway on a kitchen stool. They had begun to argue the instant my prisoner laid eyes on the younger man, and with the lights turned up, their physical resemblance and manner made it clear that they were close relations.

I could understand less than one word in fifty, but I thought that the elder—father? uncle?—was berating the younger over his failure to overcome us when he'd had the chance. The younger was not only protesting the accusations as unjust, but seemed to be near to losing his temper entirely. The animosity, and the frustration, appeared to be an ingrained part of their relationship.

Holmes and I watched them, Holmes possibly understanding more of their words, I definitely hoping for some clue as to where to begin when it came to sorting this out.

Holmes ran out of patience first, slicing into the argument with a razor-sharp voice. "Where is my son?" he demanded. *Où est mon fils?*

Both men broke off to stare at him, then back at each other. As wordless replies went, this one was unambiguous. They had no idea what he was talking about. When the older said something, he might as well have been holding up a cinema speech card printed with *What does he mean?*

"Your partner, then," Holmes broke in again. "He took Damian away from Ste Chapelle, earlier this evening. Where would they be?"

They recognised the name Damian, but otherwise exhibited the same confusion—though perhaps I might hold one thin end of this particular thread of evidence. I reached inside my bag for the sketch of the lascar, holding it out to the younger man. "This man. Do you know who he is?"

The two heads bent together over the page, another discussion rising up in the language that was not Hindi. "If you were to speak French," I suggested, "this might go more rapidly."

The younger, as I'd thought, was fluent in the local tongue. The older was less so, but he could manage, with a thicker accent and simpler vocabulary.

Both agreed: "We don't know this man."

"What are your names?"

The older started to object, but the younger held up his hand in exasperation and said, "I am Stéphane Dupont. This—"

"Sanjay," the older snapped.

"Yes, all right, my other name is Sanjay, although I never use it in this country. This is my father, Rishi Dupont."

"You're from Chandernagore?"

"We are. Although again, I have not lived there since the first year of the War. Paris is my home now."

Grumbles from the senior Dupont indicated that this was one of their ongoing points of contention.

Holmes spoke up, directing a question at the elder man. "What was your father's name?"

"My father? He was Rajiv—Rajiv Dupont."

"And your grandfather?"

"Why do you ask these things? I have done nothing."

"Please, M. Dupont, answer my questions."

Reluctantly, and under the impatient urging of his son, he replied. "His name was Ram. Ram Dupont. Although my grandmother always called him Richard."

I cut in with a question. "Your grandmother—was her name Sophie?"

"How do you know that?"

Ram had died in his forties, but his harridan of a wife had lived on, apparently long enough for this man to know her.

I continued. "Your grandfather had a brother, Krishna."

The man's face snapped shut, instantly confirming all kinds of suspicions. "I don't know."

"Yes, you do. He died long before you were born, but I can't imagine Sophie not telling you all about the wickedness of her brother-in-law, and the little French girl he brought home with him from Paris."

"No one ever talked about an uncle, or his daughter."

"M. Dupont, you really shouldn't try to lie, you are very bad at it. Yes, Lakshmi was his daughter." And I could think of only one reason why he would claim not to know about this episode of family history. "Did your grandfather Ram kill his brother, Krishna?"

His jaw dropped, his mouth working in an attempt to shape a protest, but before he could start to bluster, Holmes delivered a question of his own.

"Did your father blackmail an English woman into committing suicide?"

"I— Blackmail? An English woman? What are you—"

His protest built, but when I glanced at Stéphane, I saw that the incomprehension on his face was giving way to a look of dismay. He, too, could see that his father had something to hide. "Papa, what is this?"

"It is nothing, these two are mad, they've come here to rob us."

"Of what? There's nothing here."

I answered him. "Your father is looking for some jewels that were given to Krishna's daughter, Lakshmi, some eighty-six years ago."

"Eighty-six *years?*" Stéphane exclaimed. "No! I mean, yes, my father is here looking for some jewels, but they were stolen from the family, not given away. And it was not *that* long ago. It couldn't have been. Unless there were two robberies."

"Theft is what your father told you. It may even be what he believes, since his grandmother Sophie seems to have drilled it into him. But in fact, they were freely given to Krishna's daughter by his mother as *stridhana*, an inheritance, the day after he died. The day after Ram killed him, in order to take control of the company. Isn't that right, M. Dupont?"

But Dupont had himself under control now, and was giving no ground. The jewels were most definitely stolen, he insisted. Why would they have been given away to a French child? She wasn't even Krishna's daughter, merely a woman's attempt at getting herself a rich man. Because the Duponts had been rich, oh yes! Before those jewels went, and the business took a turn, and then the indigo market failed—but if they'd had the inheritance, if that [some word I could only guess at] had not tricked her way into Krishna's affections and robbed the family blind, they could have re-built. And now they were being accused, not only his grandfather but his father as well—what would his poor grandmother think, she who had held the family together all those years! A woman wronged by France, a woman to whom he had sworn to maintain the hunt for justice—yes, on her dying bed he had sworn to her that he would never rest until he had restored the family's honour and position.

The only accusation he had overlooked, I thought, was the question of how his grandfather Ram had died. Perhaps the causes were natural. But if my speculations about Ram's end were correct, and the man had died of violence, either his grandson did not know it, or was not aware that the wicked Lakshmi's devoted servant, Arjun, had returned to India not long before the old man's death.

Stéphane was now looking frankly appalled. "Papa," he broke in, nearly a moan. "This is absurd! This is not at all what you told me.

What have you done to these people? What has happened to this man's son?"

"I have done nothing!" Dupont's rising voice had finally disturbed the neighbours, one of whom pounded a fist on an adjoining wall. He paid them no mind. "How could I have done anything to that man? We looked for him in that town, but you went back without me to the little village, and said you didn't find him. How would I have found him if you didn't?"

"Is this true?" Holmes demanded of the son.

"I . . . I don't see how he could have gone back on his own. I suppose he might have, while I was at work this week, but he never said anything. I told him we could hire a private detective, but the man we talked to wanted money first, and I, well, I'd cleaned out my savings bringing him out from India, and I couldn't pay the man until I got my salary this morning."

He swiped his hand across his face and, taking no further notice of his father's sputtered protests, turned to Holmes and me. "I do not understand this, but I swear to you, I thought I was helping my father look for some family jewels that had been stolen when he was a young man. I'd always known about them, all my life he's had this . . . well, an *idée fixe* about them. About our family's lost reputation in general, and the jewels were a part of that. When he wired to say that he now knew who had stolen them and that they were in Paris, I thought perhaps if we could find them, even if they were worth a fraction of what he imagined they were, it might restore his sense of worth. The Duponts were important people in Chandernagore, although there's not much left of their glory other than a crumbling old house. I suppose I also thought that, if there were a few nice pieces, enough to make his old age more comfortable, it would save me from . . . well."

Save me from having to go back to India and care for him, his face said.

"But Papa," he continued, "what's this about blackmail? And *murder*? Do you know anything about this?"

"They are lying."

"It doesn't look to me like they are."

"There was no murder. A man died, his brother took over Dupont Indigo. And ran it very well, until the foreign dyes came in. That is what killed my father and grandfather, losing a large part of their business. That and the jewels."

"What about the blackmail?"

"It was not blackmail. And my father did not kill the Vernet woman."

The name echoed through the room. I looked at Holmes, but he showed no reaction other than the intensity of his glare at the man. At his blood relation.

"Then what was it?" his son pressed. "Papa, you have to tell me." The older man held a stubborn silence, but the younger pushed back. "Papa, tell me what happened, or I shall put you back on the ship tomorrow and never see you again."

"Not here. Not before these people. Who are you, anyway?" he snapped at Holmes.

"We are the people who decide if you are arrested or not. Who choose whether or not your family's reputation will survive."

The second threat proved more dire than mere incarceration. Sullenly, Rishi Dupont slumped back in his chair and began.

CHAPTER FORTY-EIGHT

"You will understand," Dupont began, "that I do not know all that took place. When I was a child, I spent a lot of time with my grandmother Sophie. She was old, nearly seventy when I was born, and she had little to do but tell stories to my sisters and me of when our family mattered, both in India and beyond. She would tell how our ancestors had been among the first to come and make a home in Bengal, back when Calcutta was the poor relation of wealthy Chandernagore. How the British, who ruled all of India, would come to consult on important decisions. How our indigo had been the prize of the ladies in the King's court in Paris.

"When my grandfather's older brother, Krishna, was nineteen, he was sent to Paris to learn the business and to find himself a French wife. He learned the business, but instead of coming back with a wife, he brought back a child, who he said was his illegitimate daughter from a liaison with a married woman. She was from a family of painters named Vernet, and her husband discovered that the child was not his."

"Lakshmi," I said.

"Yes. I do not know what her European name was. But she was a trouble-maker from the day she appeared. Disobedient, dis-

respectful, wild—she took to the streets like some low-caste urchin. She was pretty enough, with distinctive grey eyes, and looked
almost French, but my grandparents despaired of her. Plans were
under way to get the girl safely married off, when suddenly Krishna
died and the girl ran off with one of the servants, who stole the
family jewels and sailed away with her. They thought she would go
back to her mother in France, so we had our representatives there
keep an eye on the Vernets. But although there were rumours of
her presence, we could not find her. The family finally decided that
she had either died, robbed by her servant, perhaps, or gone somewhere like America.

"But then, many years later—thirty years, at least—our representative in Paris attended a ball in London and met a woman
with grey eyes who was said to be a Vernet. He sent word to my
father. He did not believe it at first, but my grandmother sold one
of her necklaces for him to sail to London—and there he found
her, hiding out in the English countryside. He found some dance
she was going to and arranged to meet her, and told her that he
was not interested in ruining her life but that he wanted the stolen
jewels back.

"And the next thing he knew, the madwoman had drowned herself off the coast!

"Before she died, she'd told my father that she had the jewels
hidden, but there was no sign of them, not so much as a rumour.
My grandmother was very angry with my father, but what could
he do? So, over the years, the responsibilities of our Paris representative have included keeping watch on the Vernet family. When
I came to oversee the Paris office—what was left of the Paris
office—I discovered that one of the Vernets had died and left some
boxes in the *École des Beaux-Arts*. I bribed a guard to get me in to
see them. There was a letter pinned to the front, saying who the
boxes should be given to, but without any details. The guard was
upset when I read the letter, and panicked when I tried to open the
tops, but after finding a trunk with nothing but old paint stains,

and a box with old clothing, I thought it was unlikely that valuable jewels would have been stored with such rubbish. The best I could do was add a letter of my own, asking that a telegram be sent to the Chandernagore address as soon as someone came to claim the boxes.

"I have been waiting twenty-five years. And then the cable arrived last month."

I stared at him. "Eighty-six years after the jewels went missing, and still you came?"

"I vowed to my grandmother, and to my father, that I would not rest until the family had its wealth again."

"And when you got here and found that the boxes had been sent to Damian Adler, you ordered your man to break in and search the crates."

"What man? I told you, I have no 'man.'"

He was as definite about it as he had been the first time. Which meant that the lascar was not working with the Duponts—but before I could focus on the significance of this, he continued.

"Sanjay and I went to the town where the boxes had been shipped for Adler to pick up. We asked questions, and found that he lived in a small village nearby. Sanjay was afraid that if the both of us went to a place that small, the artist would hear, so he went alone, on the day of the village market, to find him. But either we had been told wrong, or the villagers did not trust him, because they only said nonsense. And we did not have the money his detective wanted, so instead we returned to the search in Paris. I thought perhaps, if Adler had found the jewels, he might have already begun to sell them in the jewellers who specialise in antique and exotic pieces."

I looked over at Holmes. After a moment, reluctantly, he nodded, to say that yes, Dupont was telling the truth.

"You can't imagine the jewels are still sitting somewhere, waiting for you?"

"Why not? They have to be somewhere. My father found no

sign that Lakshmi had worn them in England. His father had found hints and traces of them here in France, but not the good pieces, and certainly not the entire hoard. The sly girl must have either given them to someone, or hidden them herself before she married. When they are found, we will be here to claim them. I have to," he cried. "The walls of my house are crumbling, a banyan tree has rooted in the ballroom, one of the ceilings has fallen in. My wife has had to take in lodgers!"

Obsession is the triumph of emotion over logic. This man's obsession was clear: despite all evidence to the contrary, Ram's grandson clung to the belief that the jewels would surface, and restore the family's palace, status, and honour.

But not the great-grandson. There was no fanatic's gleam in the eyes of Stéphane Dupont. He looked merely weary, as fed up with his father's preoccupations as any bored European adolescent.

"This has to stop," I said. The younger Dupont looked up, saw that I was speaking to him, and gave his father a wary glance.

I then turned to Rishi. "The jewels are gone," I said, my voice absolutely flat. "They are not in those crates that were sent to Damian Adler. There was no key to a deposit box, or instructions to a vault, or a hand-drawn map to a treasure island. If any Vernet ever had them, they were broken up and sold long ago. This century-old animosity between two brothers has been the ruin of your family, and will only drive a wedge between you and what remains of it. M. Dupont, you have done your utmost to fulfil the vow you made to your father and his mother. It now has to end."

As the three of us sat and watched, we saw the first thread of doubt weave its way into the man's life. The fixation would take time to loose its hold on him, but with luck, his grandmother's fanatical influence would let him go. He closed his eyes and drew a deep breath, then another.

And nodded. When he opened his dark eyes, he seemed both bereft and relieved, and would not look at his son. "I will go home," he said.

"I—" Stéphane began, stopped, and started again. "Would you like to wait, just a few days? It would be . . . I would enjoy simply seeing my father, for a time."

Then he remembered, and his eyes went to Holmes. "Unless . . ."

Frankly, I did not know what charge might be brought against the man, although there was no reason to say so aloud. Not while Holmes was fixing Dupont with his most unyielding gaze. "I will not bring forth an arrest, *if* we see no further sign of interest in my son and his family, or in these mythical jewels. However, any indication that they are still of interest, and—"

"Agreed," Stéphane broke in, then turned to his father.

"I will make no further pursuit of the matter," said Rishi.

And with that, we took our leave.

CHAPTER FORTY-NINE

had wrenched my ankle again in tackling Rishi Dupont, and lagged behind Holmes down the dim stairway. *Sophie,* I was thinking. *Sophie was the one with the long memory. Sophie the one Lakshmi needed to watch out for.*

"Do you think you'll ever tell them that you are a relative?" I asked at his back.

"Perhaps to the son. If his father shows no further signs of this unhealthy preoccupation."

"Gems have a way of taking over the human imagination, don't they? Even those that aren't prised off the forehead of a Hindu god. How many famous stones are said to bring bad luck? The Hope Diamond, the Koh-i-Noor, the Delhi Purple Sapphire. I suppose they are no more inherently conducive to ill fortune than a bag of gold coins, but—"

We had reached the ground floor, the dimmest portion of the stairway, and I nearly walked into Holmes, who was standing with his head bent.

"Where the devil is the boy?"

"What boy?"

"Damian," he snapped. "Or had you forgot he's missing?"

"No, of course not, I just hadn't—"

"If that blasted 'lascar' isn't working with the Duponts, then where did he come from? Who else is involved in this madness? I shall have to turn Mycroft loose on the matter, shan't I?" He stormed across the empty foyer, leaving me to catch up with him on the street outside.

"Holmes, I wonder . . ."

He glared at me. "What is it?"

I must be wrong, I thought. *Spending all this time, teasing out the message of a compelling voice, puzzle and history at once, I took the next step and laid my own meaning onto hers. If Holmes hasn't seen it, it can't be there.*

Then I looked at him and thought: *Could he be too close to it?*

It was, frankly, a shocking idea, that Sherlock Holmes might be too close—too emotionally involved—with a matter to be objective.

He'd read the journal—yes, it was only my translation, and he was being swept along by other events and apprehensions, but surely that would have been sufficient to read any clues that were actually there?

No doubt I was somewhat obsessed. I'd lived with Lakshmi's journal so intimately over the past days, to the exclusion of all other distractions, that I would readily admit my own degree of . . . shall we say, preoccupation, with her life and her adventures. Holmes might be the woman's son, but when it came to her journal, he had only just met her. He had not spent sixty or more hours first pulling apart her personal code, then translating it, and spending every hour along the way puzzling over its meaning. Since I'd pulled it from the crate of paintings on Tuesday evening and the successive images of her life had begun to flicker past, I felt that I knew Lakshmi Dupont—Louise Vernet-Lecomte, Louise Holmes—better than any person alive.

Obsessed? Possibly. Probably? Had I any reason to link the journal with Damian's fate? Any real reason, other than half-perceived meanings and vague suspicions?

A man had come into Damian's house with a knife. Six days later, the same man came and took him away. I could be putting Damian's life in danger, by following a series of what might be nothing more substantial than coincidences and misperceptions.

On the other hand, did we have anything more definite?

I made a decision.

"Holmes, I do not know where Damian is. But before we summon Mycroft or the French police, I'd like your permission to try something. Think of it as testing an hypothesis. I need your patience while I'm doing so, though I'll happily explain once I have an answer. You can spend time with the journal itself," I suggested. "To see if you agree with my translation."

He was not deceived by my attempt at a red herring. Then again, he'd done the same to me countless times over the years. And if he had no faith in my judgment, where would that leave us?

"How long?" he asked.

I felt light-headed—although whether from relief at his trust or dread at the idea of failing him, I could not have said. I cleared my throat. "An hour. Perhaps two."

He grunted and stalked out onto the silent streets, back to where we had left Damian's motor.

This was a waste of time. We should go and speak with the *Préfecture de Police.*

Instead, I took out the ignition key and followed Holmes.

CHAPTER FIFTY

We motored in silence through the pre-dawn streets. It being Sunday, all was still, but for a burst of neon and motorcar head-lamps when we went by one of the all-night Jazz clubs. I had confirmed my scattered idea of the route through the city on the remnants of the Baedeker's map, but in fact, once I had found the Boulevard Haussmann, it was merely a matter of following the directional signs towards the Pont de Neuilly. The closest I came to any traffic was a trio of sleek motorcars filled with Young Things, racing the circle around the Arc de Triomphe. Once their shrieks faded, all was quiet again.

Holmes did immerse himself in the journal. I waited for him to react, to see the possibilities I had glimpsed, but he gave no sign of it. I told myself that, given a short time curled up with his tobacco to digest the material, his thoughts would have brought him to the same . . . not conclusion, it was far too thin and jumbled for that. But he would have reached it. And in a far shorter time than I had.

I told myself that I'd not only lived and breathed every word of the journal for days, to the exclusion of all else, but I was not re-quired to set aside concrete truths known since I was eleven years old. I could well imagine myself in his position, learning that facts I had built my entire life around now needed to be re-arranged and built anew. I had been through a similar process myself, in California the year before.

While he read, I reviewed what I knew—and what I suspected—about our destination.

I was taking us to Nanterre, once a village, now a suburb in the northwestern part of the Paris sprawl. Like the rest of the city, Nanterre had changed immensely since the July Revolution restored Louis Philippe to the throne, a year or so after an indigo exporter named Krishna Dupont carried his daughter away to India. Three miles from the city's edge, five from the Arc de Triomphe, Nanterre was just one Seine bridge from the centre of power—a bridge that had existed in one form or another since the seventeenth century.

The solitary hill within this loop of the Seine had become a part of the city's defences in the 1840s, when the star-shaped fortress of Mont-Valérien was built to defend Paris against a growing Prussian threat. Before that, back when Lakshmi was Louise, and living with her mother, the hillock was a patch of wooded ground with a cemetery, a chapel, and the remains of a Trappist monastery inhabited by one or two old and silent monks.

In her memoir, Lakshmi later wrote, *We could set off one way to see the hermitage on the mountain . . .*

Not far from the monastery, when this loop of the river had been more farmland than suburb, the Empress Josephine bought a run-down mansion as a surprise for Napoleon when he came home from a campaign in Egypt. She spent a fortune restoring Malmaison, turning it into one of the most beautiful gardens in Europe, filled with exotic animals, curious plants, a heated orangery, and a vast collection of roses.

. . . or another if we wished to walk in the footsteps of an Empress.

The town of Nanterre has a cathedral, built on the site of an ancient chapel to Sainte Geneviève, whose prayers, in the fifth century, had saved Paris first from Attila's Huns, then from Childeric's Franks.

Or a third way—and with that thought, here came the church itself. Surely, I thought, surely the sainte patronne *of Paris would reach out and keep me . . . but her chapel went by as well, silent and uncaring.*

On a map, the fortress of Mont-Valérien, the gardens of Josephine at Malmaison, and the chapel of Sainte Geneviève in Nanterre village formed a near-perfect equilateral triangle.

Once across the Seine, I turned in the direction of the hilltop fort, now catching the first light of sunrise. Holmes noticed the brightness, switched off the torch, gave a curious look at our surroundings, and returned to the pages.

I was aware, past my growing nerves, that it was going to be a beautiful autumn day. I was also aware that I was soon going to be testing the patience of the man sitting beside me—in a way that heaven knew I found annoying when he did the same to me. Another hour, I thought. I would not push him past that.

I left the main road and began to quarter the lanes and by-ways that curled around the obstacle that was Mont-Valérien. It was slow work, and I was forced to reverse from time to time out of dead-ends and too-narrow tracks. Wandering dogs and the occasional Sunday labourer or farmer out to milk his cow eyed us with suspicion. Early church-bells called the faithful, while the occasional whiff of coffee called to the rest of us. After twenty minutes of this, we had nearly reached Malmaison. Holmes glanced up twice, and said nothing—with increasing emphasis. I doggedly crossed back over the larger road to work my way in the direction of Nanterre proper.

Finally, he closed the journal to study the meaningless garden walls and tile-roofed houses edging past our windows. "Would you care to tell me what you are looking for?"

But as if his complaint had been the key, the touch of doubt to light the magic—there it was. A glimpse, above a high wall, in the roof of a house that was almost precisely at the centre of that equilateral triangle.

My heart leapt—in hope, in a sense of accomplishment, in an unworthy feeling of victory over Sherlock Holmes. I said nothing, merely pulled over and shut down the engine.

And prayed.

Holmes bent his head to see out of the window. One eyebrow rose. He gave me a glance, then opened his door and climbed out, crossing the lane to stand before a high iron gate set into a stone wall half-hidden by ivy. He looked at the house. I stayed where I was for a moment, and watched.

I cannot even begin to describe the expression on his face. He remained worried and irritated, but for a moment, he was also surprised. And amused. And slightly melancholy.

I realised with a jolt that Holmes, framed now by the motorcar's windscreen, was creating a final image for the zoetrope of his mother's life.

He stood gazing at an old French house with an eyebrow window set in its ancient red tiles and a rose vine that climbed halfway to the roof's peak.

I could smell the scent despite the distance, she wrote.

The same eyebrow window that was seen by a frantic child being carried away from her weeping mother. A child who would go on to study the play of sails against a blue sky, and meet a lantern that danced, and witness a top-hatted man's contemptuous assault on a stevedore. Who would puzzle over an uncle's conversation with a *Thuggee* leader, and see both the violent death of a beloved father and the daguerreotype of an uncle's travels. Who would buy a ticket home for a beloved servant, then encounter a pair of blue eyes. Who would know the beach-side pleasures of a family, and learn fear and despair at a festive evening of dance. Who would pick up a pen and write the letter that ended it all.

And now, half a century after that letter had been sealed, a grey-haired man stood in the lane where a carriage had once waited and studied that same window, breathing in the fragrance of the blowsy, late-season blossoms of a rose vine with a trunk as thick as his arm.

The zoetrope's dancing figures had circled back to where they began.

I got out of Damian's motor and walked over to where he stood, taking his hand in a rare display of affection in a public setting.

For a few beats of the heart, he forgot the burden of apprehension. Then it came back, and I felt his hand withdraw.

"You can't imagine that somehow Damian managed to find—" he started to say, only to be interrupted by the door coming open. Out stepped a tall, thin figure: a young Sherlock Holmes, the resemblance even more striking with Damian's transformation from full beard and unruly hair to pencil-thin moustache and neat trim.

Holmes was staggered: Literally, he took a step back. A small step, but then he turned upon me a look of untarnished respect. "I see how you found the house, but I fail to spot how you knew he would be here."

He worked the gate's latch and started towards the house, but any explanation from me would have been overrun by Damian's voice, more animated than I'd ever heard it.

"Good Lord," he called, "I *am* impressed! How on earth did you find me? I didn't even make it to Ste Chapelle! And yes, yes, Father, I see it on your face—you told me to stay put. But I thought of something else the LaRues could send down, and when Théo went into town yesterday morning, I asked him to put in a trunk call to them. They told him you hadn't even come home yet. Which meant I wouldn't get the sketchbooks until Tuesday or Wednesday at the very earliest. I was, well, furious. You'd promised! I tried not to shout, as I was telling Aileen, but pretty much everyone in the house could hear me. Including Jules—you met him, he was France's first fighting ace during the War. And he said, 'Why don't I run you up?' I told him no—but then I thought, *Why not?* And I was careful. I cabled the LaRues, but only said enough to make sure I wasn't shot as an intruder. You like my disguise? I thought it would take more than a shave, but once the beard came off, I wouldn't have known myself in the mirror. Though I did borrow a pair of tinted lenses and a hat.

"Tell you the truth, I'm not sure how Arjun recognised me when I came out of the station, but he did. And when I'd read the letter, and saw the painting, it seemed more important than my sketch-books, and nobody at the house was really expecting me. So, I came here first."

He gestured with his hand at the house around him.

"Arjun?" Holmes asked.

"Painting?" I said.

"Oh, of course," Damian said with a self-critical roll of the eyes, "you don't know. He's the—"

But we were not to hear what Arjun was or why a painting mattered. Instead, Damian's extraordinarily light-hearted chatter cut off as something drew his attention from inside the house. He turned, his arm rising as if to welcome a bird onto his fingers. A hand emerged from the darkness. It rested on his, and a tiny figure, ancient and delicate and tough, stepped out, then straightened, squinting slightly with the brightness of morning.

Her hair was pure white, thin as floss, around a face whose brown was not entirely from the sun. Her nose was sharp, her fingers twisted by rheumatism. Her eyes, though faded with age, were steel grey, the rarest colour of all. One got the impression that those eyes missed little, and when it came to foolishness, forgave less.

But then she smiled, and her face might have been welcoming a miracle.

Holmes made a noise in the back of his throat. I looked up at him, and watched realisation dawn. He looked . . . shocked. Bewildered. Vulnerable. And young—for an instant, his eyes were those of an eleven-year-old boy. And for an instant, I despised the choice his mother had made.

She spoke then, her voice deeper than one would expect from such a figure, her English without accent as she addressed the man at my side.

"Hullo, my son. I am so very glad you found me."

CHAPTER FIFTY-ONE

L ouise Vernet-Lecomte Dupont Holmes, one hundred years old on her last birthday, sat on the terrace with her dazed son, her adoring grandson, and the young woman who had married into this singular family. Then, as we seated ourselves on chairs arranged to take advantage of the morning sun, another piece of the puzzle appeared.

He came out of the house with a gleaming silver tray of cups and coffee, a man from North India with the beginnings of silver in his black hair. His clean-shaven face showed the faint marks of childhood smallpox. A scar the shape of a crescent moon rode below his right cheekbone.

Damian's "lascar."

Holmes climbed warily to his feet. It was all well and good to have theorised that the man was not an enemy, but a theory was no good until it was proven.

The man stopped dead, although the porcelain did not so much as rattle. "Ah," he said. "I wondered if you'd seen me in Nîmes. Was it when I had to hurry out of the building after your son?"

"It was."

The man resumed his movement towards the mosaic-topped

table, smiling. "And then you lost me somewhere on the train. I'm still not sure how you managed that."

Considering that the man had climbed through a window with bare feet, in rough clothing, and with a machete in his hand, he now cut a figure both amiable and elegant as he laid out the cups and saucers on the table.

"That explains the fingerprints," I said.

The non sequitur brought a glance of polite bafflement, so I elaborated. "I found fingerprints on the machete. It took a while to figure why a man who brought such a weapon into a house would then drop it with great precision into the ground outside."

The lascar in the linen suit straightened in surprise. "Weapon? No. A tool, certainly, needed to get the shutters and window open, but it was barely sharper than a butter knife."

"May I introduce my friend Arjun Ghosh," said the old woman.

First Lakshmi, now Arjun—one might think that, being married to Sherlock Holmes, I would be well accustomed to meeting the eminent, but to be honest, this felt a bit like sitting down to tea with the gods.

"I've been showing your face all over Paris," I told him. "'Arjun.' Named after a . . . great-great grandfather?"

"Merely great," he corrected me, eyes crinkling. "The men in my family tend not to marry young." He had a warm smile, and as he proceeded to pour the coffee, the ease of his manner and the cut of his clothing made it quite clear that he was more than merely the hired help.

"The earlier Arjun was your servant," I said to Mme Holmes. "Who helped get you out of India."

"My friend," Mme Holmes amended. "And that of my father before me. I surmise that you found my image-journal." She was speaking to Holmes, but he tipped his head towards me.

"Not I. My . . . your . . . Russell, here, found it and broke your code. I merely read it."

"I'd hurt my ankle," I felt compelled to explain, "so I stayed behind, when Holmes went after Damian." I turned to Damian, to say, "I hope you don't mind, I dug through the crates from the *Institut* after Holmes left, and found a coded journal. So I set about translating it. I didn't have much else to do."

Damian shrugged off the infringement of his privacy, but the sharp grey eyes on the other side of the table fixed on me, as if weighing the value of any young woman who had nothing much to do. And then for the second time, disconcertingly, the severe gaze went soft, and Mme Holmes laughed, a full-throated sound from such a delicate figure. "We didn't intend to alarm the boy, but I was . . . concerned. It was a very long time since I'd left the journal. So many years. When I learned that Damian had claimed my uncle's possessions at last, I thought that in fairness, I should give you all at least *some* time to work on it before I came forward. But then I got word of men from India asking questions in the village, and I knew it could only be my cousins. I fretted about the journal. Who knew if it was even still there, after all this time? In the end, Arjun decided to go and see, and remove it to a safe place if he thought it seemed vulnerable."

"And went dressed as a lascar, machete in hand," Holmes commented. I was glad to see his composure returning.

"I have apologised to your son," Arjun said. "And I do so now to you. I would have been in and out without a soul knowing, but for a sleepless child. As for my appearance, I wore clothing that permits the most silence and ease of movement. I did have a suit and Western shoes hidden in the motorcar around the corner. If anyone noticed a figure in *kurta-pajama* running away from a house, they would not recognise him as the man in the suit at the wheel of a motorcar."

Damian snorted. "Scared the dickens out of us all. And when I came out of the train station in Délieux, I nearly—oh, but that reminds me!" Damian leapt up and pulled an envelope from his pocket, handing it to Holmes before striding across the terrace to the house. Arjun, with a last critical survey of the coffee settings, followed him.

Holmes extracted a letter of two pages, read it closely, then handed it to me.

I knew the handwriting. It had changed, over some thirty years, but by this point, I knew it as well as my own. She had written:

Dearest Damian,

This letter has been handed to you by a person you have every reason to mistrust. I pray you have not immediately summoned the police, or attacked him outright, but instead have paused long enough to hear his words, and thus read what I have to say. Please know that he and I both beg your pardon, and trust that this letter goes some way to setting your mind at rest.

Perhaps you remember, from your long-ago childhood, an old friend of your mother's she called L? (You thought it was Elle.) I met your mother four months before your birth. I helped her then, and I helped her afterwards, when she needed to establish a new home. Irene had no family here in France, and her friends were primarily associated with her life on the stage. After you were born, I became like a family to her—and to you. She had friends, old and new, and thus you had many honorary grand-mothers and aunts. You called me *Grand-maman Elle*.

What you did not know, what I do not believe she ever told you, was that I was—I am—your *grand-maman*, in fact. For rea-sons too complicated to explain here, I was parted from my own family, and could not claim you openly as my own, actual grand-son. But as one of a number of "honorary" grandmothers? I was free to have the pleasure of watching you grow, and if I took care not to be seen by those who might know me, I could be a part of your life.

I last saw you at your mother's funeral. You were grown, a fine

young man, and although life and the War threw problems at
you, there were only so many things that even an actual grandmother could do. So I kept my distance, depending on mutual
friends to bring me news of you.

Now, however, things are changing. Explanations need to be
given before time has run out. It would also be a great joy if I
could lay eyes on you again.

The man who has given you this, the man who scared you
witless by sneaking into your house the other night (another
complicated explanation I owe you!), is also like a grandson to
me—although in his case, the link is of affection and history, not
of blood. We both imagined that he could come and go that
night without being noticed. When you walked in and switched
on the light, he nearly fell back on an explanation.

But he decided, for good or for ill, that my story was not his
to give, and so he fled, hoping that his lack of intimidation
would convince you that his was a fluke trespass.

I am so, so sorry it was not taken in that way.

By way of reassuring you that I am who I say, my young
friend will now hand you a painting, a pair to the one your
mother loved, and that he tells me is still on your sitting-room
wall. It shows the three of us: Irene and I, with you on her lap at
the age of a few weeks.

I can understand if your alarm lingers. If that is the case, we
shall with luck meet before long. But if I have gained your trust,
I invite you to come with Arjun now, that you might meet me
again after these long years.

> Your loving grandmother,
> Louise Estelle Vernet-Lecomte
> Dupont Holmes

Damian had returned with a small framed painting, which he
lay on the table in front of Holmes.

Holmes blinked. "Well," he said, "this is a day for surprises."

I looked over his shoulder, and recognised—not this painting, but a similar one. "There's a third version of this in the boxes from the *Institut*," I told him. "Unsigned, but it's clearly by the same artist—Émile Vernet-Lecomte. It shows just one of the women, the older one, sitting in a window with her back to the room, holding the baby."

Unlike the other two paintings, in this one the women were facing the artist. The figure on the right looked to be in her seventies, an earlier version of the woman sitting across from me now. The other took a moment to recognise, since most photographs I had seen of her were in full stage makeup and costume. Here, Irene Adler wore a late-Victorian tea-dress, loosely draped and intended to be worn at home and without a corset. The way her arms held the infant declared her the mother, although she was older than one would expect, well into her thirties.

"That's Mamá and me," Damian said. "With one of Mamá's good friends that I knew as *Grand-maman Elle*."

"L for Louise," that lady said.

"And Lakshmi," I put in.

"Neither of which names," Holmes added, "did you wish publicly linked with Mme Irene Adler." I felt like cheering at the return of his incisive tones.

"Very true. Even before your brother turned to . . . his current profession, I knew that the chances of Irene being found out were too high to risk."

I waited for Holmes to seize the opening. Waited for him to demand all the things he deserved to know. *Why did you leave? Why stay dead? Why did you not trust . . . ?* Instead, he focused on the *How*.

"Madame, who are your spies?"

The aged face retreated into a slightly guarded expression. "Spies?"

"How did you know the boxes had been claimed? Did someone from the *Institut* notify you?"

"Ah, that. Yes, indirectly. My bank sends an anonymous annual gift to the *Institut de France*. In return, they receive notice of any activity—any at all—regarding the Vernet family and its bequests."

"So, you learned that an Adler had appeared, and that the crates would be sent to the Délieux station for him to claim?"

"That is what I was told," she said carefully.

"What you were told, but not what you knew. Who are the 'mutual friends' who send you news of the household? Someone who knew in August that the boxes had arrived, but that Damian had yet to find the journal. Someone who knew on Saturday that Damian was on his way back from Carcassonne, but did not know when he would arrive. Damian is convinced it cannot be one of the LaRues, but I do not see who else it could be."

"It is not the LaRues," she said. "Not directly."

And I had it. "Madame's brother, Pierre."

Her nod of approval was like a reward. "Pierre, yes. He has been my, as it were, man on the ground for a long, long time. I was living in Spain when I learned of my son's relationship with an American singer. I was pleased for him. Then some months later, when I heard that he had returned to London without her, I went to Montpellier to find what had happened. It did not take long to see that she was with child, so I decided to risk introducing myself, and ask if I might be of help. I was relieved," she said to her son, "not to find it a matter of abandonment on your part, but of independence on hers. I found Irene Adler a woman after my own heart."

I felt Holmes react to that. But I also felt a faint note of iron in her words. Her declaration of camaraderie with Irene Adler was only casual on the surface.

"With Damian due," she went on, "Irene and I looked for a quiet retreat, where we might keep ourselves out of the world's eye.

We found the house in Ste Chapelle. I joined her there for a time, until Damian was grown enough to need friends and tutors more than grandmothers. The LaRues were neighbours, and happy to supplement Gervais' income with what Irene paid them for their help. Pauline's brother, Pierre, was only a boy, but he was always half in love with this exotic American who came to earth in his little village. When he was sent home from the War so badly injured, I encouraged him to stay in the little house she had built for him, and remain as the watchman. And yes, some of the watching he does is for me. I am, after all, Damian's grandmother."

Mme Holmes looked fondly down at the painting. "I would see them every few months—I travelled a great deal, but this house has always been my home, and Nanterre is not that far from Ste Chapelle. It was a gift, to watch my grandson grow up. And I found Irene a great pleasure. Although in case you were wondering," she said to Holmes, "I did tell her that she should let you know you had a son. It seemed unfair for me to reap all the benefit. But of course she then in turn urged me to tell you that . . ." She broke off, and I filled in the words. That I was alive? That I had lied to you, day in and day out, for decades? That I had turned my back on my family? That I had—yes—*abandoned* those who loved me? "To tell you that I was here," she chose to finish.

"But by that time, I had many reasons not to come back from the dead. Just as Irene had reasons not to open the door that she had closed.

"In the end, she decided that Damian himself could choose, when he turned eighteen. She was already ill when she told you," she said to him, "although you wouldn't have seen it yet."

"I did see it," he responded. "I just didn't realise what it meant for a few weeks. She went fast. Gone by Christmas."

"A heartbreak, for all of us. And then came the War. I was out of the country for most of 1918 and 1919. When I returned, I discovered that Damian had been arrested, that you had been told and had cleared him of the charge, and that he had then disappeared.

It took me nearly a year to catch a rumour of you in Shanghai," she told her grandson—which frankly astonished me. Even Mycroft hadn't found Damian. "But you seemed happy, so I kept my distance, as I have done since you returned to France. I will admit that I come to Ste Chapelle on market day, every so often, to see that lovely child of yours."

"I look forward to introducing you," Damian said.

She gave him a sad smile. "That may need to wait until we are sure that any threat from my family in India has been . . . nullified."

"I believe you'll find that Russell and I have taken care of that problem," Holmes told her.

The old grey eyes widened. "How?" Neither exclamation nor disbelief, merely a demand for information—I could see where his mind came from.

"No violence. Or, not much," he amended. "A judicious threat, a bit of playing two men against each other, one or two outright lies. Caution would be wise for a short time, but I am confident the risk is small."

And now she permitted herself to show emotion, with a look of wistful hope. "I should greatly enjoy meeting my great-granddaughter, face to face. I have spent far too much of my life at a distance from those I love. Gleaning the small satisfactions of distant glimpses and reports from one's, as you say, 'mutual friends.' For fifty-three years, I have followed you and your brother: at school, your careers, your friendships, your trials. I cannot count the number of times when I nearly came out into view. Most recently when I read Mycroft's obituary last year. I was much relieved to find it merely a smoke screen."

She gave her son a quick smile, then folded her hands together, her aged face open and calm. "However, you, my dear son, will no doubt have questions more pressing than your mother's sly ways of keeping watch on her family. Where would you like me to begin?"

I could think of dozens more questions, from *How did you hide your true nature, there in rural Berkshire?* to *What have you been doing for the past half century?* and *How could you bear the pain?* But while their discussion about Irene Adler had involved me slightly, by the proxy of marriage vows, this was too starkly personal for a wife to intrude on.

I stood, brushing off my hands unnecessarily. "I'd like to use the, er," and turned to the house without waiting for permission.

And as I went through the kitchen door, I heard that of all my own questions, Holmes chose none of them.

"Begin at the end," I heard him say. "Your . . . 'suicide.'"

CHAPTER FIFTY-TWO

Holmes

Holmes was aware that his history with women was mixed. As a young man, he had tended either to discount them as weak and in need of protection, or distrust them as cunning and requiring a close eye. In his middle years, he had become aware that both attitudes might be signs that he was overlooking the evidence, and he started to work at seeing what was actually there, in a woman's behaviour and motivations, rather than what he expected to see. And then Russell dropped into his life, and turned everything on its head.

Sitting across from this small, fragile woman who had given him birth, he felt as if he were facing the subaltern of a platoon of gentle Amazons, all those women who had passed before his barely comprehending eyes. The clients who hired him, then walked head-high into great danger. Those who listened to his imperious advice, their faces saying that he had not comprehended the depth of their problem. Those who had risked their lives, their freedom, and their sanity for the sake of husbands or children. His long-time housekeeper, Mrs Hudson, who lived through years of his informal house arrest with her pride intact. Irene, the adventuress suspected of coercing a King, who had given his young ego a sharp kick in the shins. And Russell, who had forced his attention and respect from the first hour of their meeting. He had recently begun to suspect that the feminine approach had unsuspected strengths that might—very occasionally—edge out the masculine.

When he was eleven, he had hated this woman sitting across from him, for her cowardly desertion that left her husband and sons bereft. Later, he pitied her, first for giving way to her shameful desires, then for failing to find a solution to blackmail other than the one that she chose. Hatred and pity had both faded with the years, leaving him melancholy, for her and for those left behind.

What he felt now, though, was . . . interest.

"I read your 'suicide' account in the journal," he said. "It was clearly intended for Mycroft or me, as you cannot have anticipated a person such as Russell. Have you anything to add to that account?"

She studied her hands. "I do not remember in precise detail what I wrote, all those years ago, but I hope I conveyed how difficult the decision was for me. I knew what it might do to you and your brother, to say nothing of your father. But I also knew what it would unquestionably mean, were I to stay. I had to weigh the consequences of my leaving against the impact on you three if I were to stay and confront matters, in a setting such as England was at the time.

"I'm also not certain if I gave sufficient emphasis to my conviction that Rajiv, the cousin who threatened me, was capable of great ruthlessness. His father, my uncle Ram, was single-minded and utterly heartless when it came to getting what he wanted. I came to suspect him of killing my father—I'm sure I put that into the journal. That night at the Grenville-Paton's ball, when I looked into Rajiv's eyes, I saw Ram, and I knew that my cousin would not hesitate to tear my family to bits.

"So I admitted to him that I had stolen the family's jewels. I—"

"Sorry?" Damian sat forward. "What jewels are those?"

"The details are in the journal," Holmes told him. "For the moment, suffice it to say that my understanding of the reason for my mother's suicide was considerably off the mark. It involved some jewels gone missing, from her relatives in India."

"You told me you had family in India, *Grand-mère*," Damian exclaimed, "but this begins to sound like a Victorian novel."

"Please, let us cover that aspect of the situation later," Holmes said, then turned back to his mother. "You admitted your guilt, to Rajiv."

"Yes, and I decided that if he thought your father knew nothing about them, if I took every scrap of blame, he would take himself home and not indulge in some spiteful revenge. I told him I would have to retrieve the pieces from a bank in Paris. Instead, I spent my last days with you boys and your father, and then disappeared. After an anxious three weeks in a boarding house, I finally got news of an unidentified drowning victim, who came to shore down the coast from where I'd apparently gone in. I bribed the coroner to place a necklace your father had given me around the poor creature's neck. I was fortunate, in that her build and hair were not too different from my own. The only person I had to fool was your father, and he could scarcely bring himself to look at the body. Once the funeral had taken place, all the ends were tied off. I left England. Had you two been younger, I'm not sure I could have made that choice. But Mycroft was at University already, you were headed for school—and I of all people should know how superfluous a mother could be, if one has a father's love and attention. I knew your father would give you that, so I made you all as safe as I could, and then I trusted to the future."

"Does Mycroft know?"

The expression on her face was complex. It began with surprise, then moved to doubt, before stopping at pity. "Oh, that would be a miserable thought for you, wouldn't it?"

"Does he know?" Damian shifted in his chair, as if to object to the anger in Holmes' voice, but neither of them looked at him.

"Your brother does not. So far as I am aware," she corrected herself. "And I believe I would have heard."

She was not lying to him. *But,* Holmes thought, *if my bloody brother had any idea that Mother survived and kept it from me, I shall strangle him with my bare hands.*

He sat back, steepling his fingers, trying to consider this woman as he would any other potential suspect. She gazed back at him, pragmatic, cool, speaking the unvarnished truth. She was not begging—for forgiveness, or even for understanding.

Still, he could hear the faint ring of emotion in her voice, see the tension in her clasped hands. Guilt, he thought. And fear. Not that she would admit either. She was never going to say openly that she regretted her choice. Nonetheless, somewhere in those old eyes was a woman wondering how everyone's lives—sons, husband, family—would have been different, had she chosen another path.

"What did you do after that?" he asked. And before her body could relax with the relief that crossed her face—*interesting,* he noted in the back of his mind, *how thoroughly I can read this woman*—he added, "You said you had 'many reasons not to come back from the dead.' What were those?"

The tension was back, following a flick of the eyes towards Damian. When she looked down at her hands, Holmes could tell that she was putting together a story. Not, he thought, a false one. Merely one constructed of very deliberately chosen bricks.

"After leaving England, I made a new life. I came here for a short time, to this house, where my mother and father had loved one another. No-one in England knew about it of course, and I was certain that my Indian relatives had not discovered it. However, I thought it a good time to travel, so I did. I found work that challenged and satisfied me. I made friends—some of whom helped me keep a distant watch over my two sons," she added with a tentative smile. "Others introduced me to parts of the world I would never have seen without them. I was well accustomed to moving about, in all kinds of situations. Uncle Horace—sorry, you did guess that the artist 'Monsieur' in the journal was your great-uncle?"

"We figured that out, yes."

"You knew Horace Vernet?" Damian interrupted.

"I was his assistant, for many years. North Africa and the Holy Land when I was a child, then later in Russia and Germany. England, once or twice. And when he was at home working, Arjun and I—Arjun the First, that is," she said, with a nod at the house, where sounds came from the kitchen, "—were on our own, either living quietly here in Nanterre, or travelling. We knew Ram would be looking for me, and he was sure to find me if I stuck too close to the Vernet family. So we would take off, often dressed up as father and son. I've always enjoyed the freedoms of masculine dress, and even when I grew up, I was not blessed with particularly feminine features.

"Then when I was twenty-five, I realised that my dear friend was growing old, and that his thoughts were turning ever more to the other side of the world. Sadly, reluctantly, I sent him home. And a year later, I went to a London ball and met a charming young Englishman named Holmes."

"I only wish—" Damian started, then cut off, and gave his two relatives a sheepish look. "I was about to say that I regret it took us so long to meet, that we'd wasted so many years. This from the person who never got into touch with his own father."

"My dear boy, yes, I do so look forward to our conversations. And I hope that we might come a little more out in the open. If," she added carefully, turning to Holmes, "you are correct in believing the dangers nullified."

Neither of them so much as twitched an eye in Damian's direction; both of them were intensely aware of the young man, and of the things he did not need to know.

"In a week or so, matters should have resolved. However,"

Holmes said, his voice casual but his gaze holding hers, "I might recommend locating someone in India who would be in a position to maintain a watch over your cousin's family."

She did not look at Damian before she replied. "I might be able to assist in that."

Holmes felt a smile tugging at his face. "Yes," he said. "I thought perhaps you might."

CHAPTER FIFTY-THREE

stood at one of the kitchen windows, listening to the murmur of voices, and to the flat sound of church-bells summoning the parish, and to the noises of washing-up behind me. Holmes was sitting with his back to me, but by this time, I could read his shoulders as easily as I could his face. He'd been angry for a moment, earlier, and Damian had nearly intervened. Now the tilt of his head was that of interrogation.

And then Mme Holmes cocked one eyebrow at him, such a familiar expression in that unknown face that it startled a cough of laughter from me.

The swish of water paused, and I turned away from this family—*my* family, odd though the thought was—and shook my head at Arjun, shirtsleeves rolled up and apron donned.

"An extraordinary sight," I said.

"I am grateful to be here when it happened," he agreed.

"She seems in remarkably good health," I said, belatedly aware of the hopeful tone in my voice.

He paused with his hands in the suds. "She is . . . indomitable," he pronounced, his dark eyes sparkling with pleasure.

"How long have you known her?"

"Most of my life. The partnership established by her father and my great-grandfather has lasted over the years. My father was named Krishna, after hers. He came to Paris, shortly after Mme Holmes . . . after she left England. He stayed for several years. When my brother was old enough, he took our father's place. He was here for nearly a decade before I was sent over, a boy of thirteen. After the War, I moved to Nanterre, to be closer to her."

I hesitated, searching for a courteous way to ask, *Do you know if your great-grandfather—Arjun the First—killed Ram Dupont, after Lakshmi had sent him home?* Would he even know? It was not the sort of proud heritage one might want to pass on. And I might be tempted to go on with, *He should have done away with the poisonous Sophie as well.*

Instead, I merely remarked, "Mme Holmes is a family affair."

"We have enjoyed assisting her."

"Always here in Paris?" I picked up a tea-towel and began to dry the dishes coming out of his hot water.

"Oh no. As she said, she travels. Or she did." He looked sad at the thought that his indomitable employer might be slowing.

"She said she made a life here, after England. What did she do? Did she marry again?"

"She did not. She enjoys her freedom too much. Too, in the early years, it would have been bigamy."

"I doubt that would have stopped her if she'd found a suitable partner."

"You may be right." He really did have a lovely warm smile.

"But it was over fifty years ago that she faked her suicide. Mme Holmes doesn't strike me as the sort to have spent her days drinking tea in the garden."

"She travelled, as she said. And she had many projects that interested her, both here and abroad. Before the War, when she was beginning to feel her years, she started a school for girls here in Paris, in one of the poorer areas."

It did not sound as if he was about to give me details of Madame's "many projects." However, there was more than one way to uncover clues about a person's past. Out in the garden, the conversation seemed to be going strong.

"I'd like to let them talk," I said to the man at the sink. "I imagine Madame has a library—would she mind if I were to look at her books?"

"But of course," he said, concentrating on some recalcitrant stain on a fork.

So I went snooping in my ancient mother-in-law's house.

Her sitting room was on the other side of the entrance hall, and one step inside the doorway, I could feel the diarist Lakshmi merge with Louise Holmes in my mind.

She and the first Arjun had bought this place more than eighty years ago. There was little sign of the Frenchwoman, her mother's friend, who had owned it before that. The bones of the room were French, yes: a creaking but beautifully maintained parquet underfoot, windows that had been replaced but not changed, time-black beams in the plaster overhead. But the flesh on those bones owed more to Bengal than to Bordeaux.

One sofa was a magnificent Indian *jhula*, a sort of deep, high-backed wooden bench with intricate carving and sloping arms, strewn with silk pillows in shades of orange from dark amber to fresh apricot. Facing it across a huge and equally intricate Persian carpet was a modern sofa with a back that thrust out like wings, upholstered in carnelian velvet.

Either piece looked comfortable enough to settle into with a book on a cold night.

The fireplace was by no means original to the house, being marble and carved into the shape of an onion dome, with dozens of tiny elephants, tail in trunk, marching around its edge. More whimsical than I'd have expected, from the steely-eyed mother of Sherlock Holmes.

A shawl had been laid over the back of the wooden sofa, made

of feather-weight wool with embroidery all over it. Unlike the furniture, it was blue, delicate shades of indigo, faded with age. Close
investigation revealed thinning threads and dozens of tiny repairs,
and I wondered if I had met this shawl, when *Daadi-ma* kissed it
and laid it in the child's valise.

As if to contradict its femininity, the next thing my eyes lit on
was a collection of spears mounted above the fireplace. I was no
expert in weaponry, but I could tell that each of the five was from
a different place. The one in the centre, its shaft broken off a foot
above the steel head, was at a guess from Madagascar or Mozam-
bique. The pair on either side of it looked more Asian than African,
while those on the outside of the arrangement were unmistakeably
from the South Seas. They were not tourist souvenirs, either, but
weapons with razor-sharp points. The wood of the broken one was
stained, hitting me with the sharp memory of an enraged boar, its
tusks kept from plunging into my tender flesh by a similar, fragile-
looking, far-too-short spear, in India the previous year.

The sitting room would have invited a much longer contempla-
tion than I thought I should give it just now. The joyous dancing
bronze elephant god, Ganesh; the complex arabesques of the inlaid table; the ivory carving of—could that be Lakshmi, goddess of
well-being and fertility?

But it was not art I sought, it was enlightenment. I tore myself
away and continued through the house.

The next room was a small office, efficient and spotlessly tidy. I
was tempted—and Arjun had not explicitly forbidden me—but to
rummage through the cabinet drawers was a more blatant intrusion than I was comfortable with.

Next was the library. The room felt like—it felt like home. A
light-filled space with thick, old glass filling most of one wall, some
of the panes set into doors that opened onto the garden with another, smaller terrace. A table and chairs awaited a working scholar.

The room's other three walls were filled with books. Most were
on history, geography, or travel, I saw, although there was a sprin-

kling of fiction in half a dozen languages. The fireplace here was small and simple, with two soft chairs, each with its own reading lamp and round leather ottoman. On the floor was another stunning carpet, this one in shades of turquoise, light green, and rose, the last colour picked up in the damask curtains that would cover the cold glass wall on a winter's night. A colourful North African travelling rug was tossed over the back of a settee. A well-used writing desk in one corner—its surface littered with pads, pens, and silver-framed photographs—took advantage of the light from the windows.

I walked over to the desk—again, refraining from touching any of the actual work, which appeared to be notes of a trip into the Sudan. But the photographs, openly displayed, were surely fair game. Many were of Mme Holmes on her travels. Here she was as a slim, middle-aged woman in the tight sleeves and high collars of the 1880s, her hair gathered under a wide-brimmed straw hat, posing in front of the Suez Canal. And some twenty years later, a dignified figure in her seventies next to a Roman ruin I recognised from my time in Morocco. In another, she was ridiculously young although perfectly recognisable, no more than eighteen in a virginal white evening dress, standing beside Nicholas I of Russia. The photo next to the Czar's was from the turn of the century, where she wore a shirtwaist and boater, with the pointed temples of some Indochinese city rising in the background.

Not all the photos showed this invincible lady. A few were group shots, mostly of men, again in places that appeared to be French colonies. I smiled as one caught my eye, and I picked it up to hold it to the light. General Hubert Lyautey—no, I saw, still a Colonel here, and not in Morocco where I'd met him, but in Madagascar, to judge by the weird outlines of the baobab trees in the background. He was standing with two other officers, one a young lieutenant as tall as he, the other a major who . . .

I frowned, and squinted more closely at the image—then gave a cough of laughter. The "major" was none other than Mme Holmes.

With that in mind, I went through the group photographs more closely, and found her in each and every one, though never again as an army officer. In two, she wore women's clothing, but the majority found her clothed as a man.

And here, tucked back behind a frayed history of the Andaman Islands, was a second snapshot of Lyautey—now in a general's uniform. He wore an expression startlingly similar to one I'd seen close up on the face of an English colonial governor, Edmund Allenby, who'd been all but exploding with mirth as he bent down to kiss the filthy, blood-stained hand of what was, to the eyes of the watching notables, a Bedouin lad. *My* filthy, blood-stained hand. Here, Lyautey seemed every bit as amused as Allenby had been, posing for the camera in some desert place between two figures in North African clothing. One was Mme Holmes, looking for all the world like a middle-aged Moroccan man with an equally entertained expression on "his" beardless face. The other . . .

The other was less successful in her disguise. She might have got away with those delicate eyebrows and soft mouth when she was ten years younger, but this picture was clearly of a woman in her mid-twenties dressed in a man's burnous and turban.

Isabelle Eberhardt. Lyautey himself had told me about her: born Swiss, converted to Islam, and had spent most of her brief adult life moving among the bemused locals of North Africa. Like Gertrude Bell in her Arabian Desert, Eberhardt took full advantage of the good manners of her hosts, who were too polite to challenge a mad foreign woman's choice of clothing or her interference in men's affairs. Lyautey had come across the woman while he was moving to conquer Morocco, and had used her relationship with the local people to garner local intelligence as he planned out his next moves.

Local intelligence . . .

My hand slowly replaced the little silver frame on the shelf. My feet carried me in a circuit of the room while I studied the photographs and thought about the dates indicated by her clothing in each one. Thought about the languages of the books on her shelves, and the weapons in the sitting room, and the way she occupied men's trousers and turbans with sure confidence. Remembering the games she had played with her father, and with her sons. The code she had used to write her journal. The *kurta* and *abayya*—men's clothing—in the tea chest in Damian's studio. The skill this woman had used her whole life, for disappearing in plain sight. Even from the eyes of her clever sons.

I had many reasons not to come back from the dead, she had told us. *Depending on mutual friends to bring me news,* she had written.

The guarded expression on her face when Holmes asked who her spies were.

Possibly even the reason that, once she embarked on that path, she would not have risked returning to her home, for fear of bringing outside dangers with her. Although, if she was good enough to avoid the attention of Mycroft Holmes . . . Or was this something else Mycroft had kept from us? I shook my head and returned to the kitchen, where I found Arjun arranging summer fruits on a tray.

"These 'many projects' of hers," I said. "They seem to have taken her to Madagascar, Indochina, North Africa, Polynesia. All places of keen political interest to France. And in all of them, so far as I can see from the photographs in her study, she visited at times when pressures were building towards either war or annexation."

He said nothing, merely adjusted the grapes among the late apricots and ruby-red plums.

"M. Ghosh, I am aware that France has a department in the Interior Ministry called the *Deuxième Bureau.* It is roughly the equivalent of Section 6 in England's Military Intelligence." More or less where Mycroft Holmes spent his days, although I did not tell him that.

I had many reasons not to come back from the dead.

Arjun opened the top of a packet of dates and began to arrange them among the fruit. He seemed to be smiling to himself.

"M. Ghosh. Is your employer . . . Was Mme Holmes . . ." I drew a breath, and tried again. "Is she a spy?"

He looked up then, as overflowing with delight and mischief as an Indian version of General Allenby. He said nothing. But his hand rose, one long index finger coming to rest across his mouth, nose to chin. Clever eyes shining, lips closed now and forevermore.

Well, I thought. *This is certainly going to make for an interesting conversation, when next we see Mycroft.*

AUTHOR'S NOTES

Holmes and India: Laurie King is not the only Sherlockian to have noticed the thread of India that runs through the stories by Arthur Conan Doyle. And as is required by the principles of Holmesian scholarship (known as "The Game"), tiny details from the Doyle "canon" become foundations for a preferably vast and impressive edifice of interpretation. Such forays into academia occasionally even reach publication before collapsing under the weight of their own fancy. One of the more thoroughly engineered articles is Thomas Cynkin's "Was Sherlock Holmes Raised in India?" (*Baker Street Journal*, vol 70, no 3)—which, despite evidence to the contrary in this current volume of the Russell memoirs, nonetheless manages to put forward some thought-provoking explanations for such things as the detective's Buddhistic methods of meditation, his specialized knowledge of swamp adders and Indian tobaccos, and his remarkable failure to mention having passed through India on his way from Europe to Nepal.

On words: The vocabulary of a story like this can easily become so complicated as to be a distraction. Hence, "roti" and "chapati" are used instead of *"paratha," "luchi," "naan,"* or any of the myriad varieties of Indian flat bread that are eaten at different times in various parts of the country. Similarly, the simple "turban" covers the range of men's headgear, from loose to tightly formal. Various words, including place names such as Chandernagore, Calcutta, and Bombay, here preserve the spelling used in Mary Russell's era.

The matter of lascars: Race, prejudice, and skin color are touchy matters. There have always been people who disregard the whole idea of "race"; and, one fears, there always will be people for whom it matters. Many people of color, especially from America, found some relief in 1920s Paris, but the intersection of caste and color in India has a long history. Similarly, the "lascar" in British society was regarded by the white population in much the way the "Lascar scoundrel" of Conan Doyle's "The Man with the Twisted Lip" is presented, as "a man of the vilest antecedents" (although, in fact, the man proves a reliable confederate for the person who actually hired him—that person being a white man happy to deceive even his own wife).

The Vernet genealogy: The extended Vernet family is every bit as convoluted as it appears in this story. "Claude" was known as Joseph, "Antoine Charles" as Carle, "Jean Émile"—or sometimes, "Émile Jean"—is dropped from before the name Horace. "Fanny" was the name of Camille's mother and her daughter; Horace Vernet's first wife and elder daughter were both named Louise; his second wife and younger daughter (who was born to the first) were both Maries. To complicate the "Louise" question further, Camille's son Émile named his daughter Camille Elisabeth Louise—and, to top matters off, some genealogies give Camille a son named Louis, born in 1812, while others give her a daughter named Louise born in 1815. Under these circumstances, who would be surprised if Camille had another daughter in 1825, and named her Louise as well?

This is why Laurie R. King gave up academia and went into fiction, where the demands of footnotes are considerably fewer.

The art in Holmes' blood: In "The Adventure of the Greek Interpreter," Arthur Conan Doyle has Sherlock Holmes revealing to Dr Watson (a man he has known and lived with for several years) that he has a brother who is also very clever, musing that "art in the blood is liable to take the strangest forms," and explaining that the artistic bent came with "a sister of Vernet, the French artist." Doyle does not specify which of the many Vernets it was, but Mary Russell knows it is Horace.

Horace Vernet was famous for his remarkable powers of observation and incomparable memory. He would meditate long into the night on a painting, then attack it without studies, notes, or hesitation. His ability to block out the world was phenomenal, as was his willingness to put up with all kinds of discomforts in order to research a painting.

The 1839 photographic/painting expedition to North Africa that Arjun discovers and Lakshmi joins took place more or less as described. Horace Vernet, then fifty, was accompanied by the artist and recent convert to daguerreotype, Frédéric Goupil-Fesquet (twenty-two), along with Charles Burton (twenty-six), Vernet's nephew by marriage. Details of their voyage can be found in Goupil-Fesquet's 1843 illustrated publication *Voyage en Orient fait avec Horace Vernet,* or in the excellent two-part article by Michèle Hannoosh on "Horace Vernet's 'Orient': Photography and the Eastern Mediterranean in 1839" from *The Burlington Magazine,* April and June 2016 (see the University of Michigan's website).

Horace Vernet's *Arabs Travelling in the Desert* shows the three men on camel-back, with a certain young servant boy looking on bemused in the background, while his 1835 *Self-Portrait with Pipe* presents Vernet looking distinctly Holmesian.

This Vernet led a tumultuous life even before he met young Lakshmi, having been born in the Louvre palace, then carried to safety three years later across the Tuileries courtyard amidst a hail of bullets during the French Revolution. His aunt went to the guillotine when he was five, and many of his paintings were thrown on the flames by the February Revolution of 1848.

And yes, he and his colleagues very probably sent back intelligence reports on their travels.

About Irene Adler: The "hiatus" of Sherlock Holmes from 221 Baker Street is generally agreed to have taken place between May 1891 and April 1894 (in Arthur Conan Doyle's "The Final Problem" and "The Adventure of the Empty House"). Montpellier is mentioned, along with Nepal, but the record was silent on such matters as India, his mother, and any contact with Irene Adler beyond the Conan Doyle short story, "A Scandal in Bohemia"— until the Mary Russell memoirs began to come out. Damian and Estelle Adler are introduced in *The Language of Bees* and *The God of the Hive*.

ACKNOWLEDGMENTS

This tale of family links and influences owes much to the author's own wider family, the community of people who surround and support the person who actually flings words on the page. As always, the hard-working folk of Bantam Books/Penguin Random House make me look good: Hilary Teeman and Caroline Weishuhn, Allison Schuster and Emma Thomasch, Kim Hovey, Melissa Folds, Carlos Beltrán, Rachel Kind, Kara Welsh, Jennifer Hershey, Kelly Chian, Mark Maguire, Pamela Alders, Pam Feinstein, Davina Bhanabhai, and a thousand others, from management to shipping. Thanks are due to Recorded Books, who put the words into readers' ears, especially Brian Sweany and the voice of Mary Russell, Jenny Sterlin.

Behind the scenes, I owe more than I could ever return to my friends, cheering section, beta readers, and reference library for all things Russellian, Team LRK: Alice Wright, Merrily Taylor, Karen Buys, Sabrina Flynn, Erin Bright, John Bychowski, and all "The Beekeeper's Apprentices" on Facebook. To Les Klinger, who knows his Beekeeper and is happy to share. My blessings on Mary Alice Kier and Anna Cottle from Cinelit, who keep the faith; on Alec

Shane from Writers House, who always has my back; and on Sue from Interbridge, who keeps me online.

Bless, too, the booksellers and librarians, determined to keep back the dark and put words into the hands of readers.

And for all you readers, who clamor for Russell, yet support the other voices in Laurie King's head: thank you, for bringing me to 2024, which marks thirty years since the first of the Mary Russell and Sherlock Holmes memoirs came out.

ABOUT THE AUTHOR

LAURIE R. KING is the award-winning, bestselling author of seventeen previous Mary Russell mysteries, a new series featuring SFPD cold-case Inspector Raquel Laing, the contemporary Kate Martinelli series, the historical Stuyvesant & Grey stories, and five acclaimed standalone novels. She lives in Northern California, where she is at work on her next Mary Russell mystery.

Facebook.com/LaurieRKing
Instagram: @LaurieRKing
Twitter: @mary_russell

ABOUT THE TYPE

This book was set in Caslon, a typeface first designed in 1722 by William Caslon (1692–1766). Its widespread use by most English printers in the early eighteenth century soon supplanted the Dutch typefaces that had formerly prevailed. The roman is considered a "workhorse" typeface due to its pleasant, open appearance, while the italic is exceedingly decorative.